SAFE HAVEN:

REAP OF THE RIGHTEOUS

CHRISTOPHER ARTINIAN

ISBN-10: **198689911X**
ISBN-13: **978-1986899116**

DEDICATION

To all those who fall but refuse to stay down. To all those who stand when the tyrannical demand you kneel. The greatest weapon is the will to do anything for the ones you love.

ACKNOWLEDGEMENTS

First, last, always and forever, I want to thank my wonderful missus, Tina. She's always there to put me on the right path, and she never lets me down. I am so lucky to have her.

Thank you to the awesome Dean Samed - a magical artist who can give you a universe in a single cover.

And finally... A huge thank you to all of you. I will never take a reader for granted. Time is something we can never get back and for someone to spend theirs reading one of my books leaves me in a state of humbled gratitude. Thank you so much!

CHRISTOPHER ARTINIAN

1

The sea mist engulfed the small motorised dinghy as it chugged across the still morning water. Samantha Fletcher, Sammy to all who knew her, sat at the back of the boat with tears streaming down her face. There had been ever since she was given her instructions and set adrift fifteen minutes earlier. For a girl of eight, she had an old head on her shoulders, but with the sound of gunfire and explosions behind her and the frightening realms of the unknown ahead, all she could do was act her age.

She had been out in the dinghy a number of times with Mike, and he had taught her how to start and stop the motor as well as steer, but she had never been out in fog. She hated crying, she hated the part of her that was still a frightened little girl, and at this precise moment in time, there were more reasons to cry than not. She switched off the motor and crawled over to where her older brother lay. Sammy shook him.

"Wake up Mike," she begged. When he didn't, she draped her arm across his chest, nestled her head into his shoulder, and sobbed herself to sleep.

*

The dark interior of the lorry smelt like rotting meat. The women huddled together in small frightened groups, crying, begging for mercy to unhearing gods. The only light came from holes in the siding caused by stray bullets. Lucy and Emma had been through a lot together. They had developed a sisterly bond during their journey from Leeds to the northwest of Scotland, and not just because Lucy and Mike, Emma's younger brother had fallen in love. The terrors they had fought, they had fought together. The horrors they had seen, they had seen together. The losses were mourned and the victories were shared, and now they were like blood. They sat shoulder to shoulder in a corner of the lorry. They had been joined by Beth, another survivor from Leeds and Sarah, a teacher at a deaf school who had befriended them.

"Where are Annie and John?" Emma whispered to Beth as the lorry juddered over a pothole in the road.

"Sarah and I hid them, her kids and a few others with the librarians under the stage in the village hall. I'm hoping they didn't find them, but we were rounded up pretty soon afterwards."

"Why didn't you stay with them?"

"Because we knew you wouldn't run and hide. We knew you'd need help." She paused. "Where are Mike, Sammy, and Jake?"

"Jake ran off. We don't know where he is. Sammy and Mike are on a boat heading across to one of the small islands," said Emma, the whisper hiding the fact that her voice was breaking with sorrow.

After a long pause, Beth asked, "How did you get Mike to agree to that?"

2

This time it was Lucy who spoke, but not to Beth. "That look on his face. I can't get it out of my head. That look of betrayal."

Emma took hold of her hand. "He'd be dead now if it wasn't for you, Lucy."

Lucy turned her head towards Emma, her look was distant. "What if that was the last time I ever see him? What if the final memory he has of me is betraying him?"

"What happened?" asked Beth.

When Lucy didn't speak, Emma replied, "We had to drug him. He wanted to fight. He wanted to..."

"But there are hundreds of them," replied Sarah.

"You haven't really seen Mike when his back's against the wall, but he... He becomes...emotional."

"It was the right thing to do," Beth reassured the pair of them. "He'd have been killed in seconds. These men are merciless. I saw one of them crack Calum Macdonald's head open with the butt of their rifle. He was nearly ninety for God's sake, he was no threat to them."

The image of the old man floated like a ghost in front of them all as the drone of the engines took them nearer to their nightmarish future.

*

Privates Hughes, Private Barnes, and Private Shaw were the only remaining survivors from the original squad of troops that had made the journey north from Candleton. Shaw had taken a stab at leadership but wasn't up to the job. He had made an enemy of Mike and lost the respect of the rest of the group, but now he was fighting

3

hard to prove himself to be a valuable asset. Hughes was the unofficial leader of the small group. He was the most experienced soldier and the voice of reason. It was because of this that Mike had asked him to help lead the expedition around the Inner Hebrides with Mike's gran, Sue, and Jenny, another Candleton survivor. She had been a successful hotel owner and businesswoman, and she was the obvious choice to help lead negotiations. Raj and Talikha, along with their Labrador Retriever, Humphrey had been instrumental in the group's escape. It was in their cruiser that they had travelled up the west coast. They were the ones who had brought the group to safety. Now, one a vet and one a veterinary nurse, they spent most of their time ferrying supplies using their newly acquired yacht. For the past few days, their cargo had consisted of people.

Even though it felt like something of a vacation after the turbulent times that had gone before, this small delegation was doing crucial work. They were setting up a trade route, they were re-establishing communication with islands that had thought themselves forgotten to the outside world, and more importantly, they were forging alliances. When they had first set foot on the small island of Jura at the beginning of their journey, it had been with trepidation. They had not known if the place had been overrun by RAMs or whether the people would be hostile and untrusting. Their fears had been misplaced though. The infection had not reached the island and the people were so grateful to hear news from the outside that representatives from Lonbaig were treated like heroes. Sue had brought small amounts of produce as samples of what could be traded, but she was given much more in return by grateful islanders. This was the beginning of something new, something strong, something powerful. The old world was gone, but what was being forged now was something elemental and pure.

It was something hopeful.

As the seven of them sat around the breakfast table relishing the bounty that Talikha had prepared, their moods were buoyant. Their journey was coming to an end as they headed back to Lonbaig. Life was never going to be normal again. But that didn't mean that it couldn't be good.

*

Mike had been awake for several minutes before he managed to open his eyes. When he did, all he saw was grey, all he felt was a cold, uncomfortable dampness shivering through him. He closed his eyes, his breathing remained heavy, and his thoughts fuzzy. He waited a few more minutes and then opened them again. The greyness was still there and now...now there was something else. It felt like he was being rocked, ever so gently. He forced himself to take in a deep breath and caught the unmistakable smell of the sea. He tried to find a memory, something that led to his current situation. He delved beyond the fogginess, searching...hunting—what was the last thing he remembered?

"Mike?" his thoughts were interrupted.

He moved his head to see where the sound had come from and immediately, the fuzziness washed over him again like a wave. He fought to gain control and saw his little sister Sammy. Her tear stained-face was staring up from his shoulder. It did nothing to abate his confusion. He tried to speak but couldn't. It was almost like he'd been drugged. Then that single thought rang in his head:

It wasn't like he'd been drugged—he had been drugged!

He remembered turning to see Lucy with an empty syringe in her hand, a look of panic on her face, the warm feeling rushing through his veins. He slowly moved his fingers up to his neck and felt a small spot of dried blood where the needle had gone in. Lucy had drugged him. But why?

"Mike?" Sammy pleaded this time.

"I'm okay...just groggy...give me a minute," his words scratched from his dry throat as he tried to regain his train of thought. He and Lucy had been in bed. There had been a fevered banging on the door. One of the villagers had told them of two armies... "Where are we?" he asked urgently, adrenaline beginning to surge through him, countering the remaining effects of the anaesthetic.

"I don't know. We kept going until I couldn't hear the guns any more. Then I turned the motor off." Her tone was apologetic. "Jake ran away," she cried as if confessing some terrible deed.

"What do you mean?"

"I was trying to listen to what you were arguing about in the kitchen. When you started shouting, he must have got scared and run off. Lucy went to look for him, but couldn't find him and then Emma told me I had to get you to safety." Her words were interspersed with sobs. When she finished, she broke down, and Mike held her close. Five minutes passed by and the cold mist slowly began to lift. Behind it there was the suggestion of a blazing sun, today would be a hot day.

He kissed Sammy on the head and slowly sat up, pulling her to an upright position as well. "Don't worry, we'll find Jake. I know he's only six, but he's smart. I'm sure he hid away somewhere."

"Do you think so?" she asked.

"I know so. We're survivors in this family. You'll see. He'll be waiting for us when we get back there." Mike hated lying to his sister, but right now, lies were much easier than truths.

"Emma gave me this," she said, handing Mike a compass.

"Right," Mike replied, starting the motor. "Let's go find our brother."

*

A horn sounded from up ahead, and the lorry stuttered to a halt. It suddenly occurred to Lucy that she couldn't remember the last time she had heard any gunfire. Other vehicles pulled up behind and doors creaked and slammed. She could hear shouts and laughter over the wails and cries of the women in the lorry. A heavy bolt lifted, and the door swung open. Light flooded in, and the women near the door backed away from it like frightened animals. Four men stood with rifles aimed into the lorry, while two more ushered a large group of crying figures up a hastily erected step ladder.

"Fuckin' hell, were they the best you could find?" scoffed one of the men.

"They'll be alright for working the fields," laughed another.

"Too right. Waking up next to that'd give you nightmares," he said as laughter erupted from the others.

When the final woman stumbled into the lorry, the step ladder was removed and the door slammed shut again. The sound of chains clanged against the metal before vehicle doors banged shut. Two men, obviously the ranking 'officers' lit up cigarettes at the side of the trailer.

Lucy, Emma, Beth, and Sarah peered through the bullet holes and strained to listen to what they were saying.

"That's it. Fry and the Boss are going to be over the fucking moon. These crofters and fishermen, they knew how to fucking hoard, I'll give them that," said one of the men as he took a long drag on his cigarette.

"Oh my God!" whispered Beth, as the men continued talking.

"What?" asked Lucy.

"Fry...that fucking madman from down in Candleton."

"It can't be him," replied Emma. "He's dead."

"Did anyone ever make sure? Because it's a hell of a coincidence don't you think?"

"Oh shit!" said Emma and Lucy simultaneously.

"Did you find any juice, the trucks are running low?" asked one of the raiders.

"Red Diesel. Fucking gallons of the stuff," replied another.

"Sweet. Right, we'll get filled up, then head back. It's just past eleven now, we should be back at base by seven or eight."

"Like I said, we staked this area out well. Stick to the route and we'll be fine." Gordon McKeith had travelled throughout the highlands several weeks before, posing as a trader. All the time he had been cataloguing what each village had, how each village could be used to his advantage. Now came the harvest. Food, seeds, equipment, fuel, alcohol, building materials, women for the whore houses and for servitude, it was a bonanza, he would be a hero when he made his return, but more importantly, he would have status with Fry and The Don, and nothing was more important than that.

When the vehicles had refuelled and begun to roll again it was Sarah who spoke. "I don't know if this is of any use, but when they opened the doors I took a good look. I think we're on the road to Inverness."

"Great, anybody fancy a shopping trip? asked Beth"

"Screw this. We're getting out of here," Lucy said, turning to Sarah. "How long do you think before we reach Inverness?"

"Maybe forty minutes or so."

"Okay, listen, if we try and make a break for it in the open country, the ones they don't kill, they'll just round up. If we make a break for it in a city, they won't have the stomach for it."

"You don't know that," Sarah replied.

"Inverness will be swarming with RAMs, the cost of catching us will outweigh the benefits a thousand times over. They've got our supplies, getting killed for seventy or eighty women wouldn't make sense," she said, this time looking towards Emma and Beth who were following her every word.

"Wait a minute," Sarah said in a louder voice. Realising she had caught the attention of some of the other women, she continued in more hushed tones. "How do *we* survive the RAMs? More importantly, how do we break free in the first place?"

"If we're going to do this, we all need to be in it together," Lucy said as if it was the most natural thing in the world.

"Do what? In what together?" Sarah asked.

Lucy grabbed a strap dangling from the side of the container and got to her feet. Emma and Beth joined her. Sarah looked on confused, but eventually rose too.

"Ladies. Listen to me." The inside of the container became hushed. "Most of you know me. Most of you know how myself, Emma, and Beth came to be here." The women stayed quiet, their sobs and moans temporarily subdued. "We have just two choices. We either stay in this truck until it reaches its final destination - I can't even begin to tell you what a nightmare awaits us at the end of this journey - or we escape and make it back to our homes."

"What homes?" one of the women called out. "Th-They killed my husband, they set fire to my house," she said beginning to cry again. "What is there to go back to?"

The woman's teenage daughter wrapped her arms around her, to comfort herself as much as her mother.

Lucy couldn't see detail of the woman's face in the dark, but she could hear the pain in her voice. "You're right. What we'd be going back to is a big question mark at the moment. But we're a community. If nothing else, we have each other. If your house is turned to ashes, together we can build a new one. Whatever hardships lie ahead of us, let's face them together on our own terms."

"They stole our supplies. They took what little livestock we had," yet another frightened voice shouted out. "We'll starve to death if we go back."

This time Beth stepped forward. "We've got crops in the ground. There are fish in the sea. There's fruit in the forest. We can survive."

The hard voice of a middle-age woman broke through the dark. "What if we don't want to survive?"

Lucy took over again. "Then they've won. In your heart of hearts, if you think there's nothing left worth fighting for or if in some twisted way, you think you deserve this fate, then stay here." She held the strap up in her hand, "Or take one of these lashings, tie it around your neck and hang yourself now. But I know we need to fight. We need to find strength in each other, get back to our homes, and rebuild." She paused waiting for someone else to shout out, but nobody did. "You women talk among yourselves. This decision is yours and yours alone, but my friends and I are getting out of here, and you can come or you can stay. But whichever choice you make, you need to make it soon."

2

The fog had lifted fully by the time Mike steered the dinghy into shore. His little sister had been silent for most of the journey back. She was scared, she was worried about Jake, but most of all, she was confused. The intentions of adults were perplexing to youngsters. Mike looped the rope around a large black rock and helped his sister out. He took hold of her hand to reassure her as they walked back to the house. There was no sign of raiders or damage to the house. As he walked through the gate, he noticed that Daisy, his gran's goat, did not come rushing up to him as was her custom. In fact, there was no sign of Daisy at all. He let go of Sammy's hand and signalled for her to stay put as he stooped to remove his knife from its ankle holster. He quietly pushed down the handle on the door and allowed it to swing open. Deathly quiet greeted him from within. He searched the entire house, then went back to the door to collect his sister.

In the kitchen, the cupboards had been emptied.

Drawers had been pulled out and smashed on the tiled floor. There was not a grain of food left. Mike sat down on the corner of the table as he surveyed the damage. Sammy stood, tears welling in her eyes.

Mike could feel his blood boiling inside him. He could feel his hands beginning to tremble as rage consumed him. He took a long deep breath, clenched and unclenched his fists once, twice, three times. He had to control himself for Sammy's sake. He had to remain level headed. All he wanted to do was find the men who had done this and literally rip them limb from limb. That would come later though. He would get revenge for this. Taking his sister and Lucy...making Jake run...he would make them pay for all of it. But first of all, he needed to take back control.

He knelt down in front of his little sister, hugged her tightly, and then pulled back. "Listen to me, Sammy. I don't have a right to ask you this but... Right now, you're the only person I can rely on in the world. I know you're only eight, but you're more intelligent and capable than most adults I know. I've got a lot to do, and I need to know that if I ask you to do something, you'll do it. I need your help more than I've ever needed anybody's help in my life. Will you help me, Sammy?" She swallowed hard, fought back the threat of tears and nodded. He kissed her on the forehead and smiled. "I love you, Sammy. Never forget that. I love you more than you will ever know."

"What do you want me to do?"

"I need you to stay here and start tidying up. This is our home. We need a bit of order to it."

"I want to help find Jake," she said, beginning to get upset once again.

"Sammy, you'll be helping to find him by staying here. The only point of reference Jake has is this house. If he comes back here and finds us all gone, he's going to think we've abandoned him. I need you to stay here, so if he comes back, he won't go wandering off, okay?" Sammy nodded. "Now, I'm going to stay in sight of the road at all times, so if there are any of those men still around, I'll know and I'll come back, but just in case; if you hear any vehicles, go to the cupboard under the stairs and hide there." Sammy nodded once again and Mike smiled to reassure her.

He returned to his feet and headed out of the kitchen. His smile immediately turned to a menacing grimace.

Ever since they had arrived at his gran's house, Mike had been demanding that the villages should develop a defence strategy. He had been arguing constantly for some cohesive plan to deal with raiders, but everybody had called him paranoid. Time and time again they told him that no one would travel this far north to steal the few scraps they had. So, Mike had begun to make plans of his own. He had drawn up schemes for defending the entire stretch of coast but now it was too late for those whose lives had already been taken. What he was sure of, though, was that he would never let it happen again. No matter how few of them were left, no matter how much dissension he encountered, he would implement plans to fortify their stretch of coast.

In the bedroom, he moved the pine-framed, double bed to one side and peeled back the rug. He levered up a few ill-fitting floorboards revealing his rucksack. The rucksack had rarely been off his shoulder on the journey to Scotland. It had saved his life and the lives of his friends and family countless times, and now it was time to call on its services again.

He grabbed one of the straps and pulled it out of its resting place, replaced the floorboards and rug and then moved the bed back. He sat down for a moment looking at it, recalling the battles he had fought to get his family up here. Finally, he unzipped it. He pulled out a pump-action shotgun, a box of shells, and his preferred weapons, two machetes. How many RAMs had he killed with those? He flipped the rucksack onto his back like someone putting on his favourite jacket. He carefully positioned the machetes in a crisscross pattern, so he could get quick and easy access as well as a good degree of momentum when he withdrew them from the rucksack. Then he loaded the shotgun, put a few more shells in his pocket and the remainder of the box in the backpack.

He thought the raiders would be long gone by now, but if they weren't, he wasn't going to take any chances.

*

The lorry noticeably slowed as it negotiated the roundabout.

"Okay," said Sarah, leaning against the door. "About 200 yards and there's the other roundabout. That's where we need to make our move. As soon as we hit the ground, we head down into the city."

Lucy and Emma looked at each other. The plan was already set, they knew exactly what they were going to do. Emma pulled up Lucy's top and tore away the Glock pistol and spare magazine that had been taped to her back just underneath her bra. Lucy did the same for Emma. Neither winced as the thick gluey plastic peeled off their skin. Their minds were somewhere else now.

"This is it," said Lucy in a louder voice to the rest of the women. "Remember, follow Sarah and Beth, we're heading to the Home and Garden Depot on Bridge street."

The women closest to them who could just make out what was going on in the dim light suddenly understood. Up until this point, the escape plan had been just a fantastical plot, Lucy and Emma had not shared the finer details, just in case the lorry had stopped at any moment and an interrogation had taken place. Now though, just seconds away from the plan going into action, a more positive feeling in the lorry became palpable.

Beth crouched down and raised her trouser leg. She pulled out a hunting knife, readjusted her trousers and rose to her feet. "Your brother taught me everything I know," she said to Emma with a smile.

"Let's hope he taught you enough."

The lorry began to slow again.

"Now!" Lucy shouted as Sarah pushed hard

against the doors. Lucy fired four deafening rounds through the thin metal shattering the bolt on the other side. Both doors budged six inches as Sarah continued to push against them, just enough for Lucy to see the thick chain, sealing them in the container compartment. Despite the jerky motion of the vehicle, Lucy took careful aim and shot two more rounds, shattering the heavy iron links. Sarah quickly pushed the doors open wide.

It all happened in a matter of seconds. At first, the driver and passenger of the truck full of raiders behind them couldn't comprehend what was happening, but as the doors swung open revealing a woman down on one knee and carefully aiming a gun in their direction, it became clear. Lucy fired four rounds and both men were dead before they could so much as duck. The heavy green army truck veered, hit a crash barrier and then turned the other way sharply. The momentum proved too much for the change in direction and it toppled over. The vehicles behind had little time to react and began to pile up with deafening crunches and shrieks of tearing metal. The lorry they were travelling in kept going for a few seconds more before jerking to a sudden stop.

Lucy and Emma peeked out of the doors and realised they hadn't crossed the roundabout, they were actually on it. The doors of the cab opened and closed as the driver and passenger got out. The engine was left running in case they needed to make a quick getaway. They had heard the shots, but they were at a loss as to where they had come from. They had their rifles at the ready and scoured roadside shrubbery looking for an ambush, desperately trying to understand what had caused the carnage that was still amassing behind them. Other vehicles in the convoy began to slow and stop as they too became aware of the unfolding destruction.

"You see anything?" shouted the driver as he walked down one side of the lorry while his passenger walked down the other.

"Nothing," the other replied.

"Change of plan," said Lucy, just loud enough to be heard. "We're going to take the lorry. Em, take the passenger, I'll take the driver. Beth, Sarah, as soon as we're out, close these doors and get everyone down on the ground. Tie them together or something until we get where we're going. We're going to sustain a lot of fire." Before anyone had a chance to discuss it, the two women had jumped down to the tarmac. They looked at each other as they took positions at their respective corners, then Lucy mouthed, "Now".

Neither of the raiders were looking in their direction and both were down before anyone even registered the sound of the shot. The two women heard the doors slam shut. Men from the vehicles up ahead ducked as they saw the two men fall. Because Lucy and Emma were crouched low, they could not see them, and like their fellow raiders, they thought the attack was coming from the roadside. Lucy and Emma heard frightened shouts as more and more raiders dismounted from the vehicles ahead of them. The two women used the underbelly of the lorry to creep along out of sight.

Suddenly, there was a huge explosion from

behind. "Get down," screeched one of the raiders as searing heat washed over the convoy.

"The fucking diesel," shouted another as a bigger eruption sounded.

Lucy and Emma instinctively covered their heads as they heard debris hitting the roof of the lorry and scattering over the road beside them.

Lucy yelled over the noise. "This is our chance!"

The doctor scrambled further up the underneath of the lorry, hoping Emma would do the same. As they reached the cab, they quickly rolled out, opened the door and dived in. While the raiders were still covering their heads on the ground, Lucy crunched the gear stick into first, pulled off the handbrake, and the lorry juddered off the roundabout and down the hill towards Inverness.

Gordon McKeith was in the front vehicle, he had been leading the convoy home to a victorious welcome, but now, the convoy of fifty vehicles carrying, men, fuel and supplies had been reduced to less than fifteen vehicles and one burning mass of torment for any human caught in it. He had not cowered as the diesel had exploded, he had just watched in disbelief. It took him a moment to understand what was happening, when one of his lorries, the one carrying all the women they had collected for the men's entertainment, veered off the roundabout. But then as he focussed, he saw a woman with long brown hair in the passenger seat, frantically looking around, searching for any potential danger.

His blood began to simmer through his veins as he watched the lorry chug away, and the cowards he had brought with him, still on the floor covering their heads.

He heard one of his lieutenant's shout "The women are escaping!" then too slowly, rifles were raised and shots were fired. He looked down to where the women were heading, the streets were moving. Dozens, then hundreds of undead were pouring onto them. The explosions acting like a chorus of echoing dinner bells, telling them food was abound.

McKeith realised what he had to do - run.

He could not go back now. He would be publicly executed for such a colossal fuck up. The best he could do was run and hide. He would find a small corner where no one knew him, somewhere he could live out his days. He turned and walked back to the Land Rover.

"Are we going after them, Gord?" asked his passenger as he emerged from cover behind the Land Rover.

McKeith just looked at him blankly and climbed back into the car. The passenger was about to do the same, but the Land Rover's tyres screeched and it tore away, quickly blazing a trail into the distance. The man stood there bemused for a moment, then realised, he had been left in charge. He looked towards the lorry as it headed towards the masses of RAMs crowding the streets, then looked towards the men and what remained of the convoy.

"They're finished, Diesel's pouring out of that

thing," he shouted down the line as the raiders looked towards dozens, then hundreds of massing RAMs with more and more unease. "Let's get in our vehicles and go."

He walked down to the transit van, which had been the second vehicle in the convoy and commandeered the passenger seat. The driver nervously climbed in and watched through his mirror as the other raiders quickly returned to their vehicles. Two more explosions sounded, as wagons carrying red diesel in unprotected plastic containers ignited. He looked beyond the men to the huge plumes of black smoke rising from the wreckage behind, then engaged first gear and moved off. There was a feeling of dread in his stomach.

*

Mike climbed the craggy hill above the main road to Lonbaig. The cairn at the top was Sammy and Jake's not so secret den. He stood on top of a rock and surveyed as far as he could, looking south towards the village he saw smoke rising. He turned to the north and saw more plumes.

"Jake!" he shouted at the top of his voice. "Jakey!" he yelled again.

He stood still barely breathing, just listening for a response. He turned 360 degrees, hoping to see movement, hoping to see anything but the smoke plumes that signalled destruction. Mike climbed down from the rock and slumped onto a mound of dry earth. He sat there looking out over the calm sea.

Just the day before, he and Lucy had snuck away to one of the many small sandy beaches. They had made love in the afternoon sun and then gone for a swim in the bracing water. They had held hands, watching this same sea, marvelling at how lucky they were. And now...and now that familiar feeling was back with him. That dread that lurked in the pit of his stomach; would he ever see her again? He hadn't seen what the raiders had done first hand yet, but the smoke plumes gave him a sense of what lay in Lonbaig and the other small villages and enclaves. His instinct was always to fight. Even in this case, he would have charged in.

The raiders were nothing if not pragmatic. Male villagers were unlikely to be of their persuasion, so it made more sense to kill them rather than to try and recruit them. Females were like a currency. They would be kept alive for...

Mike broke off his thoughts. He didn't want to think about what they would be kept alive for.

He leant forward, resting his elbows on his knees. Lucy and Emma had made sure he survived for a reason; the first one being to protect the family. Before he could do that, he needed to find Jake. He was just about to stand up when a sharp pain stabbed him in the back. He jerked around quickly and found himself face to face with a vicious beast.

"For fuck's sake Daisy!" he said to the goat as he began rubbing his kidneys. "All the fucking people who come in and out of Gran's place, you lick their hands and let them stroke you, but me... If you're not fucking biting

22

me, you're trying to gore me!" Daisy just stood there, eye to eye with Mike, slowly rotating her jaw, as she munched a succulent mouthful of grass. She paused for a second in mid-chew and then barged Mike again. He scrambled to his feet and let out a big sigh.

"It's a good job I'm a vegetarian you little bastard, otherwise I'd have you on a spit."

Daisy let out an angry bleat and began to trudge away. Mike noticed the rope she dragged behind her. He looked at the end of it. It had not been cut or chewed, so somebody had taken the time to untie her. He picked up the end of it and tugged, trying to get her to change direction so that he could get her back down the hill, but she was stubborn. He tugged a little harder, but she kept walking.

Despite his differences with the goat, he quickly developed the feeling that she was trying to show him something. He allowed himself to be led. They walked a short way over scrubland and heather. Daisy stopped dead in her tracks and bent down to chomp another tuft of grass. She stood there chewing, and Mike began to wonder if this had just been another power play by the goat to prove to him who was boss, when he saw something turquoise between two branches of a thick bush. He dropped the rope and walked across to find Jake just sitting there, eyes staring wide into the distance, dried tear stains on his cheeks. Cuts and scratches scarred his face, arms and legs as if he had been crawling through brambles.

"Jakey... Jake?"

There was no response. Mike reached out and touched his brother's arm. There was still no reaction.

"Jake. Jake, look at me!" The young boy just continued to stare into the distance. "Jake!" Mike yelled this time, but to no avail.

Mike knelt down and snapped his fingers in front of Jake's eyes. Nothing. He looked across towards Daisy who was in the same spot, still chewing happily.

Mike let out another heavy sigh and got to his feet. His muscles flexed as he pulled his younger brother up and positioned him over his shoulder like he weighed no more than a bag of flour. He walked across to the goat and carefully bent down to take hold of the rope, making sure he didn't lose his balance.

"Maybe you're not so bad after all girl," he said to her as the three of them began to make their way back down the   hillside.

3

"Deja vu anyone?" Lucy asked as she took a corner at speed to avoid ploughing into a horde of charging RAMs. The wheels screeched and she and Emma heard muffled screams as the lorry nearly tipped. "I think they took out a tyre, or maybe two. This isn't handling like it should." She looked at the wing mirror and saw the army of creatures in pursuit. "Shit! Look at the gauge. I think they got the tank too," she said as they squawked around another bend. Just then, a red warning light flashed on the dashboard. "You've got to be kidding me?" said Lucy, as the oil light started flickering.

"Over there, Lucy. The industrial estate," Emma said, pointing. "Do you think we can lose them?"

"I'll give it my best shot, sweetie," she said, ramming the gear stick into third and flooring the accelerator.

The engine rumbled as the lorry hurtled down

the street. Emma could see the struggle Lucy was having to hold the wheel straight as the flattened tyres dragged the vehicle. They took another bend, and then a sharp right. Lucy checked the mirror again, they had lost them for the time being, but she wouldn't be happy until they had found somewhere to hide. The lorry was becoming harder to steer by the second and the fuel wouldn't last more than a few minutes before it ran dry.

"Didn't Sarah mention the Home and Garden Depot?" Emma asked.

"Why?"

"That's it, there?"

Lucy looked at the fuel gauge again. The dial was on red. She turned onto the industrial estate that Emma had seen and passed the entrance to the huge DIY centre.

"What're you doing?" cried Emma.

"We don't want to park where we can be seen from the road. Not by those things or anyone else," she said as they passed a sign for delivery vehicles.

The engine began to splutter just as the lorry navigated its way around a corner and into a huge loading bay. It barked one final cough before cutting out forever and the large white vehicle stuttered to its final resting place. Lucy let out a deep breath. Perspiration dotted her forehead.

"Nice work," Emma said as she looked around the desolate loading bay. She began to get out, but Lucy grabbed hold of her arm.

"Listen to me. This is down to us. You and me. We're going to get back home. We're going to get these women back home, but we need to be smart and we need to be strong. They're scared, and they'll believe it's all hopeless. We've got to show them it's not." She looked at Emma's face and saw a glint of unease. "Sweetie, we've been here before, and we thought taking our own lives was the way out. It wasn't. The way out was fighting, fighting and not giving up. From now on, when we're in a tight situation, we've got to ask ourselves WWMD?"

"What's WWMD?"

"What would Mike do?" she replied with a smirk. Emma let out a small giggle. "We've got to get back to him, Emma," Lucy said more seriously this time. "I have to see him again. I have to tell him I'm sorry."

Emma took hold of Lucy's hand. "If you hadn't done what you did, he'd be dead now. He's the most hot-headed person I know, but he's not dense. He'll realise what you did was to save him."

"That's sweet of you to say. But I need to make it right." For a moment, Lucy felt the urge to cry, but she quickly gained control. "Come on, we need to get inside and get safe."

The pair climbed out of the cab and headed to the doors of the container. Emma lifted the bolt and daylight rushed into the lorry, revealing seventy-five terrified women.

"Listen," Lucy said, bringing the frightened mutterings to a halt. "We need to get inside quickly; we're too exposed outside. Stay quiet, do as we say, and you'll be fine."

She nodded to Beth and Sarah who immediately climbed down and began to help the other women while Emma and Lucy climbed up onto the loading dock to look for a way in. There was a small frosted glass window towards the end of the dock. It was six feet off the ground, but there were plenty of discarded materials around to build some makeshift steps.

Emma stacked a couple of boxes and climbed up to it. She held up three pieces of thick cardboard to the glass and punched hard. "Fucking bastard," she yelled as she cradled her fist in her other hand. The glass remained unblemished, as she grimaced and tried to numb the pain.

Lucy ran back to the cab of the lorry and looked underneath the driver's seat. There was a large, grimy crowbar laying on the carpet. She grabbed it, climbed back onto the loading dock and ran to where Emma was still shielding her hurt knuckles.

"Move sweetie," she said as she swung the heavy black tool. The glass splintered but did not shatter as she anticipated. "It must be reinforced," she said taking subsequent swings.

Eventually, it caved, and Lucy reached in to release the catch and lift the window open. She brushed the shards away and climbed inside. Emma climbed in after her, still grunting from the pain of her hand.

Beth and Sarah had got all the women out of the lorry and were helping the final few up onto the loading dock. They walked past the enormous padlocked roller shutters to the small opening that Lucy had created.

Lucy and Emma looked around the dimly lit storeroom as the first of the women began to climb in. Most of the racking was empty except for a few boxes of till rolls and some old EPOS terminals. As they headed into the room, further away from the source of light the small window provided, they instinctively withdrew their weapons. The room was narrow but long, and if this had been just a stationery cupboard as the last remnants on the shelves suggested, it gave an indication as to how big and busy the DIY superstore must have been before commerce came to a grinding halt.

The pair paused at the door looking towards each other in the dimness.

"That's everybody in," called Beth as she climbed through the window and down onto the sturdy plastic crates below.

"Remember, stay quiet, and follow our lead," said Emma as Lucy turned the handle to the door.

The pair headed through the opening simultaneously, each raising their weapons to shoulder height. The sun's rays poured through the huge skylights of the silent warehouse. They advanced, keeping a careful watch for movement. They headed through the heavy plastic doors and onto the shop floor, pausing to make sure all the women were still following. Beth was the last through. She was carrying the crowbar and had it held high ready for action. The group slowly moved towards the front of the store, scanning their surroundings, alert for any sight or sound that seemed out of place. They reached the tills.

"Drop your fucking weapons!" roared a gruff voice as armed men in military uniforms sprang up from behind the cash desk.

More rose from behind the customer service desk, then the sound of running feet heralded the arrival of more still. The women were completely surrounded and some began to scream uncontrollably. Lucy's face flared, neither she nor Emma lowered their guns.

"I said drop your fucking weapons!" the voice shouted again. This time its owner walked forward. A tall, muscular figure pointed his rifle directly at Lucy. "I won't tell you again."

Emma and Lucy lowered their weapons and carefully placed them down on the floor. Two men broke rank and went to collect them while the rest of the rifles stayed aimed at the group.

"Stop your fucking caterwauling as well, otherwise I'll stop it for you," he shouted, and immediately the terrified screams turned to confused and muffled sobs.

"Who are you people?" Lucy demanded.

"We're your absolute worst fucking nightmare," replied the man.

*

Mike had taken Jake back to the house and carried him up to bed. He explained to Sammy that their little brother was in shock, and she needed to stay with him in case he came around, while he went into the village to look for survivors. He hated the thought of leaving them, but he had no option.

His original plan had been to drive down in his gran's camper van, but on finding it completely siphoned of fuel, he ended up taking a bicycle. The last thing he wanted was to go on a seven-mile bike ride, but in the absence of all other transport, he didn't really have an option. The black smoke hadn't abated since he first saw it. He hoped there were survivors. He hoped he could find some clue as to where the raiders had taken Lucy, Emma and the others, and he really hoped he could find some motorised transport. After fifteen minutes of cycling flat out, he arrived at the outlying houses of the village. Doors had been kicked in and he saw two lifeless bodies lying face down on a lawn. He dismounted and walked across to them.

They had been shot in the back of their heads. He lifted the face of one to see it was his gran's friend, Dean Marsh, a sixty-five-year-old retired English teacher who suffered crippling arthritis.

What kind of cowards were these raiders?

Mike's stomach turned in disgust. He stood and walked back to his bicycle. As he advanced further down the road, he saw the old post office in flames. The building had been standing over two hundred years, and within a few hours, it had been consumed by the treacherous deeds of these lowlifes. As he approached the village hall, he climbed off the bike and withdrew his shotgun.

"Hello!" he yelled at the top of his voice.

He waited for something, for anything; a sound, a movement. But nothing came. He walked up to the entrance. The safety glass had been booted in, the posters taped to the back of it, shredded by the splinters. He pushed the door open and walked inside. His trainers squeaked on the varnished floor.

"Hello!" he shouted again, but again he was greeted with silence.

He looked around. Plastic chairs had been toppled over and doors to adjacent rooms broken in as the raiders hunted for anything they could use, anything they could loot. He pulled one of the plastic chairs to its feet and slumped into it. He slid the rucksack from his back and carefully placed the shotgun down in front of him.

Mike sat forward, resting his elbows on his thighs and placing his face into his hands. He felt helpless. The soldiers, his gran and his friends were whereabouts unknown, the village that was their home, their safe haven had been decimated. His brother was catatonic but worse than all of that, Lucy and Emma had been taken. Mike knew what happened to women when they were taken, it was something he did not want to think about, but the circumstances dictated he must.

The despair fluttered inside him for several minutes, but then the despair turned to something else. Something familiar, something frightening, something powerful. Over the past few weeks, he had grown complacent, he had grown comfortable. Life was good, he was with a woman he loved and his family had been safe, his complacency had softened him, but now rage was beginning to simmer.

He jumped to his feet and picked up the chair, flinging it with all his might across the hall. Its legs broke through the safety glass at the top of the entrance door and it stuck there frozen, like a piece of modern art. He flung the rucksack back over his shoulder and picked the shotgun up, pumping it violently. He didn't know how he was going to do it, but he knew that he would not stop until Lucy and Emma were with him again.

He began to march back out into the morning sun when he heard a muffled thud from behind him. He jerked around and raised the shotgun. He slowly headed back into the hall. It sounded like it had come from the back, near the stage.

"Hello?" he shouted. He lowered his weapon.

If there was someone hiding, it wasn't going to be a raider. He listened carefully, but there was no further sound.

"It's Mike. Mike Fletcher. I'm by myself, the raiders have gone. Is there anybody in here?"

A black wooden panel fell forward from the side

of the stage and a figure stumbled out. It was Ruth. She looked bedraggled and worried lines streaked her face, but there were no signs of tears.

"Oh, Mike," she said, rushing forward with open arms.

The pair hugged tightly. It was an unusual friendship that had started when Mike had broken into her library in the North Yorkshire market town of Skelton. Despite an awkward start, Mike had taken a liking to Ruth and her two colleagues, Richard and David. They were all quirky and socially inept, but he had a sense for understanding good and bad and these people were definitely good, kind, and decent. As they hugged, Mike saw more people emerging from the cramped conditions underneath the stage. Richard and David came out next, followed by Dora, one of the deaf girls from Sarah's school. She was holding hands with a fellow pupil and formed a chain of eight as they all clutched each other hard, frightened to face the outside world alone. Next to come out were Beth's siblings, Annie and John, and then eleven more children Mike had seen in the village, but couldn't put names to.

Ruth broke the embrace, and she looked at Mike's face. "Where's your family?"

Mike broke eye contact and looked down. He exhaled deeply and then told her. By the time he had finished the story and Dora, who was the only one of the children who could lip-read had translated it for the others, he was back in Ruth's arms. As awkward as she was with relationships she felt a motherly bond with Mike which neither understood, but both were grateful for.

Mike pulled away. "They've taken everything by the looks of it. Food, fuel... anything they could get their hands on. You need to come back to the house with me. We've still got Daisy, she can provide milk. We've got the boat," he said turning to Richard and David. "You two can catch fish. There are mussels on the rocks down at the shore and there's food in the forest you can forage. I didn't check Gran's polytunnel, they might not have got down to that. You can't see it from the house."

"Don't you mean, we, Mike? You keep saying you. Don't you mean we?" Ruth asked.

"I've got to find them, Ruth. I need to get them back."

"Mike, that's insanity," almost dismissing what he said. "There were hundreds of those men, all heavily armed. It would be suicide."

"I don't need to go to war with them, Ruth. But if I can track them down, I might be able to figure a way of getting our people back."

Ruth brushed her hands over her face as if trying to wash away a waking dream. "Dear God Mike, you need to think about this. Sammy and Jake need you. We need you!" Her plea fell on deaf ears; he had already made up his mind. "At least wait until your gran and the soldiers come back... please Mike. I don't think you've had time to think it through." She looked at him, desperately trying to catch his eye, but he was staring beyond her and into the future. The next time she spoke, she sounded like a school teacher telling off a pupil. "I mean, honestly, what are you thinking? How can you possibly go after these people? You've already said all the fuel's gone. You need to stay here, wait until the yacht returns, and then form a plan with Hughes, Barnes, and Shaw."

"Ruth. We don't know when they'll be back. The only hope I have is trying to find a vehicle that still has some fuel in it and head out now. I need to try and pick up a trail while there still is one. I know which road they took, and that's something. A slim chance is better than no chance at all."

Ruth let out a deep sigh. She knew it would be impossible to try and talk Mike out of going after his sister and Lucy. "But how Mike? How can you go after them if you've got no means of transportation?"

Mike's shoulders sagged. He knew that was the single biggest problem. His best intentions meant nothing without a viable vehicle.

"What about Angus Macdonald?" Richard, one of the other former librarians, said, stepping forward.

"Who?" Mike replied.

"Angus Macdonald. I bet the raiders didn't get as far as him. There's a dirt track to his place that runs at the back of the campsite. He doesn't even have a water main. He's got his own well. He's a funny old sort, cantankerous, swears like a drunken sailor, but I take him books once a week, and we seem to get on.

"Does he have a vehicle, Richard?" Mike asked, not interested in the old man's biography.

"I think he has just what you're looking for, Mike."

Within minutes, Mike and Richard were heading up the track behind the campsite. Mike had given instructions to Ruth and David, and the small group were heading out of the village, the older ones, protecting the younger ones from the horrifying sights where ever they could. Most of the children were traumatised, but Ruth and David had spent the last few weeks working closely with all of them as their teachers. A bond of trust had built up and given them all a stability which many of them had lacked in their lives before the disaster.

"Let me do the talking Mike," Richard said with uncharacteristic authority in his voice. "He can be difficult, but he's a good man. I just don't want you to rub him up the wrong way."

Mike smiled to himself. A few weeks before when they had first met, Richard had been scared of Mike. It reassured him to realise that he had grown in confidence. He had lost weight and grown a goatee. The man had come into his own, and all it took was the apocalypse.

After half a mile or so, the pair reached a clearing in the heavily wooded surrounds, Angus was already in the garden. He was sitting in his wheelchair with a book on his knee trying to fight off the need to nap. As Richard creaked open the wrought iron gate, Angus jerked his head up in surprise. "What the fuck are you doing here? You only came yesterday. And who the fuck's that with you?" he said in a slurry voice.

"Hello, Angus," Richard replied.

"Hello, Angus, hello, Angus. I can never get any fucking peace around here. If it's not her jabbering away, there's always some bastard coming up from the fucking village wanting something or other."

"Angus, pipe down," Richard demanded. "Listen, where's Christina?"

"What do you want to speak to her for?" the old man asked.

"I need to speak to both of you, urgently. Now where is she?"

"She's in the house somewhere, probably concocting some foul-smelling stew to poison me." He turned his head towards the doorway. "Christina?" he shouted but to no response. "Christina?" he shouted again, but still to no avail. "Christina, we've got fucking visitors," he yelled one final time before beginning to cough violently. "She's probably got her hearing aid turned off again. She keeps doing that. Tells me nothing I say is worth listening to anyway."

A much younger looking woman stepped from the doorway out into the beating sun. She was drying her hands on a tea towel and smiled at the two visitors despite only recognising one of them. Angus was still coughing as she came out. She looked towards him and just rolled her eyes.

"Hi, Richard, who's this with you?" she asked.

"Hello, Christina. This is Mike Fletcher, a friend of mine. Listen, something terrible has happened."

Angus brought his coughing under control and looked towards Richard with a serious expression on his face. Christina stopped drying her hands and froze. Neither of them had known Richard a long time, but they knew he was not one for hyperbole. If he said something serious had happened, then it had.

Richard laid out the full story for them. By the time he had finished, Christina had flopped down on the doorstep, her legs too weak to take her weight.

"All dead you say?" Angus said distantly, wishing he could disbelieve what he had been told, but knowing it was true. "My brother. My brother Calum. him too?"

"I don't know, Angus, but we haven't seen any other survivors," Richard said. "I don't know how you managed to miss it. The noise was..." He looked towards Christina and her hearing aid, then to Angus, who had aged ten years in a matter of minutes, and he broke off.

"I'm sorry for your loss," Mike said, interrupting the mourning that had already begun behind the old man's eyes, "but I really need your help."

The old man looked up at him. "How on earth could I help you?" he asked in a much softer voice now, gesturing towards his wheelchair.

"Richard told you they kidnapped nearly all the women who could be of use to them...well I need to find them. I need transport," Mike said, not breaking eye contact with Angus.

"And what will you do when you find them?"

"Whatever I have to, to get them back."

Mike expected the old man to scoff at him, to dismiss him, but instead, he turned his head to the doorway. "Christina, take Richard and this laddie to the garage. Give them whatever they need."

"Do you mean..," she began.

"Whatever they need," Angus interrupted.

The three of them headed around the house to the large double garage. Inside there were two cars and a motorbike with a tarpaulin carefully draped over it. Mike peeled back the cover to reveal a black motorcycle, it looked like it had never been used. "Wow!" he said looking at the Kawasaki Ninja ZX-14 and almost salivating. "This belonged to Angus?" his voice rising in disbelief as he reached the end of the question.

"It was going to be a present for our grandson on his twenty-first birthday, but he got killed by a drunk driver a week before," she said, summoning strength from within to endure the painful memory.

"Your grandson? You and Angus are man and

wife?"

"Yes. Why?" she asked a little puzzled.

"I just thought you were his carer or daughter or something," he replied.

"You seem like a pleasant young man, so I won't pass that on to Angus, but let's just say the years have been kinder to me than to him," she said with the beginning of a smile on her face.

"He really won't mind if I use this? I mean with it holding so much sentimental value."

"Angus doesn't say things he doesn't mean," she replied turning to Richard. "It sounds like you could use a vehicle as well. And some food. If you wouldn't mind giving me a hand, I'm sure we can find some new potatoes and a few other bits ready for harvesting."

"Go ahead Richard, I'll make my way down and tell Ruth what's going on before I set off," he said.

"You're going now?"

"The sooner I set off, the more chance I have of finding them. Look after everybody Richard, and thank you, Christina." The woman looked down sadly. The young man's bravado did not affect her like it had her husband. She firmly believed, they would never see him or the bike again.

*

Within just a few minutes, Mike had thanked Angus and set off. He had caught up with the group walking the seven miles to his gran's house and explained that Richard would be along directly and would ferry them in the 4 x 4. He had thanked Ruth for taking charge, and they had hugged before he gave David a lift to the cottage.

When they arrived, Jake was still catatonic and Sammy was talking to him softly, having placed a wet face cloth on his head.

"How is he, Sammy?" Mike whispered.

She brushed away a tear from the corner of her eye, sniffed and said, "he's still the same."

"Come with me a second," he replied, taking hold of Sammy's hand and leading her out of the room, while David took over sitting vigil. He gave a child-friendly account of what he had seen and explained that Ruth and the children were heading to the house. He then went on to tell her his plan. When he had finished, he paused, waiting for her to start crying or screaming.

"Promise me you'll bring them back," she said calmly.

He knelt down and placed his hands on her shoulders. He looked into his little sister's eyes and saw his own. This was one of those times in life when trying was not enough. This was a time for doing. He took a deep breath. "Sammy, I promise you, I will bring them back."

4

More and more figures assembled around them pointing rifles in their direction. The tall man with the gruff voice dragged Lucy and Emma from the rest of the group and marched them away. Two other men, their weapons trained on the women, followed them.

Emma and Lucy had a sinking feeling in their stomachs. They had made a dramatic escape from their captors only to wind up captive again, but this time, they had no escape plan.

"Where are you taking us?" Emma demanded.

"Shut up and keep walking," said the tall man as he pushed Lucy through a door. The sign read staff only, and as soon as they walked through, darkness enveloped them in the narrow corridor. The two women gulped. They were pushed through another door and one of the soldiers flicked a torch on revealing a staircase. Although Lucy's impulse was to fight and flee, that wasn't a realistic option. She might be able to save herself and even Emma, but what of the women downstairs? They ascended the steps and then went through another door which led into a large brightly lit room. The windows looked out into the loading bay, which explained why their break-in had not been a surprise.

"Keep walking," barked the gruff man as they headed towards another door at the far end of the room.

Emma thought about Mike, how she wished he was here with her now. Then she thought about how his life had taken on new meaning with Lucy, how he had begun to change because of her. She stopped walking. "Look, let her go, you can do what you want with me, but let her go." Lucy reached out and dug her fingers into Emma's arm.

"I said keep walking," the man shouted this time and poked both of them in the back with the muzzle of his rifle.

Emma span round in a fury, and grabbed a tight hold of the rifle before the gruff man even had time to react. She swung her fist hard, knocking him off his feet. Blood exploded from his nose and lip simultaneously as a look of pure shock swept over his face. Not wanting to lose the impetus, she leapt on top of him and began pounding away at his face, unafraid of what consequences awaited her.

Lucy immediately ducked, grabbing her knife from its ankle holster. She stayed low and lurched towards one of the other men, sinking the blade into his thigh causing him to scream like a hurt child. The third man, who looked very young, panicked; he fumbled with his weapon, pointed at one woman and then the other, then lowered it again. The facade of being a tough guy no longer one he wanted to maintain.

"Jules, Jules," he yelled again, almost crying this time. The door at the end of the large room burst open and four men and four women all wearing military uniforms came running out, pointing their sidearms at the skirmishing figures.

Lucy withdrew the blade from the man's thigh and pivoted around, clutching the knife to his neck and taking hold of the rifle pointing it in the general direction of the approaching group.

"Drop your weapons or he buys it, followed by one of you," she barked.

"Jesus fucking Christ!" blurted the woman leading the group. "Lower your weapons," she ordered the others, who obeyed straight away. "Do you mind taking the knife from my brother's throat please?" she asked politely. Her voice had an Irish lilt, and in the space of a couple of sentences had gone from being authoritative to placating.

"Your brother?" Lucy and Emma were both taken aback. They had expected the worse when they had been led away by the three men. They had expected to be raped and tortured, but seeing the assembled group, half men, half women and more conciliatory than aggressive, they were puzzled. "Who are you people and what do you want with us?"

"We don't want anything with you other than to find out why you broke into our place and get you the f— get you out of here," the woman replied. "Now, please take the knife from my brother's throat."

Lucy felt the frightened breathing of the man she was holding at knifepoint. She looked around at the faces behind the Irish woman. Some were older, much older. These weren't raiders, they were survivors. She decided to take a calculated risk. She reached down to the man's belt and unbuckled it.

"What are you doing?" he screamed, terrified this American psycho was going to torture him further.

Lucy looked towards the leader of the group. "Do you have any bandages or medical supplies? I need to see to his wound before he loses too much blood."

"You're a doctor?" the woman asked, amazed.

Lucy nodded while helping the young man onto the floor. She took off the belt and carefully removed his trousers as he let out a whimper. She wrapped the belt around his leg above the wound to stem the flow of blood. "The cut's not too deep, I didn't hit anything major, but I'm going to need to suture it."

"Get her what she needs," the woman said to the others in the group as the room sprang into a hive of activity. She looked towards the unconscious figure with the pummelled face. "And can someone see to Andy?" she asked, looking to one of the older women. "In the meantime, please come with me," she said directly to Emma. "Nice work you did on my brother."

"That was Lucy, not me, and anyway, he had it coming. He was lucky to get away with just a cut," Emma said not feeling the need to justify their actions.

"Not him, the other one," she gestured back to the battered unconscious figure who was being dragged across the floor for Lucy to look at after she had attended to her own victim.

"How many brothers have you got?"

"Three, the third is the one who screamed like a girl when you took out the other two," she replied.

"You must be so proud," Emma said with a smirk.

"You have any brothers?"

"Two."

"I'm guessing you love them more than anything, but that doesn't stop them from being a constant pain in the fuckin' tits."

"One of them's only six and he's adorable, but it sounds like you've already met the other... My name's Emma," she said extending a hand as they entered the office from where the group had emerged.

"Aren't we fucking formal now," smiled the

woman extending her hand and curtseying. "Delighted to meet you, Emma, my name's Julia, but everyone calls me Jules," she said in an affected English accent before falling back into her friendly Belfast one. "So, do you mind telling me, who the fuck are you? And what the fuck are you doing here?"

Like Lucy, Emma got an immediate sense that these people weren't a threat and that they were just like them, floundering in a world that had gone to hell. She told Jules a potted version of the entire story, right from the outset in Leeds up to breaking into the store. Towards the end, Lucy had come into the office to join her, escorted by an older woman who remained by the door, as if on guard.

"Fuck me," Jules said as Emma finished. "It sounds like you've been through the mill and then some."

Emma and Lucy nodded. "What about you?" Lucy asked. "Were you conscripts?" she asked nodding towards the uniform.

"Fuck, no," Jules replied. "Well, a few of the blokes were. I was the deputy manager of this place, and for some reason completely fuckin' beyond me, everybody thought that was a good enough reason to elect me to be the group leader." She pinched the cloth of her shirt. "The togs and the guns we got from a quartermaster's depot just out of town. That was back when we still had fuel for the vans."

"You didn't think about trying to get out of the city?" Emma asked.

"We thought about it, but we were finding more people every day. There were a lot of innocents just trapped in Inverness, desperately trying to survive. We found them and took them in. We made a conscious decision to give it a week and then head out, maybe up to Wick or Thurso. But then things went from shit to fuckin' shit. A group was out scavenging when they got hit by a party of raiders. A few made it back, but some of them were badly injured. The night after that, we found that one of the women we had brought in had died in her sleep and turned. She must have been bitten or scratched or something." She looked away from the two women mournfully. "Fuckin stupid. I should have made sure everybody we brought in was checked for bites and scratches." She looked up towards Lucy and Emma. "Just so you know, we'll be checking you and everyone downstairs if you stay." She looked away again. "Anyways, you can imagine what happened. More than a dozen of us were attacked and turned before we got it under control."

Jules looked away and gulped hard. Emma and Lucy both said nothing but felt terrible for the woman and her group.

"We thought, surely things can only get better," continued Jules. "Then three nights ago we got attacked by fucking rats. Rats can you believe? Thousands of the little brown fuckers." She looked back towards the two women. "Y'know, you see a man you care for get bitten and come back to life, only to take a bite out of someone else. You think you're never going to see anything more horrific. But let me tell you, watching a friend get picked clean by an army of fuckin' ridden, shit eating rodents is an image that will haunt me until the day I die."

She paused and the room fell silent. "How did you get rid of them?" Emma asked, wincing as she remembered back to an episode she and Mike had encountered in Skelton involving a massive horde of vicious rats.

Jules maintained her silence for a moment and then continued. "One thing we're not short of here is household goods. One of my brothers, as fucking stupid as he is, had the idea to use aerosols as flame throwers. Fuckin' idiot nearly blew one of his friend's hands off with one of those ten years ago. Who'd have thought the same thing would have saved us that night? We managed to beat them back, but they've come every night since. Not in the same numbers, and they haven't killed anyone else, but some have been bitten and fallen ill." Her eyes were heavy as she looked at the two women. "I don't know how much longer we're going to be able to survive."

"You've still got guns, don't you think it's at least worth trying to make a break for it?" Lucy asked.

"A, we've got hardly any bullets for the guns, they're mainly for show, and B, weren't you fuckin' listening? We've got too many sick people now."

Emma was now the one who looked distant due to something Jules had said. "The people who were bitten by the rats. Where are they?"

"They're in one of the meeting rooms with the rest of the sick and injured, why?"

"When Mike and I were in Skelton, we came across rats that attacked the RAMs." Emma immediately saw Jules's brow crease, "RAMs, that's what we call the infected. If a rat still has flesh or blood from a RAM on its teeth when it attacks a human, it's likely that they'll become infected."

"Oh Jesus fuckin' Christ!" Jules put her head in her hands, then looked up to the older woman who had been stood by the door. "Get all the rat-bite victims separated, get them in another room, now," she ordered. The woman left immediately. "I don't know how much more of this I can take," Jules said, gulping hard.

Lucy walked across to Jules and crouched down in front of her. "Look, you've done something incredible to keep these people safe for as long as you have. The cities are too dangerous to live in now. I'll take a look at your sick and get them ready."

"Get them ready for what?"

"Get them ready to travel. You're coming back with us."

*

The engine cut through the serenity like a chainsaw through butter. Well in advance of the bike's appearance, animals fled to safety in fear of what terrifying beast could make such cacophony. To Mike, the sound was like music. He was tearing through the countryside at over 140mph and each second brought him closer to the possibility that he might find Lucy and Emma.

It took Mike less than fifty minutes from the beginning of his journey to reach the outskirts of Inverness. He slowed down and stopped, well before reaching the city, wheeling the bike quietly along the road. He halted where the tree line broke. From his elevated position, he had a good view of the once thriving place. He reached into his rucksack for the binoculars and scanned the landscape. His attention was drawn to a plume of black smoke. There had been a multiple vehicle pile-up. Some of the vehicles were reminiscent of the type the raiders had used in Candleton, civilian buses and cars with grills and metal sheets welded on for protection. One thing they couldn't protect the occupants from, though, was fire and the flames were still burning. If anyone had been alive at the time the fire had started, they would have long since been burnt to a crisp.

The pile-up hadn't just caught his attention. As he panned out, he saw several RAMs, milling around hoping something edible would miraculously appear from the wreckage. He angled the binoculars a little further up the road and saw two figures lying dead. He couldn't make out a huge amount of detail, but it looked like there were dark purple patches on their green clothing. He placed the strap of the binoculars over his head, pushed down the kickstand on the bike and stood for a moment, pondering.

In many respects, Lucy and Emma were unrecognisable from the people they had been as little as a few weeks ago. The trials they had endured had made them virtually fearless. They were formidable, to say the least. If there were two people who had the ingenuity and capability to escape those raiders, it was them.

Mike brought the binoculars back to his eyes. He counted sixteen RAMs around the wreckage. He couldn't take that many out in one go, but if he could lure a few away, that might give him enough time to take care of the remaining ones and examine the site.

Since arriving at his gran's house, virtually everything had been ruled by committee. His gran was the matriarchal figure who everybody looked to for guidance. If someone wanted to go on a supply run, it had to be discussed and a plan had to be drawn up. If someone wanted to fish a little further out than normal, it had to be discussed and a plan had to be drawn up. Something in the manner of what Mike was about to do would have been discussed over and over, before being flatly turned down. The familiar adrenaline rush made a little smile appear on his face.

Mike fired the engine back to life and began to head towards the crash site at breakneck speed. He was still a good distance away when he noticed most of the RAMs had broken their watchful gaze over the wreckage and were beginning to head towards the sound of the engine. He slowed down and readied the bike to head in the other direction. When the RAMs were just a matter of a few feet away he began moving again, this time much slower, tantalising the beasts with the promise of fresh meat. Like the pied piper, he led them away from the wreck. After half a mile, he veered left into a lay-by, the creatures still followed him, it was then that the bike erupted back to its former glory, heading out of the lay-by and tearing back the way it had come, leaving the RAMs almost standing still in comparison.

As he powered back down the hill and to the crash site, he noticed three creatures remained around the burning wreckage. He reached into his backpack and pulled out one of the machetes. As the first beast ran towards him, he veered and swung the shining blade.

Mike remembered back to the first RAM he had seen up close. It had been his stepfather, Alex, his best friend. His first feeling had been fear, but as he looked into the grey dead eyes and felt the cold flesh underneath his fingers while he tried to fend off the creature that was intent on killing him, the fear turned to hatred. It wasn't hatred for Alex, but hatred for the virus, for this disease that had turned Alex and billions like him. The hatred had turned to anger and he vented it through killing these monsters.

The machete sliced through the grey cheeks of the RAM and carved through the brain and skull. The bike was already heading towards the next creature as the top of the first one's head somersaulted through the air, intermittently releasing globules of tissue and congealed blood. The body of the beast collapsed to the floor. Mike repeated the technique for the other two RAMs, the momentum from the bike proving more power than his muscular arms ever could. He veered off the carriageway and up the grassy embankment to avoid the heat of the licking flames, then he rejoined the road at the other side. He stopped at the far end of the large roundabout, knocked down the kickstand and cut the engine.

He knew he wouldn't have long before the beasts were upon him once again, so he worked quickly. He knelt by one of the fallen figures he had seen from a distance and pulled the man's shirt open. It was still damp from the blood. He had indeed died from a gunshot wound. Mike looked back to the other side of the roundabout. A lorry was on its side. The flames were slowly working their way towards it, but for the time being, it was still in one piece. It blocked the entire carriageway as it had veered then toppled. The question was why? Mike could feel the heat from further back as he approached the cab of the truck. The windscreen had shattered, and there were several small holes that had made the glass crack. Bullet holes. He booted the fragile screen in and pulled out the broken bodies with the same compassion he would show for a bag of cement. He flung them on the tarmac and immediately saw red holes. They had been shot too. Mike leaned into the cab and pulled out two rifles. He checked the bodies for spare magazines, put them in his backpack, and then something else caught his eye.

"Fuck me!" he said lifting a grenade from the pocket of one of the dead men. He placed it gently into his rucksack, flung both rifles over his shoulder, and stood searching the area for any further clues.

Nobody had survived the carnage at the back of the overturned lorry. There must have been vehicles in front because there were clear skid marks, a sure sign of an abrupt stop. If Lucy and Emma had somehow managed to capture the truck, they would have done it where they had options. A roundabout was the perfect place. There were four exits, Mike ruled out north and south immediately. One was blocked by a raging fire, and one had probably been blocked by enemy vehicles. The east exit would have been the easiest, but it headed away from the city, and the city was the safest place for them to go. The raiders didn't have a problem fighting and killing unarmed villagers, but RAMs, they were something else. They wouldn't wade into a city with their numbers diminished as they were just so they could take back their female entertainment.

Mike ran back to the bike and headed down the west ramp, ten metres from the bottom he saw a small line of something black. He immediately put the kickstand back down and dismounted. He looked back beyond the burning wreck and could see the RAMs not too far back now, but he would be gone before they got close to him. He bent down to take a close look. He stretched his middle finger out and gently touched the blackness. He brought it up to his nose. Oil. He looked a few metres further, there was another dribble. The lorry was leaking oil. He would be able to follow it to its resting place before it finally ran out. He climbed back onto the bike and began to follow the oil trail.

He travelled a couple of hundred metres before stopping and cutting the engine. There was a familiar sound, but much louder than he had ever heard before. It couldn't be. It was. The sound of not dozens, but hundreds of RAMs. He couldn't place where it was coming from, it seemed like it was all around him, it seemed like he was drifting in a sea of their noise, their growls.

It was probably the sound of the engine that was riling them. "Shit," he spat.

He looked at the bike but knew if he continued on it, it would be game over. It had got him this far, but it would be the death of him if he took it further. He wheeled it onto the pavement and into a bus shelter. If he needed it again, he knew where it was, but the rest of his journey would have to be on foot.

The rifles were heavy on his shoulders, but if he made it to Emma, Lucy and the rest of the women, they could be the difference between life and death. He looked behind. The distance he had made since the roundabout along with the few twists and turns would have been more than enough to flummox the RAMs that had been chasing him. He advanced to a crossroads, still following the leaking oil trail, the menacing drone getting louder and louder with each step he took. He gripped the side of a building, once a carpet showroom, now just a relic. He dreaded what was waiting for him around the corner. Mike ducked low and edged his head out, the sound immediately increased in volume, but there was no movement and no sign of any RAMs. He looked up and down the street. There were long abandoned car showrooms, a ransacked petrol station and a few fast-food restaurants, plenty of places for RAMs to lurk out of sight of the road. He stood up and headed around the corner, immediately picking up the oil trail once again. He began to run, eager to get off the streets.

His eyes darted from side to side as he went, peering through crud covered showroom glass, looking for the slightest movement behind industrial waste bins, but he saw nothing despite the constant noise of a number of RAMs he didn't even want to estimate. The area became more open-plan the further he ran down the road, he could see beyond the street he was on, up another carriageway and across to a large industrial estate.

He squinted into the distance to see the huge colourful sign of the Home and Garden Depot. Without realising it, a smile formed on his lips. He knew Lucy and Emma were a lot more intelligent than he was. If he was escaping with a truck full of unarmed women, the first thing he'd want to do is arm them. This wasn't America, you couldn't just walk into a sporting goods store and arm yourself with guns, the best you could do over here was equip yourself with weapons for hand to hand combat. Provided the huge DIY superstore hadn't been looted already, that would be the logical place to go. That would be where Lucy and Emma would go.

He began to run faster, realising that the growling drone was diminishing. Wherever it was coming from, he was moving further away from it. As he carried on following the trail of oil, he became more convinced that the DIY superstore was where the lorry had headed. He came to a large roundabout and rather than looking for the trail, he ran directly across it to the third exit, in the direction of the store and the industrial estate. He immediately picked up the oil trail again. He allowed himself a grin. He was right. He was going to find them.

As he approached the gigantic store, he noticed there were no vehicles in the car park. That made sense, they wouldn't want to advertise the fact they were here. He slowed down a little, he had been running for quite some time and the weight of the two rifles and his backpack were becoming more noticeable.

The volume of the huge gathering of RAMs

wherever they were had decreased further, giving him a small amount of relief. Only a small amount, because he knew that when they headed back out of the city, there was the chance that they could run into them, but that was a nightmare for later. Right now, he had to find Lucy and Emma.

*

Lucy and Beth came out of the makeshift infirmary and headed back into the office where Jules and Emma were still talking. "I've examined the five who sustained rat bites. None of them are displaying any symptoms I would associate with turning, but their wounds are infected and unless we can get them some antibiotics, they might not make it.

Jules looked forlorn. "Virtually every place in town has been ransacked."

"If we can get them back to Lonbaig, I've got drugs that can treat them," Lucy said.

"That's if the raiders didn't take everything," Beth added.

"I stashed everything of value. There's no way they'd find it."

"I've told you, there's no way of getting out of here. The whole city is overrun. It's all my fault. I should have got us out when we still had fuel for the vehicles."

"Baloney, you did good here, Jules. You did better than good. You gave people a chance who would never have had one by themselves. We'll figure something out. We've been in tighter scrapes than this, we'll figure something out." Lucy reassured her.

"Jules we've got trouble," yelled a voice from the other room.

"Oh, there's a fuckin' switch," she said, sighing deeply and pulling herself up out of her swivel chair. "What is it now?" she said marching past the three new arrivals and heading towards the window.

The three friends followed her out, lingering just a moment. "Sarah and all the women are being fed downstairs. If nothing else, they've got a good supply of food and water here. Honestly, what do you think our chances are?" Beth asked, looking first towards Emma and then to Lucy.

"Honestly…better than they were when we were in the back of that lorry," replied Lucy.

"That's it?"

"I'm not going to lie to you, Beth. Without transport, we're stuck here, and when the food runs out… We're going to have to go out and find working vehicles. It's not going to be a walk in the park."

This wasn't news to Emma, but Beth's face drained of colour.

"Lucy! Emma!" Jules shouted.

Lucy and Emma, followed by Beth, walked

towards the small crowd assembled at the window. The Venetian blinds had been angled down and all the figures were watching the loading bay below. As the three women approached, Jules turned to them.

"I hope you know how to use those guns, because we've got company," she said.

The two women reached around to the back of their jeans like it was second nature, pulling their Glock pistols out ready for use.

"What is it?" Emma asked.

Jules glared out through the narrow slits. "There's a bloke with a shotgun, tough-looking bastard; looks like he's scouting the place out. There'll probably be more behind him. He's checking out the lorry you pulled up in. Now he's looking at the bullet holes on the side. Okay, now he's stepping back, taking in the back of the building. He's looking at the canopy over the loading bay and the office windows. Now he's climbing up the outside of the lorry cab. He's taken the rucksack off his back and flung it onto the canopy. Now he's done the same with the shotgun... The mad fuckin' bastard, he's just leapt from the top of the fuckin' lorry onto the loading dock canopy. Jesus, this guy's fuckin mental."

Lucy, Emma, and Beth looked at each other in the subdued light. Suddenly, the man Jules was talking about sounded very familiar.

"Let me see," Lucy demanded as she and Emma squeezed in next to Jules. "It's Mike!" Lucy said, almost shaking with excitement.

"You know this guy?" Jules asked turning to Emma.

Emma's voice erupted with joy as she spoke. "Jules, Y'know that pain in the tits I was talking about? You're about to meet him."

"How the fuck did he find you here?"

"My brother can be quite resourceful when he needs to be," she said, the smile not leaving her face.

"Oh man, he is going to be so pissed that we drugged him," Lucy said, remembering the look of betrayal on Mike's face, despite the overwhelming feeling of joy that had swept over her. Then, she snapped to her senses. "What the hell are we doing?" she asked and roughly pulled up the blinds and opened the window.

Mike had climbed onto the canopy at the far end, and for the moment they had lost sight of him. Lucy leaned right out, the stillness of the hot afternoon air becoming electrified by her excitement.

"Mike," she yelled, waving her arms. It took him a second to locate the source of the shout, but then his feet began to thunder across the corrugated steel roof towards her. He shoved the shotgun into his backpack and without missing a beat leapt up, grabbing a tight hold of the window sill and pulling himself through the gap using his powerful arms.

He looked at Lucy, then Emma, almost not

believing his eyes. The shock quickly turned to elation, and he pulled both of them into him. Emma clutched him, her joyous tears running onto his shoulder. He had his arm tightly wrapped around Lucy's waist, and she took hold of his face, kissing him feverishly.

"I found Jake on the peak behind the house...he's in shock, but he's alive," Mike reported.

The two women remained silent but held him even tighter. After a minute, he let go and went across to Beth, embracing her firmly, he pulled away, keeping a warm and reassuring hold of her upper arms. "Annie and John are safe."

The uncertainty about her younger brother and sister had been eating away at her ever since she left them, but hearing this news was like having a huge weight lifted from her.

Although Mike had known other people were in the room, he hadn't acknowledged them. His attention had been on the ones he loved and cared for. Now, he began to look around at the assembled men and women. They wore military uniforms, but he could see they were not military personnel and they were not raiders. They possessed the looks of people who were scared, who were on the verge of being beaten.

Emma stepped up to her brother's side and turned him towards Jules. "Jules and her people are coming back with us."

Lucy and Emma looked at each other. They had

made the decision, knowing it would be hard, and dangerous, knowing that it defied reason, but also knowing it was the right thing to do.

Mike turned to look at all the tired and harrowed faces, then he looked towards Emma and Lucy. "Alright," he replied shrugging his shoulders.

5

Fry sat back on the plush burgundy leather sofa and took another satisfying suck on his cigar. Part of him was furious that the raid had gone so badly - the terrible loss of men, vehicles, fuel, and supplies - but there was part of him that was laughing inside.

He was the right-hand man to a gangster, affectionately named by the local press in the northeast prior to the apocalypse, The Don of Durham. As a crooked police officer, he had done his bidding before the days of the infection and since. Fry had garnered a reputation as a terrifying and unrelenting sadist, and the men feared and despised him. But recently, things had changed.

Fry had been sent north of the border at the behest of The Don, to create a Scottish base for their operations. During the crisis, they had thrived, creating a black market for sought after goods. They had recruited willing and weak henchmen, and when Fry and The Don felt the time was right, they struck, taking over villages, towns and cities. The armed forces had been too badly depleted to put up any real resistance, so The Don's army of raiders soon became the dominant force. When the remainder of the British Armed Forces were called south in a last-ditch effort to save the capital, that was when The Don and his men began to wreak real havoc, spreading almost as fast as the virus that had started this apocalyptic catastrophe.

Fry had plundered a village called Candleton, which had a unique geography and could have been made into a fortress and a solid base of operations in Yorkshire. He had desperately wanted it for himself and was enraged when instead The Don had handed the rule of the village to a man called Potts who had been his daughter's current pet. Lorelei was a constant thorn in Fry's side, but a move against her would be a move against The Don. And as much as he fantasised about holding his hands around her throat and watching her eyes turn red as she spluttered and choked to death, he chose not to do it.

Soon after Fry moved to Scotland, Lorelei had returned to her father's side in the northeast. Potts had been killed and the army she had taken with her had been cut in half through continued attacks by RAMs. Their original base, in Sodburgh then fell without a strong general there to organise the men, and so, The Don's entire empire had crumbled. They had all fled north to join Fry in Loch Uig.

All the men who had despised Fry began to realise he had been the one keeping them alive. He had been the strength behind The Don's operation. When Gordon McKeith had gone to The Don with his plans to raid the surviving villages and farms in the Highlands, Fry had protested, saying it wasn't a sensible move. Eager to win back the respect of his men and restock their dwindling food supplies, The Don had flown in the face of Fry's advice and empowered McKeith to head the raid.

TJ, who had been Fry's own right-hand man, but unlike Fry had enjoyed a good level of camaraderie with The Don's troops, informed Fry that serious dissent was brewing in the ranks. Unless something was done soon, there would be trouble.

The encampment at Loch Uig had been disorganised when Fry first arrived, but he had soon brought order to it. It was home to over three thousand souls. The vast majority of them were The Don's soldiers, but women kidnapped from plundered villages numbered in the hundreds, providing various degrees of servitude to the camp. Although enslaved whores kept most of the troops content, some men had decided to make more permanent arrangements. Women who had a man of their own wore a pass or were given a tattoo to signify they belonged. If they were touched by anyone else, it would be death to the man who laid hands on them.

"Penny for your thoughts," Juliet said, as she slumped onto the sofa and laid her long brown legs across Fry. Up until meeting Juliet, Fry had despised women. He used them to fulfil his physical needs and treated them as a tradable commodity, but Juliet... Juliet was a kindred spirit. She was a powerful force, easily turning adversity to her benefit. Her smooth dark skin and stunning looks tantalised him, her sense of humour made him roar with delight, and her hunger for power made him feel that he had found the one thing he had been looking for to take the next step.

He was under no illusions as to her attraction to him. She was young and beautiful, he was a grizzled warhorse with scars inside and out, but she saw the strength in him and that was the only aphrodisiac she needed.

"You know my thoughts, sweetheart," he said snapping out of his daze and sweeping his hand up her smooth, silky legs.

"Some party," she smirked, looking across the dining room.

The room had been prepared days before at The Don's request. The homecoming of McKeith and his men would have been a huge celebration.

But now, The Don sat at the head of a table with just a few cronies keeping him company. He was never one to pass on an opportunity to eat, drink and be merry, so even with no returning heroes to toast, he decided to throw the party anyway. Lorelei, as always, was in a state of inebriation, wrapping her lips around a young soldier who would doubtless be her next toy. Although the sycophantic fools poured drinks and tried to make merry, there was an air of foreboding in the room.

The large country hotel where they had taken up

residence was luxurious. It was reserved for The Don and a select and favoured few. Fry had been offered the chance to move in, but he had preferred the privacy of a large house on the outskirts of the small town, where he could talk to Juliet until the early hours of the morning, planning...plotting.

The generators chugged away, providing electricity for the so-called celebration. Coloured lights and music did nothing to disguise the defeated air that surrounded The Don. He raised another glass to the people at the table, they all raised one back and feigned good humour, but even a child could see there was none.

"How about you and me go back home and have a little celebration of our own," Juliet said, moving Fry's hand up her thigh and underneath her short white skirt.

He loved the feel of her skin underneath his hand and looked towards her longingly in the dancing coloured lights. "Come here," he commanded.

Juliet dropped her feet to the floor and swivelled around so Fry could hold her in his arms. She draped her long legs over the sofa and wrapped her arms around him. He stubbed out his cigar in a plant pot and cradled her head in his hand pulling her mouth towards him. The nicotine flavoured kiss lasted more than a minute and Fry's free hand roamed all over Juliet's supple body. When the kiss ended, their faces remained close. Although some found his thick Glaswegian accent hard to understand, Juliet did not. She hung on his every word as though he was casting a spell.

"There is nothing I would like more than to take you home and have some fun sweetheart," he said smiling. Juliet's face lit up excitedly, her broad grin making Fry smile himself. "But, tonight's the night."

The smile left his face. His eyes, which a second before had been filled with carnal mischief, were now stone-cold...icy. Juliet's grin widened further.

He bent down and his hot breath whispered into her ear, "Tonight you'll go to bed a princess and awake a queen."

*

Mike and Lucy held each other tightly. The night before they had been in their own room in a comfortable bed. Now they were stretched out on a fire blanket high up on some metal shelving. This was the norm for life in the Home and Garden Depot since the rat attacks had begun. The legs to the huge steel shelving units had been greased making it virtually impossible for the rodents to climb. That did not stop them from trying.

Mike, Lucy and Jules sat with their legs dangling over the edge of the shelf. The fading summer light still provided enough illumination for them to see what was going on. The day had been spent working in earnest. Jules's organisational skills and forward-thinking had impressed Mike, Lucy, and Emma. She had taken good care of her people, given the limitations she faced, and they were more than willing to obey her commands.

The Home and Garden Depot was the biggest of

its kind in the Northern Highlands, it supplied to the trade as well as private customers. It had a small fleet of delivery vehicles, six transit vans and twelve bigger box vans. Displaying a level of paranoia that immediately ingratiated her to Mike's heart, Jules had insisted that the vehicles were parked in the loading bay of the toy superstore next door, giving the illusion that their own premises were completely devoid of life should a casual observer pass by.

The vehicles had little fuel to begin with, but after a few daring "smash and grab" raids around town to find provisions over the past few weeks, they were all just running on fumes. All but one of the vehicles were now parked in the Home and Garden Depot's loading bay again, and three of them had been loaded up with all but a smattering of the group's food and water supplies as well as vital tools, seeds and materials that could help rebuild and sustain life back on the stretch of coast that was soon to be home for all of them. They had kept one vehicle in the neighbouring parking lot just in case.

While Jules, Lucy, Emma, and Sarah had been coordinating the logistics of this operation, Mike and Beth had been demonstrating how to make crude spears out of broom and mop handles. They had dismantled garden shears and shown people how the remaining long-handled blades could be used to deadly effect against an assailant, living or otherwise. They explained how a strike to the brain of a RAM was the only sure way to bring one down, and the creature's bodily fluids were as deadly as their bites. The frightened faces of the men, women, and children slowly grew with confidence as the pair spoke with a calm expertise.

In the afternoon when they had broken for dinner, Mike had gone to check on the loading operations, and Beth had taken it upon herself to tell stories to Jules's people about the daring feats they had undertaken to reach Scotland. When Mike had returned, the confidence level had grown even more. By the end of the day, the vehicles had been loaded and the rag-tag army was fully armed and had undergone their first induction.

Jules winced as she took a drink of vodka and passed the bottle to Mike. "I can't thank you enough for letting Andy have one of those rifles. He'd have never fuckin' shut up about it otherwise," she said, her Belfast accent becoming thicker the more she drank.

"It doesn't matter to us, Sweetie. The four of us who can shoot are all armed, so we had a rifle going spare," Lucy replied, taking the bottle from Mike.

"Don't get me wrong," continued Jules almost as if Lucy hadn't spoken, "I love my brother. I love all three of them, but sometimes it's like I'm looking after fuckin' children." She paused waiting for the bottle to be passed back down to her. She took another hefty swig. "It's been like looking after a fuckin' warehouse full of children." She put the bottle down beside her and leant forward to look at Mike then at Lucy. "When your lorry first showed up today, I thought——raiders, this is it, it's all over now... And it's a fuckin' terrible thing to say, and may Jesus forgive me, but there was a big part of me that felt relief...relief that I didn't have to be responsible any more. These people made me their leader, but I'm just a fuckin' retail manager. I used to go out with the girls on a Friday night and get pissed, most of the time I'd be working the next day, and I had to do it with the mother of all hangovers...but I had no aspirations beyond that. I didn't want too much responsibility, I wasn't that ambitious." She paused again, picked up the bottle and took a drink. "You coming here today...you saved me...you saved all of us."

"We haven't done anything yet, sweetie. You can thank us when we're back in Lonbaig."

"Yeah, well, I see it differently. So what you have done or you haven't done, I thank you anyway," she said holding the vodka bottle up and taking a final drink in salute to them both. "And now, I'd better get down before I start seeing two of everything," she said smiling. She took tight hold of the rope which had been attached to the strong metal frame of the shelving unit. Jules looked around the small area that had been cordoned off with sheets of cardboard to give the occupants privacy.

"It's funny, I used to complain to my landlord all the time that the walls in my flat were like fuckin' cardboard. I suppose I didn't know when I had things good did I?" With that, she shuffled off the edge of the shelf and shimmied down the rope to the floor, greeting the tenants of the lower shelves as she went.

Mike and Lucy leant over the edge watching her as she went down. Even though she was clearly tipsy, she still had the presence of mind to get on her tiptoes and place the rope carefully onto the tall first shelf just in case they were visited by rats in the night.

*

Stifled sobs and moans could be heard from all over the large warehouse as the women from Lonbaig and the rest of the coastline finally had time to come to terms with what had happened to them and their families. They had been kept busy all day making ready for their escape, but as darkness and quiet crept over the large echoing building so did the realisation of what they were escaping back to.

Mike and Lucy laid still, listening to the sadness spread like a cold. Eventually, Mike turned onto his side. "You did good today," he whispered into Lucy's ear.

She turned onto her side and draped her leg over him, leaning in so she could whisper without being overheard by the tenants of one of the neighbouring shelves. "I thought I'd lost you. I thought you felt I betrayed you."

He pulled her even closer to him. "If I'd tried to fight, I'd be dead now. You saved me. The more time we spend together, Lucy, the more I realise I need you. I have so many demons floating around in my head, but when I'm with you, they're all kept at bay."

Lucy moved her lips up to his and they shared a long and passionate kiss. When they pulled away, they smiled at each other in the dim candlelight.

"The thing is though, when we get back home, I'm going to need some of those demons to help make that coastline into a fortress," said Mike. "I've had my little holiday from reality now. Despite the nightmare that has gone on around us, the last few weeks with you have been incredible. I was excited to wake up every morning to learn what the new day would bring. But to make sure that I can feel that again, I need to know that I can give you safety, that I can offer everyone safety..."

"That's not just on you Mike," she whispered.

"I realise that, I know it's not just my responsibility, but it's something I feel I need to take charge of. You and Emma are born leaders, you have the intelligence and respect to get people to do what needs to be done. But to deal with these raiders...as much as intelligence, we need primal brutality and a complete lack of compassion. And whether I like to acknowledge it or not, when they need to be, those are real strong suits of mine."

"That's not true, Mike, you're a good man, don't put yourself down like that."

"I'm not. I can't change the DNA I inherited from my dad, any more than you can change yours. The thing is, though, I can put it to good use for us, for all of us." He leaned across and kissed her again.

"What do you make of these people?" Lucy asked, gesturing into the darkness, past the edge of the metal shelf they were lying on.

"They seem decent, they seem scared, just like the villagers in Candleton and Lonbaig."

"It won't be the same when we go back. Something's been taken from them. Something's been taken from all of us."

"Then we'll build something new. We can't bring back the people who've died, but we can make sure that it doesn't happen again."

The pair returned to their backs, staring at the candle's flickering reflection on the shelf above them. They let the sad sounds envelop them for the moment, then Mike reached out to take Lucy's hand. The guilty comfort it gave them both relaxed them enough for them to close their eyes. It was unlikely they would get any sleep on this night, but at least they could rest, together.

Emma and Sarah had taken a top-shelf on the racking, giving them a full view of the warehouse if they chose to lean over and take it. The sounds rose from the tortured depths below, but their own voices remained secret to the rest of the occupants of the building.

"I hope the kids are okay," Sarah said.

"You don't need to worry about them. Dora's there, and as much as they drive me mad, Ruth, Richard and David are responsible people, they'll be able to deal with anything that happens." Emma looked out into the darkness, hoping her words were true. She rubbed her hands over her face and then sensed something that made her turn on her side and look at her companion. Emma saw tears in Sarah's eyes.

"I'm really not cut out for this."

Emma edged closer to her, making the heavy

metal racking creak a little with the movement. "Sarah, seriously, don't talk like that."

"It's true. I wanted to be brave. I wanted to help because I knew that's what you'd do, but, I was just in awe of you. I felt like a frightened child as I watched you and Lucy," she admitted, finally wiping a tear streak from the side of her face.

Emma moved closer still, and Sarah turned her head to look in her direction. "Listen to me. When we set off from Leeds, there wasn't a second that went by where I didn't feel like peeing myself because I was so scared. Mike on the other hand, he was just unbelievable, right from the outset, because he knew that if he didn't step up, we were all finished. The more I saw him do, the more I wanted to get involved, but the fear inside me kept pulling me back." She paused, searching Sarah's eyes for understanding. "Then, when those soldiers knocked Mike out, that was it. It was down to me or we were all dead. I had to swallow all my fear and my doubts, roll my sleeves up and get on with it. And when I did, I found I was capable of a lot more than I thought I was." She paused again. "I see a lot of me in you, Sarah. When you beat your fear down, you'll be able to take on the world," she smiled, and Sarah smiled back. "Now try to get some sleep, it's going to be a long day tomorrow."

*

As the night wore on, the numbers in the dining room slowly dwindled. Lorelei had wandered off with another young man who she would use until she got bored of him. All of The Don's *friends* had staggered off to find their respective rooms in the luxury hotel, where they would slumber in comfort until morning. Juliet had bid Fry goodnight with a long passionate kiss. She had then been escorted home by Fry's most loyal soldier, TJ. That had been half an hour earlier. Now, only Fry, sat on the luxurious sofa, puffing another cigar and swirling cognac around the bottom of his glass. He went unnoticed by The Don as two young women, high on whatever the drug of choice was that evening, fawned over the ugly fat old man like he was some young Hollywood icon. The music still carried on, and it was that in conjunction with The Don's own intoxication that allowed Fry to remain unnoticed.

Fry took a sip of his cognac as his eyes slowly narrowed. His thoughts went back to the time that he had first approached The Don. He had offered to lose evidence in a case that would have put the gangster away for years. That had been the beginning of a lucrative relationship for Fry. They had even formed an uneasy friendship in all those years. But now, The Don had become a liability.

Raucous laughter erupted from the table as one of the women disappeared underneath it, while a second pulled her top off and began to jiggle her naked breasts in front of The Don. At the other end of the large dining room, a door opened and TJ and four other men quietly entered unbeknownst to the three revelling figures at the table. TJ looked towards Fry and nodded deliberately and slowly as if it was some kind of pre-arranged signal.

Fry's ginger and grey whiskers parted as his lips broke into a wide grin, displaying a mouthful of yellow teeth. He gulped the remaining cognac from his fragile glass and carefully placed it down on the table beside him. He edged forward on his seat and took an exaggerated suck on his cigar which he exhaled releasing an explosion of blue smoke into the already heavy air in the room. Extinguishing the remaining stub, he stood.

As Fry paced across to the table, the young woman re-emerged from underneath it, wiping her mouth and laughing hysterically. The Don's own guffaws nearly drowned out the music. The Don was so preoccupied with the dancing breasts of his companion that it took him several seconds to break his eyes away from their hypnotic movement and realise that someone was standing by his side.

"Alright Fry," said The Don, still smiling widely. "Are you calling it a night?"

"No," he replied smiling warmly, "but you are."

A confused look swept across The Don's face for a second. It transformed into a contorted snapshot of fear as Fry tightly grasped a handful of the older man's pathetic comb-over and with his other hand took the long-bladed hunting knife that TJ had handed him. Fry angled The Don's face towards him and sawed into the sagging flesh of the fat man's neck with the serrated edge. The women immediately began to scream and started running away only to be stopped by TJ and the other men. The Don's pained cry became a loud gurgle as the knife tore through the bloody sinew. Arterial spray covered Fry' face, running down his beard, turning the ginger to a glistening dark red. Fry's eyes danced with a youthful excitement as the moment he had fantasised about a thousand times before had finally arrived. He felt a pang of sadness as The Don stopped struggling, and his eyes closed for the last time. His sadness wasn't for the passing of a long-time associate, but for the fact that he couldn't kill him again. He only had one chance to enjoy the sensation of seeing life bleed out of The Don, how he wished he could bottle that feeling and drink it at will.

It took him the best part of a minute to separate The Don's head from his neck. By the time Fry was finished, perspiration had begun to dilute the warm red blood that painted his face. He pulled the head away from the body with an aggressive yank and held it high. It hung almost comically, suspended by nothing but the few hairs of the old man's comb-over. Blood continued to drain from it, occasionally landing on Fry, but he was not repelled. It did not disgust him to shower in the blood of a man he once called his friend.

TJ looked on, smirking at Fry's obvious enjoyment, but the other men looked uneasy. It was one thing to be happy to go along with killing The Don, but none of them expected the execution to be so graphic, so barbaric.

The music still pounded away through the speakers, but the party was now officially over. He looked across at TJ, "That's enough music for tonight, don't you think?"

The room became silent apart from the terrified sobbing from The Don's two female companions. Fry looked around at the assembled men. "Unless any of you want those two, send them to the Whore Pit," he commanded in a menacing shout. There had been a brothel for the men in New Sodburgh which had been nicknamed the Whore Pit. When Fry had moved north of the border to take command of the new outpost, the idea and the term had followed with him. In this new world, Fry and those like him saw most women as nothing more than currency. Most women. There were the odd few who were something more, like his new queen, Juliet.

"What's next boss?" TJ asked, as soon as the room fell silent.

"We're not going to get much sleep tonight." He held the head up in front of him like he was looking at a goldfish in a bag won from a travelling fair. "Because of this piece of shit, we lost two strongholds and fuck knows how many men. Unless things start getting better, the men are going to be deserting in their droves. You and me, we're going to turn the tide TJ, starting right now." He searched his friend's eyes for understanding and loyalty. Happy that he did indeed see both, he then looked back to the dangling head. "First thing's first, though. I have to go give Lorelei the terrible news." Fry's mouth curled into a devilish smile. The blood dripped from his whiskers, over his lips and onto his teeth. TJ looked on, giving nothing away, but feeling a sudden shudder down his spine.

6

The Home and Garden Depot was in total darkness when a sudden noise awoke all its inhabitants. Each night when the rats had come, they had found another way into the huge warehouse and tonight was no different.

There had been silence, followed by a loud crack, as if something had given way, then the small scrambling feet and excited screeches had begun to echo around the cavernous building, quickly followed by fearful cries.

Small lights flicked on and candles were lit as everyone realised they were under attack. The familiar sound of breaking glass, followed by sudden whooshes made Mike realise, Molotov cocktails were being thrown. He carefully moved to the edge of the shelf to get a better view. Although he was high up, he could see some of the rats, burning. Their bodies writhed in agony as the flames enveloped their rough brown fur and then consumed their flesh. The size of the creatures made him feel uneasy. He knew that rats tended to grow according to their environment and conditions. If there was a large supply of food and few predators, they were likely to grow to a reasonable size, but some of these were the size of small dogs.

"Fuck me," he whispered, almost hypnotised by the river of furry bodies that was scurrying below. "Look at the size of these things."

When he got no response from Lucy, he turned to look at her. He could see in the dim candlelight that she hadn't moved. She was still lying flat on her back, a tear had run down the side of her face and her whole body was quivering. Mike immediately moved across and cradled his left hand underneath her.

"Lucy, what's wrong?"

She looked at him, ashamed, "Rats. Mike, I'm terrified of rats."

"It's okay, I'm here, I won't let anything hurt you."

"You don't understand, I mean I have a real fear of rats, Musophobia, Suriphobia, Murophobia. Call it whatever the hell you want, my parents sent me to a shrink for it after I found one in our basement. It didn't help."

She looked straight at him, and he saw that her eyes were filled with the tears of a childhood nightmare. Mike moved in and kissed her on the forehead. He sat up and gave himself more room on the narrow shelf by dangling his feet over the side. He reached across for his rucksack and pulled out his shotgun, a machete and the two aerosol cans he had been issued by Jules along with a lighter.

"What are you doing?" asked Lucy between sobs.

"Like I said, I won't let anything happen to you. If anything gets up here, I'll deal with it."

"Hold me Mike?" she begged.

He remained in position, dangling his legs over the side of the shelf and watching the events below. Mike extended his hand back for Lucy to hold. "I'll hold you later. If I let my guard down, I'm not keeping my promise." He squeezed Lucy's hand tightly and then let go again, torn between wanting to comfort her and having the necessary freedom to move quickly. "Sis, are you okay up there?" he asked, looking across the aisle and up to the next level of shelving.

Mike could see there was a small lantern glowing, but could barely recognise outlines of figures in the light. "We're fine. Beth, are you alright?" Emma called across to the shelf just down from her.

"Oh yeah... Great," she replied.

Mike continued looking down and saw a number of the rats trying to ascend the metal racking only to be foiled by the greased legs. His respect for Jules etched up a further notch as the rats soon lost interest and skidded away with the rest of the pack. His eyes followed their route as they scurried and weaved around the flames on the ground and towards the front of the DIY megastore.

He squinted into the relative darkness where many of the rats disappeared into a structure he didn't remember seeing before he bedded down for the night. It was built from pallets, a large garden shed, racking, tarpaulins and heavy cardboard boxes. There were discarded jars and cans scattered about. The rats that didn't enter ran up the outside of the makeshift dwelling and feasted on scraps of food. The construction came to life as hundreds of excited brown, furry creatures feasted on the bounty that had been left for them. The shanty building throbbed with terrifying ferocity as the white breezeblock of the cash office it was built against began to get painted red with bloody spray as the vicious rodents fought each other for delicious morsels.

Mike heard agitated words from several aisles down, but couldn't make out what was being said. He looked back towards Lucy who had put her forearm over her eyes, hoping it would help block out her fear. It didn't.

"Lucy, come here a second."

"I can't Mike. Don't you understand, I can't."

"They're gone."

"What do you mean they're gone?" she said slowly moving her forearm away.

"I mean they're gone. There's something at the front of the store, I can't quite see what it is, but they've all headed there. I think they've set up a trap." Mike reached into his rucksack, pulled out his binoculars and focussed them down towards the front of the store.

Another Molotov cocktail flew towards the entrance of the structure. Mike pulled the binoculars away from his eyes before the flare burnt his retinas. When the whoosh had died down, he brought them back up and saw things a little clearer in the stronger light. He caught sight of two objects holding down a tarpaulin. "Nobody could be that fucking stupid," he said.

"What?" asked Lucy, rising to the urgency in his voice.

"They look like Calor gas cylinders," he said bringing the binoculars back down from his eyes.

"What do you mean?" she asked shrugging.

"Y'know, gas cylinders, like you use for a barbecue or a heater."

Three more Molotov cocktails arced through the air towards the structure, exploding into small fountains of flames as they landed. The entrance and the exterior were now fully consumed. High pitched screeches sent shivers into the night as rodents burnt to death. There was little risk of the fire spreading through the building as it mainly consisted of concrete and corrugated metal, but the burning fuel from the Molotov cocktails would certainly trap the rats inside.

A rifle shot rang out from further down the

warehouse. Mike and Lucy looked at each other in panic. "They are that fucking stupid!" said Mike. "Em, get down now," he shouted, as he grabbed hold of Lucy and pushed her as far towards the back of the shelving unit as she could physically move. He draped himself over her and a split second later, another shot fired, this time followed by what Mike thought the end of the world might sound like. A cacophonous explosion, followed by another and another and another, made the whole building quake. The sturdy metal shelving creaked and screeched as the thunderous roar tore down the aisles of the store. The rat trap almost vaporised. Mike and Lucy felt their shelving unit buckle a little, and both relinquished their grip on the other, ready to try and make an escape, but the movement was just momentary, and as the initial waves of the explosions died down, the terrifying displacement of air and space began to normalise. The thunder of the explosions themselves drowned out the single thing that Lucy and Mike knew would be the disastrous result of such an ill-thought out plan. The glass that made up most of the storefront had been blown into the night. The flames that had whooshed through the building were nothing compared to the ones that had broken through the front and found an abundance of fresh and nourishing oxygen to feed on. The initial flames licked high into the night sky, followed by the deafening sound.

They both knew instantly that the rats were gone, but they had just alerted every RAM in the city to their presence.

Another tremulous noise carved a sharp note of fear through the already terrifying dark as one of the huge metal shelving units two aisles over gave way. The heat and force from the explosions had buckled the steel too far. Over the clatter and crash of the metal collapsing onto the cement floor sang a chorus of petrified screams. Mike and Lucy shuffled to the edge of their shelf. Looking down the aisle they could see random splashes of fire as the waves of the explosions had found something combustible, but that was nothing compared to the blackness that lay beyond where the vast glass entrance had been. The ebony shroud would soon uncover a nightmare, no one could imagine.

Earlier in the night when the occupants of the warehouse had settled down like some weird tribe of tree people nestling into a steel jungle, there had been ladders and harnesses to help them with their ascents. Now, there was no time to waste waiting for someone to come along with a ladder to help people down. When Emma had been buried in a collapsed building back in Candleton, it had been a race against time to get her out before the air had run out. Air wasn't the problem this time. The things that lurked in the thick dark night, awakened by the blast—they were what Mike was worried about.

Once the steel had ground and clattered to an abrupt finale, the groans, screams and cries of the people who had been using it as their night time dwelling took over.

"Em!" Mike yelled into the relative darkness of their own aisle, "Get Sarah and Beth and anyone else who doesn't strike you as a clueless fuckwit and meet me next to the collapsed shelving. And be quick about it."

His words were angry and he wanted people to hear that he was not someone who suffered fools. He grabbed his rucksack and took a tight hold of the solid metal frame, ready to begin climbing down. He looked at Lucy, her face sad and scared, still not having got over the episode with the rats, still not having accepted that they were in yet another life and death situation.

"Luce," the only time he had used the name before was when they had been intimate together, but now, knowing once again that this vision of her could be one of his last, he felt the need to use it again. "I wish I could say to you to sit this one out, you've been through enough, but I can't. You and Em are the only people I can rely on one hundred per-cent. If there is just a sliver of hope that we can get out of this, I need you with me."

Lucy looked at him in the dim light and took a deep breath. When she exhaled, it fluttered like it did when someone had been hiding tears and upset. She swallowed, placed the Glock in the back of her jeans and pulled herself to the edge ready to descend straight behind Mike.

"C'mon, let's do this." The fear came out in her words, and it broke Mike's heart to hear it.

"Your brother never thought about becoming a diplomat before all this happened?" Sarah asked, confounded that Mike would come out with something so damning of his hosts.

"He's never been into the whole treading lightly thing, and to be honest, I just might beat him to finding out whose idea it was to ring a fucking dinner gong for every single RAM in the city."

The true consequences of the explosion hadn't registered with Sarah. Emma, Lucy, Beth and Mike had been in lots of situations since their journey began. They understood what attracted RAMs, what actions were dangerous or downright suicidal, and to that end, they were the people to watch and listen to. Sarah hadn't contemplated what would happen as a result of the noise and the flash and the front of the store disintegrating into a pile of webbed metal and broken glass. She felt a sudden urge to be sick. "Do you think those things, the RAMs will come?"

"The entire city is in a silent darkness, and all of a sudden, there's a deafening explosion and a beacon of flames a hundred feet high. Oh yeah, I'm pretty certain, every last one of the fucking things will be heading straight for us," Emma replied as she began shimmying down the side of the shelving unit.

By the time she'd reached the debris of the collapsed shelves, Mike was already flinging large scraps of metal to one side in order to try and find survivors. The sporadic patches of fire gave him enough light to work with, and he glanced around angrily towards the faces of the dazed and the petrified who looked on as if giving him help would make the situation more real, more terrible.

He took hold of a huge buckled piece of metal, and Emma and Lucy joined him. They grunted and huffed as the three of them lifted the weighty debris. Immediately a hand became visible, then an arm, but nothing more. As they carried the large piece of steel to the side, away from the working area, they looked at the severed limb. A few weeks earlier, they would have been horrified to see such a gut-wrenching image, but now they were different people. Sarah went across to them intent on helping, and as soon as she saw the bloody arm, she had to run to the side and be sick.

Beth and Jules got a small group working on the other side of the collapsed unit and before long, they had managed to find an old couple. They were shaken and had cuts and bruises, but that was all. Lucy went across to help them, while more people joined the ranks of the diggers. When Mike was satisfied that there were enough people searching the wreckage for survivors, he took hold of Emma's arm and led her away. Jules came to join them.

"When this is over, I want to meet the person who came up with the idea for the rat trap, but right now we've got bigger problems," growled Mike. "We won't have more than a few minutes before we're inundated with RAMs—we need to get out through the back and as far away as we can, as quickly as we can."

"That won't give us time to dig everybody out of the wreckage. I'm not leaving them," Jules said.

"Well, good luck with that," Mike replied, beginning to walk away. "We're leaving."

Some of the people from the warehouse stood behind Jules, watching on with growing concern.

"You can't leave," she said, fumbling her pistol from the back of her jeans. "You can't leave us!" she pointed it feebly in Mike's direction, tears had begun to roll down her cheeks. "You can't leave us," she said more weakly this time. "Please don't leave us." The men and women gathering behind her looked down at the ground. Jules had been admired and revered by them all, but this single night had been the straw that had broken the camel's back.

Mike looked at her, he looked at Emma, then he looked back towards Jules. "I'm sorry Jules."

He walked away as his host dropped her gun on the floor and fell to her knees sobbing. A middle-aged man and woman from the group behind her immediately went to her aid.

Emma looked at the pathetic figure, and then reluctantly followed her brother. When she caught up with him, he had found Lucy, who was being helped by Sarah as they treated the wounded. Mike took hold of Sarah's arm.

"Tell Beth to get everyone together, our people are leaving now," he ordered.

Sarah looked surprised at first that Mike wasn't asking her but telling her to do something, then, she looked behind him, beyond the wreckage and into the darkness. He knew what was out there, he knew what was coming. She went to find Beth without a word in response.

"We can't move some of these people, Mike. One of them's got a broken leg. One's got what looks like a torn ligament..."

"If we don't go now, we're all dead. It's that simple," replied Mike taking hold of Lucy's arm and beginning to lead her away. She shook her arm free and stood her ground.

"That isn't who we are Mike. We don't leave people who need our help. If we do, then we're no better than the raiders. These people might be weak now, but they can be made strong. We grew strong. We learned to survive. We can help them. We can show them what it takes."

"This is madness, we're going to be attacked any second and you're playing fucking Florence Nightingale to a bunch of..."

Lucy erupted, "A bunch of what Mike? A bunch of frightened, hurt and helpless people who didn't ask for any of this to happen to them? I can treat these people," she said gesturing to the slowly increasing line of figures recovered from the debris. "I'm staying, Mike. Do you think Hughes or Barnes or Shaw would run out on them?"

"Seriously?" he asked, fuming. "How short is your fucking memory, Lucy?" she turned away to go back to work, but Mike grabbed a tight hold of her arm and pulled her around to face him. "Where were your fucking heroes when you were tied up in the back of the ambulance or stuck in that little cupboard waiting to die?" Emma, in turn, grabbed hold of Mike's arm to try and calm him down, but he pulled it away aggressively. "Maybe if I'd have coshed someone I'd called a friend and left his family for dead, then kidnapped his girlfriend, you might think a bit more highly of me."

Lucy took hold of his wrist and angrily pulled his clenched hand away. "Stop behaving like a child Mike, you know what I meant."

"Yeah, I know exactly what you meant." Their stares fixed for a moment, and then Mike turned in the other direction. Emma went to him, but then caught his gaze and immediately backed off. She was familiar with that look and the tornado that usually followed. Mike tore his eyes away from his sister and began to look around the dimly lit interior of the building. There were people trying to find survivors in the wreckage, there were older men and women comforting children, there were looks of fear and looks of sadness. Some of the trapped were screaming, some were silent. Jules was kneeling down on the floor, almost catatonic, knowing it was all coming to an end. There was still a group of people behind her, and her brother Andy stood over her with his arms folded. Mike's eyes narrowed as he saw the rifle they had given Jules earlier on, strapped to his shoulder. He was the one who had fired at the canisters, and the chances were good, he was the one who had come up with the plan.

Mike swept past Emma, marched straight up to Andy, and before Jules's brother even had chance to understand what was going on, Mike's fist made square contact with Andy's jaw, knocking him from his feet and into the land of unconsciousness. The small crowd gasped at the brutal display, then looked away as they saw the rabid anger remained in Mike's eyes.

Jules, whose world had fallen apart in the last few minutes, got to her feet still crying. "What did you do to my brother?" she screamed, leaning forward, her hands clenched into fists by her sides.

In that instant, a memory came back to Mike. The morning he had been forced to kill his stepfather Alex, Sammy had come into the room. She had screamed uncontrollably, and asked almost the same question "What did you do to Daddy?" Mike looked at the fallen man and looked towards Jules, the anger now replaced by pity, guilt even. She was an adult who had a huge amount of responsibility thrust upon her shoulders, but for those few seconds that Mike regarded her, she was just a frightened confused little girl.

Mike stepped towards her, and she slapped him across the face. He saw it coming and readied his cheek for impact. She slapped him again and then burst out crying, collapsing against him, "Why did you do it? Why did you do it?" Only now, Mike sensed the question was no longer aimed at him but towards her unconscious brother. Mike put his arm around Jules, and she clenched his t-shirt as she hid her sobbing face in his chest. As he held her, he looked around at the broken faces. She had kept all these people together and safe, and now as they watched her unravel, so their own hope unravelled, too. He looked across to Lucy who continued to examine fresh patients.

Mike took a tight hold of Jules's shoulders and pushed her away. "Listen to me, Jules. We're going to get out of here. All of us. But I need your help, and I need it now." Jules's sobs came to a teetering halt, ready to begin again if this virtual stranger's statement turned out to be nothing but an empty promise.

"That van we kept in the other car park... we have to get to it now." He immediately began to lead her away, she looked around as if to question what the hell was going on, but then she allowed herself to be swept into the moment. Andy had scrambled back to his feet in a daze.

Mike looked around to see Emma was still following a few paces behind him. "Em, organise these people now. Once we're out of here, throw as much debris as you can up against this entrance. Get people armed and ready to fight. Anything comes through, you kill it. I'm going to try and lead them away. When you think it's safe, lead them out of the back. Get onto the A835, that was clear when I came in. Get them back to Lonbaig. I'll catch up with you later."

"Mike..," There was so much she wanted to say, but nowhere near enough time. She wanted to tell him that Lucy was scared and she hadn't meant what she said, she wanted to tell him that she didn't want him to go, she wanted to tell him, she loved him and she was proud of him. "Please...be careful."

He stopped in his tracks, "I love you, sis."

"I love you too."

*

"Lorelei, oh Lorelei, darling," sang Fry to the young woman who was in a deep, chemically-induced sleep. Light was beginning to bleed through the curtains. The hotel room looked like it had been used by a 1980s hair metal band. There were drinks cans and drug paraphernalia scattered around, and Lorelei and her companion had clearly been very active before their deep sleep as underwear and clothing littered the room. Fry bent down and looked closer at her sleeping face. She was a good looking girl, she had a surgically enhanced figure which most men drooled over, but rather than feeling sexual impulses towards her, all Fry could think of was how much he was going to enjoy mentally torturing her for all the hell she had put him through.

He went around to the other side of the bed to see a typical Lorelei selection. The man was probably a little younger than Lorelei, almost definitely not as experienced, and he slept with a smile on his face—the contented smile of an idiot. Fry took out his knife and plunged it deep into the man's throat while simultaneously putting his knee on his victim's chest and covering the man's mouth with his free hand. The victim's eye's shot open, but by the time he understood what was happening, he was already gurgling his last bubbles. Fry's weight prevented the convulsions from disturbing Lorelei too much on the luxury king size bed, but the man made enough of a ruckus for Lorelei to moan in agitation before returning to the depths of her sleep. When he was sure there was no life left, Fry withdrew his knife and looked at the treacly blood as it ran down the blade, over the hilt, and onto his hand. There was part of him that regretted not being able to share this with his beloved Juliet. What wonders that woman had introduced him to since she had come into his life, but no, Juliet would get to play with Lorelei later on, it was only right, only fitting that it was Fry who broke the news to her of her father's sad demise.

He stood up and watched as the blanket sponged the blood from the dead man, like a kitchen towel soaking up red wine. Fry smiled. He had been on the police force most of his working life, and for most of his working life, he had also been on The Don's payroll. He had money, women, and he could do and get away with whatever he wanted, but it was power that he really craved. All these years he had played second fiddle to The Don, he had reaped untold benefits, but it was the need for total control, total domination that drove him to want more. It didn't matter that the world had been ravaged by a virus, it didn't matter that undead creatures roamed the streets of the cities and towns stalking the living like vengeful parasites. What mattered was that he had power, he could do whatever he wanted without ever having to answer to anyone. He wanted the world to be at his feet.

Fry slowly moved around the bed, switching his gaze from the sleeping girl to the expanding lake of blood and then back again. He bent down once more.

"Lorelei," he said softly, "Lorelei," he repeated, once again to no avail. "Fuck this," he said underneath his breath, then moved his face to within an inch of hers. "Lorelei!" he yelled as if it was a battle cry.

Lorelei's eyes shot open in panic which intensified when she saw Fry. She frantically moved her hand back to grab her companion, baffled as to why he hadn't jolted awake with Fry's yawp. She felt something warm and wet and immediately pulled her hand out from under the covers. Her eyes were still adjusting to the dim morning light, but from its hue, consistency and coppery smell, she knew immediately it was blood. She sat upright and pulled the covers back in one move only to see the gory remains of her one-night stand. Her head looked towards Fry, then she leapt over the dead figure to stand naked on the other side of the bed. She looked down at Fry's hand and saw the crimson knife, thick droplets slowly washing over the blade's tip and falling onto the carpet.

"My dad's going to fucking kill you for this, you sick bastard!" she screamed before running to the door.

She twisted the handle only to find out it was locked. She looked across at Fry who bent down and pulled something from underneath the bed before hiding it behind his back. Her actions became more frantic, pulling at the handle and kicking the wood as she saw Fry start moving towards her. She looked around the room in desperation and finally ran to the bathroom and locked the door.

"I'm warning you, Fry," she shouted through the wood, "you come near me and there won't be anything you can do or say. My dad'll fucking crucify you!" Her voice was shaky and it made Fry's heart flutter just a little.

He had never known this spoilt little bitch to be anything other than totally full of herself, and now to hear fear in her voice, to hear uncertainty, it was empowering. He knocked on the door three times.

"Come on now Lorelei...come and play with your Uncle Fry," he said with a maniacal grin.

He heard a latch being unlocked on a window

and realised Lorelei was trying to make an escape. He stepped back and with one forceful boot, kicked the solid pine door in. The handle and lock remained frozen in place for a second before falling to the ground while the rest of the door swung inwards. Lorelei, still naked and terrified, fumbled to get the window up, but it was too late, she could feel Fry behind her. He pushed himself against her naked back, and she turned, edging into a corner, forcing daylight between the two of them. He was a powerful, muscular man, but there was no way she would give up without a fight.

"Whatever you do to me, you piece of shit, it will be the last thing you do. My dad will make fucking mincemeat out of you!" she spat.

"About that, sweetheart," he said with one hand still behind his back. "Your dad has got to leave us. But I told him he could kiss you goodbye before he went."

Her face became confused for a moment, not understanding what Fry was saying, then as he brought his hand around revealing The Don's severed head with his tongue unnaturally protruding beyond his lips. She realised her life was over. Her hysterical scream nearly deafened Fry, but if he was to lose his hearing, he could have no sweeter sound to accompany him for his remaining years.

"Now give Daddy a kiss!" he yelled, widening his eyes in excitement as he pushed The Don's severed head into the screaming girl's face.

7

Mike and Jules stood on top of the smouldering wreckage of the storefront. The pair looked out past the vast car park, beyond the dual carriageway and to where Mike had heard the rumble of an untold number of RAMs a few hours before.

"Here they come," he said, spotting the first figures emerging. "We've probably got three minutes before they get here."

"So what's the plan?" Jules asked, nervously.

"We get to one of the vans, try and draw the RAMs away from here while our people get out of the city."

"That's it?" she asked, disbelieving. "No fuckin' offence? The way your girlfriend and sister talked about you, I thought you'd be the Second Coming. That sounds like the worst fuckin' plan I've ever heard."

"You swear a lot for a girl don't you?"

"Go fuck yourself."

"Lead on," Mike said.

"Y'what?"

"Take me to the feckin' vans y'big eejit," replied Mike, mimicking her Irish accent. "You understand that?"

"Smart arsed little shit," replied Jules before climbing down the mountain of debris and breaking into a sprint towards the neighbouring superstore.

As they ran, Mike pulled out a flare from his backpack and ignited it, and a burst of bright green flame erupted into life. He began waving it around aggressively, and as more beasts emerged over the carriageway, he could see in the breaking light of day that their attention had been snatched by the bright, rapid movement.

"What the fuck are you doing?" Jules shouted.

"The thing about a decoy is it only works if it's being followed," he replied sprinting faster to join her.

"I thought we were going to get into the van first?"

"Jules, by the time we get to the van, they would already be in the store. Now stop talking and run," he ordered, continuing to wave the flare around.

*

"Right, everybody, listen up," shouted Emma. All movement and nervous chatter in the interior of the store halted, and she felt a moment's self-consciousness, but then cast it aside remembering that her brother was once again risking everything to try and keep her and those around her safe. "Get the children and the injured into the back. Everybody else, pick up your weapons and get ready to fight." She looked around to see the frightened faces in the dim light of the interior. The odd glint of fear sparkled in the flames still burning at the front of the store. "Listen to me. I know how you feel. I know what you're thinking. A few weeks ago I was in your shoes. I was scared, I was weak, and all I wanted to do was hide. But in the end, you run out of places to hide, and the only option is to stand and fight." She looked towards Sarah and Lucy who had stopped treating the injured to listen. "Right now, we need to make a stand until it's safe for us to leave. So swallow your fear, swallow your doubts and join me at the front with your weapons."

Emma looked around at the faces, picked up her rifle, flung the strap over her shoulder, picked up a spear and marched to the mountain of wreckage at the storefront without another word. At first, no one followed her, but then Sarah looked towards the injured, then looked towards Emma. If the RAMs made it in, saving the injured would become a redundant issue anyway. She picked up a wooden spear that had been made earlier in the day and went to join Emma at the front.

"That was the bravest thing I've ever heard," she said quietly as she walked up to her friend.

"Thanks, but given a choice of being in here or being out there, I'd take this option every time. You want bravery, think of Mike and Jules," she said as she began adding to the mountain of rubble, trying to build as big a barrier as she could between her and the outside.

*

"Shit, there's a fence?"

"Course there's a fence, what do you expect?" replied Jules beginning her ascent of the chain links.

"Where's the van?"

"They're around the back in the loading bay."

Mike pushed the flare through one of the holes and quickly climbed over.

"Listen to me, Jules, we can't afford to let them lose sight of us." He pulled the shotgun out of the back of his rucksack and pumped it ready for action. "Right, this is ready to shoot, you just aim and pull the trigger. When it's fired, pump it like you just saw me do and fire again. Only use it as a last resort." He picked up the flare and began waving it to make sure the RAMs didn't lose sight of them.

"What the fuck are you talking about? That fence won't hold with all those things attacking it," she said, looking out towards the sea of moving bodies, the hundreds of running feet pounding on the tarmac almost drowning out the excited growls of hunger.

"You're wasting time, Jules. Get the van and get

back here. If you're too late for me, then lead them away from here, then when you think you're far enough, put your foot down as hard as you can and just get the hell out of town." He began waving his arms around once again and skipping sideways in order to keep the attention of the advancing hordes.

Jules was frozen to the spot. "That's fuckin' madness, Mike."

"Just go, Jules. A lot of people are depending on you."

Reluctantly, she turned and ran, looking down at the shotgun as she went. This was insane. She was just a girl from Belfast, she liked going out with her mates and playing football. How the hell had she ended up here? She scanned the area as she ran, making sure there was no movement on her side of the fence. She made it to the corner of the building and paused, giving one last look back towards the flimsy chain-link barrier before disappearing. The animated figure with the flare was still dancing up and down, and as her eyes adjusted to the light more and more, she could see the size of the army of beasts heading towards him.

"Jesus, Mary, Mother of God!"

*

Emma had arranged three rows of lancers. Each row consisted of twenty-five people, each person had a sharp spear and one other weapon for close combat such as a screwdriver or hatchet. The second row was two metres back from the first, the third row, two metres back from that. She had quickly explained that if the RAMs broke through the first row, it was the job of the second to take over and so on. Her hope was that not a single RAM would appear over the wall of wreckage, but that would probably be asking too much. The small army stood in virtual silence listening to the thundering steps of the masses of beasts surging across the car park.

Emma and Sarah stood next to each other in the centre of the front row. Directly to the right of Emma stood Beth, just a few weeks earlier, a meek farm girl, now, a battle-hardened soldier. They waited, tense, nervous, edgy. The three of them kept throwing glances back past the ranks assembled behind them, to Lucy and her deputies as they frantically got the children, the old, and the injured out of harm's way.

*

As the first of the RAMs flung itself at the fence, Mike pulled out a machete from his rucksack and thrust the blade through the gap in the chain-links and straight into the creature's eye. Immediately, other RAMs smashed against the chain-link barrier, making it bow a little more with each impact. Mike withdrew the blade watching the grey face, tinged green in the light of the emergency flare, stare back at him with its one lifeless eye. The pressure from the RAMs that had already piled up behind the creature, kept it in place, not allowing it to fall to the floor. Mike took a step back, and then another. Suddenly, there were no visible gaps. The RAMs had caught up, and now the ones at the front were being thrust hard against the fence. Their contorted grey faces and bodies being squeezed like rotten meat through a mincing machine.

As more and more creatures pushed forward, what once looked like a sturdy divide became less and less secure. The metal shifted and creaked under the weight and force of the RAMs. Mike took several more steps back, each pace whipping the creatures to a greater frenzy. An explosion sounded to the back of him. He knew only too well that it was the distinctive signature of the shotgun. It rang out again. He watched as many of the RAMs heads turned in that direction, tantalised by the possibility of finding further prey beyond the lump of fresh meat that stood just beyond the fence. He hoped that Jules had made it to one of the vans. If she hadn't, it was all over. Over the cacophonous dirge of the growling creatures, Mike heard other sounds, popping sounds, followed by a grinding throb of concrete on concrete. He looked up and down the line of fencing to see two of the large stone fence posts had been uprooted and the integrity of the entire divide was beginning to crumble.

"Oh fuck!" His voice was lost in the roar of the creatures.

Another loud crack resonated in the early morning air, and as if in slow motion, the fencing began to collapse forward. The first of the creatures collapsed with it, but the ones behind climbed over them as if they were nothing more than rocks or mounds of dirt.

Mike's morbid curiosity lasted just milliseconds as the reality of the situation snapped him back into action. He turned and began to sprint as fast as he could.

He remembered when he had been back in Skelton trying to escape fifty of these things, now there were hundreds, possibly even thousands. He remembered how they didn't seem to tire, but how he had. He remembered becoming more desperate with each metre he ran and eventually making the decision to trap himself in that house, that, but for one moment of inspiration could have been his tomb. That day had been like a walk in the park compared to this ordeal.

He bolted across the enormous car park, for the first few metres not daring to look back, just trying to put as much distance between him and the beasts as possible. It was only after a few seconds that he realised at the other side was another fence, and even from this distance and in such dim light he could see three threatening strands of barbed wire adorning the top of it. Even if he made it across there before the RAMs, he would probably get caught on the barbed wire and dragged back down to a grisly demise.

The noise behind him was constant, but it echoed throughout the otherwise still morning, so Mike couldn't gauge where the creatures were in relation to him. He turned his head, catching a peek and wished he hadn't. It reminded him of a scene from one of his beloved samurai films; countless charging warriors heading to a bloody battle, except now, they were not brave samurai. They had been replaced by bloodthirsty monsters, and they weren't exactly charging towards battle as much as charging towards breakfast.

He was running in a straight line, if he changed

direction and headed towards the exit, it would mean the distance between him and the creatures to his left would close. If he ran in the direction Jules had taken, he would encounter a similar problem. He could only assume Jules had not made it. There had been no further gunshots, there had been no sound from a revving engine, although that might be difficult to hear over the rumble from behind. He was by himself and his only chance, if he could call it that, was to get over the fence on the other side and hope that would give him enough respite to build up a bigger lead. It would all be over one way or another within the next twenty seconds.

*

There were bound to be stragglers. Even these single-minded creatures were limited to some extent by the bodies they inhabited. Emma hoped that they would be few and easily manageable though. They had stayed quiet during the stampede that had taken place outside. But there were still patches of un-extinguished fire that flickered the suggestion of mealtime to the RAMs.

Emma heard it then. To her, it was a familiar sound, but to those who had never gone up against these creatures in hand-to-hand combat, it was not. The growling gurgle got louder. She listened as small amounts of rubble were displaced and then she saw it, its battered head and torn clothing slowly emerged over the mountain of debris. As it appeared, she heard sharp intakes of breath from around her. She heard the stifled screams of children from behind her; once that would have been her, but not now. On seeing living, breathing men and women, the

RAM became excited and moved down the slope as quickly as it could, snagging itself on pieces of twisted metal and stumbling over jagged breezeblocks along the way. Despite its single-mindedness, Emma wasn't afraid. It had been an old woman in life, frail and weak. Its leg was now twisted, and yes, it could be potentially dangerous, but not to her.

She realised these people around her needed a show of strength, needed to be led. She slung the rifle off her shoulder, put down her spear and pulled out her knife. Marching forward and climbing a few feet up the pile of debris to meet the lone invader, she nonchalantly plunged her blade straight through the beast's temple.

A few weeks before, fear would have stopped her from approaching the creature, and the questioning doubt that maybe there was some small remnant of the person that once was in there would have halted her from killing it. Now, though, as she watched not so much the life but the disconnection of the final current, flickering in the RAM's ghoulish grey eyes, she felt nothing.

She withdrew the knife, and the pathetic bundle of rags and twisted bones collapsed, just another piece of rubbish to add to the pile. She wiped her blade off and marched back to her position, slinging the rifle back on her shoulder and picking up her spear. She sensed the eyes of others on her, and then she heard more sounds.

These were more vibrant than before, like large animals following tracks of prey. Three more figures emerged over the crest of the debris. These looked more like the dangerous creatures she was used to. She spared a moment to think of her brother, out there in a sea of these things. Then she let that image feed her aggression, and she moved forward, goading the three creatures to head towards her. The plan worked, all three, spoilt for choice by the array of fresh meat just lined up for the tasting, headed straight towards the closest one.

Emma felt someone to the side of her, she took a quick look. It was Beth. Sarah—as much as she wanted to—was still frozen to the spot, terrified by the truth behind these soulless aberrations.

The three RAMs charged at the same time. Emma and Beth struck mercilessly, as if choreographed, their spears sunk into the eye sockets of two of the creatures. Emma booted the third back, to give herself enough time to withdraw her spear from the first, but she did not need to. As the creatures flew down to the ground another figure blurred past Emma's side and plunged a spear deep into the beast's skull. It was Rob, one of Jules's brothers. He looked towards Emma and nodded appreciatively as if to thank her for taking such a brave lead. He didn't get a chance to say anything before more menacing creatures began to appear over the top of the mound.

*

An eardrum shredding screech of tyres tore through the sound of the chorus of growls and gurgles as Mike continued to sprint towards the fence. He looked to his right and saw a white transit van careening along a footpath, barely wide enough to take the vehicle's axle. The front wheels left the edge of the curb and flew through the air landing hard on the tarmac of the car park. They juddered momentarily threatening a loss of control, and Mike's heart juddered along with them.

Jules corrected her steering and saw the grey ocean of undead faces that was threatening to overwhelm Mike like a tsunami from hell. She realised that just continuing towards him, there wouldn't be enough time for them to make an escape before the van was consumed. It took Mike a couple of seconds to realise what she was doing. Jules swung the wheel and began heading towards the oncoming army at a diagonal, then, as she nearly reached both them and Mike, she swung the wheel back and floored the accelerator, heading straight towards the fence. The distance was thirty metres at the most, but she prayed that it was enough. She nearly went through the windscreen as the initial impact struck the front bumper, and for a heart-stopping second, she thought it was all over, then the green chain-links parted like a curtain. She heard the scrape of the barbed wire as the van passed underneath it and the scrape of the fence as it dug gashes into the paint, but she was through. She immediately rolled down her window and snapped the mirror back into position. Mike was seconds away. She leaned over to open the door and kept the van going ahead.

"Move, move!" he yelled.

As he grabbed hold of the passenger door and the roof of the van, she sped up and Mike nearly lost his grip, but, it was just a momentary slip, and he soon got it back. He slammed the door, sliding the rucksack from his shoulder and into the footwell. He bent over, taking agonised breaths as the van continued to head off.

"Keep them in sight Jules," he said, trying hard to regain his composure.

Jules checked the mirror, the swarm of beasts were still following, but she was pulling away. She eased on the accelerator just a little.

Looking across to her passenger she said, "I don't know if that was the bravest thing or the stupidest thing I've ever seen, but whichever it was, I'm glad you're okay."

Mike was still bent double, his heart was pounding and his chest felt raw. He reached out his hand to the gear stick and placed it over Jules's, squeezing tightly.

"You saved my life, Jules. Thank you!" he said, still labouring for breath.

"We can sing each other a fuckin' serenade later, but in case you hadn't noticed, we're still shoulder deep in shite here."

Mike managed a small smile as he took a controlling breath and tried to sit upright. He looked across at the dashboard, the needle was hovering close to empty.

"You weren't kidding about the fuel, were you?" he said rolling down his own window to click the mirror back into place. "Right, on my way in, I dumped my bike near an old carpet showroom, it wasn't that far away from here. Do you know where I mean?"

"You're going to have to do better than that. There are loads of places like that around here," she replied, anxiously checking the mirror to make sure she was maintaining a good speed.

Mike closed his eyes for a second to remember. "It was on a corner. It looked like it had gone out of business long before all this started. I dumped the bike at a bus stop, just a few yards away."

"I think I know where you mean," she said as the van slowed to exit the car park and head left.

*

Sarah forced her spear through the chest of a RAM who towered over her. The vicious creature's arms flailed angrily in her direction, and she realised they were getting closer. Despite the spear having pierced the chest cavity, it had not encumbered the monster's advance by more than a few seconds.

Sarah's forehead creased in confusion and fear. She had heard a thousand times how these beasts had to be stabbed through the head, but she felt certain, a spear to the chest would have stopped this one. Its arms grabbed at her once again and this time she felt the breeze from the passing tips of the creature's fingers. The grey eyes punctuated only by an eerie shattered pupil made larger by the dim lantern light from behind her. The beast opened its mouth, seemingly tasting the air as each struggling second drew it closer to Sarah. The beginnings of a cry began from inside her, but then a wooden spear whizzed past the side of her head and through the beast's eye. It stopped its struggle immediately and collapsed to the floor. Sarah followed the line of the weapon and saw the end of it clasped firmly in Lucy's hand.

"The head, Sweetie, always make sure it's the head," she said, quickly withdrawing the spear and thrusting it firmly into the right eye of another advancing creature.

Most of the RAMs were on the floor dead, a couple were still in the throes of a struggle, but as the spearmen and women became more confident, they worked together quickly to put the beasts down. Lucy saw Emma had climbed to the top of the hill of rubble, leaving a trail of dead creatures behind her. It was remarkable to think that a few weeks ago, she and Emma had been stuck in a house surrounded by RAMs ready to end it all. She quickly surveyed the area, making sure there was no immediate danger and edged up the mound of wreckage to join Emma. She laid down flat on her belly by her side.

Emma who had momentarily had her head held over the peak edged back down. "There are a couple that are wandering aimlessly close to the entrance, but the rest of them seem to have taken the bait."

The pair of them looked at each other for a moment as Emma realised what she had said. The bait was her brother, Lucy's love.

"I didn't mean..."

"It's okay, I know what you meant... Listen. We're all ready back there. The ones who can't walk, we've got them on flatbed trolleys, we're getting people assembled in the back ready to go. There are some trailers in the back as well that might come in useful too. One of the older guys is going out to attach them to the vans now. She paused for a breath and then continued. "You did really good here today. You saved these people Emma."

"Mike and Jules saved them, Lucy." There was no false modesty in her statement, and she slowly got to her feet and made her way back down the mound.

8

"I think I might have picked the one with the least fuel," said Jules apologetically as the van began to splutter. They were a good fifty metres ahead of the rampaging army of RAMs now, but no distance would make Jules feel safe.

"That's good, that gives the others a better chance. Floor it Jules, we're not far away now," said Mike pushing the shotgun back into his rucksack.

Jules did as requested and put her foot down on the accelerator. The van coughed forward a little more and then spluttered to a stop.

"Okay, run!" shouted Mike, grabbing his rucksack and climbing out of the van. The pair sprinted down the road, throwing urgent looks behind them. "There's the bus shelter," he shouted as they turned onto a familiar-looking street.

Within seconds, Mike had mounted the bike like

he had been riding it all his life. Jules had never been on a motorbike before and couldn't actually ride a bicycle, but given the situation, she was more than willing to learn. The engine started and Mike pulled out of the bus shelter in time to see the street full of RAMs heading their way.

"Hold on tight!" he shouted, and Jules sunk her fingers into his chest in order to stop them from shaking with fear.

Mike revved the engine loudly, but the bike didn't move an inch. He made it growl so loud it drowned out the sound of the increasingly excitable horde that was heading towards them. Jules knew what he was doing. She knew he was waiting until the last possible second to make sure he took as many stragglers as was possible, but the sight of the bloodthirsty creatures terrified her, and she pushed her face into his back and closed her eyes tight as if she was a little girl holding onto a teddy bear for comfort.

The wheels eventually began to turn, but rather than tearing down the street at maximum speed, they kept a steady 30mph before pausing once again at the street's end. Mike saw more RAMs heading from the north. They had probably been too far away when the initial explosion at the Home and Garden Depot had occurred, but now, rather than hunting around aimlessly, they had a definite target in their sights.

The light had improved dramatically since they had first set out, so Mike didn't have to worry about any nasty surprises waiting in the shadows, but his primary concern had never been for himself or even for Jules. His concern had been to lead as many of these creatures out of the city as he could. As the bike's engine idled, the sound of the beasts became deafening once again. He took out the shotgun and fired a couple of rounds into the advancing crowd. His only reason being to alert any more RAMs that were not already on the hunt for him to his presence. Jules lifted her head, her face had drained of all colour. She looked up the street and saw the other group coming towards them and once again nestled her head into Mike's back and clenched her eyes tight. Tears began to form, and she thought about her brothers.

The bike moved off once again, the pace steady, the direction south. Each second they travelled put greater distance between themselves and their people.

*

When Emma stepped out onto the loading bay, most of the people had already been loaded into the box vans. Beth and George were coordinating all the efforts, and Rob, Andy and Jules's other brother, Jon, were loading the trailers with even more supplies.

"We're almost ready to go. George thought it was too good an opportunity to waste valuable DIY supplies now that we've got the trailers too. With what's in the transits and the box vans as well, we can probably build a new village. What's going on out there?" asked Beth, gesturing towards the world beyond the store.

"Those gunshots we heard seem to have caught the attention of the last stragglers. It's deserted."

"Listen!" said Beth as she pulled a satchel onto

her shoulder. Emma noticed the handle of a hatchet sticking out of it and smiled inwardly as she realised her brother had clearly started a new trend. "George and I have been talking with Jules's brothers. It's a waste to get out of the city and then abandon the vehicles. One of the transits has got nearly a third of a tank. Once we're a few miles out, wouldn't it make sense to park up and go on a scouting trip for more fuel? It's all rural as you head north. There must be some farm vehicles or something that haven't been drained by the raiders. We could take some jerricans and hosepipes and siphon enough fuel to get us back to the coast and then some."

"I thought we were going to have to ferry people out of here. Are you saying we've got enough room to haul everybody out in one trip?"

"We've got room to spare, we've already filled a couple of the vans with supplies."

"So, you weren't so much asking me as telling me what you were going to do?" Emma smiled.

Beth looked a little embarrassed. Although there had been no official designation, it had been clear that Emma and Lucy had been running things up to this point.

Emma nodded, "it's a good idea. We should do it." She looked the row of vehicles. "Where's Lucy?"

"She's in the box van at the end with Sarah and some of the injured."

"Okay, I'll go do one last sweep to make sure

we're not leaving anybody behind, and then we'll head out." She disappeared back into the vast retail complex while the final van was readied for the journey.

*

Fry's house was not the grandest in Loch Uig, but he was not interested in grandiosity, he was interested in practicality. It was a decent size, it was surrounded by a large garden and hedges giving him privacy, but most importantly, it had a solid fuel stove that gave him heat and hot water. He stood in the shower letting the scorching spray wash away the final streaks of The Don's blood from his scarred face.

Outside, a new day dawned. For so long, he had been held back by The Don. He had lost so much time and so many resources due to The Don's simple-minded debauchery, but now that was at an end. At eight o'clock tonight he would rally his new army. He would sound the battle cry, and he would take back this land from the RAMs and the weak. A new system of feudalism would rule, all his men would reap the benefits, but he would reign over everything. He would have supreme power. Fry felt intoxicated by its promise.

He heard the glass door of the shower open and then close behind him. Two cold hands gently came to rest on his hips before slowly working their way around his mid-section and up to the bristling grey and ginger hair on his chest.

"Morning, Daddy, I didn't hear you come in." Juliet rested her head on his back. As she pulled the rest of his body closer to her. He felt her nakedness against him and smiled.

"Have you seen the present I brought you?" he asked, continuing to wash himself, but becoming more aroused by Juliet's wandering fingers as each second passed.

"No. What have you brought me?" she asked, pulling his muscular frame around to face her. She looked down, "Is that it?" she smiled, her eyes lighting up.

"You can always have that sweetheart," he grinned widely revealing his nicotine-stained teeth. "No, I've got something special for you down in the cellar."

Juliet's eyes flared, and Fry remembered back to the first time he had seen her, lying on her back, completely disinterested in the man on top of her. Their eyes had locked and there was something in that hypnotic gaze of hers that drove him to want her, to need her. She was a kindred spirit. Since the pair had moved to Loch Uig, there had been a number of visitors to their cellar ranging from men who looked a little too longingly at Juliet to lowly members of Lorelei's entourage. A census had never been taken by The Don and desertion was nothing out of the ordinary, so rarely was curiosity sparked by a disappearance. But now, Fry had brought Juliet the ultimate prize.

"Come on, I'll show you," he said, turning off the shower and stepping out.

"Can't it wait?" asked Juliet, Fry's excitement

sending a wave of electrical impulses through her that demanded satisfaction.

"When you see it, you'll be glad we didn't," he replied, dousing his hairy body with a towel before throwing on a bathrobe.

Juliet's shoulders sank. She nearly always acted on impulse, when she couldn't, it felt like she was betraying her body. She stepped out of the shower cubicle with a pout and flung on her own robe. "This better be worth it," she said, only half-joking.

Fry smiled as he led her out of the bathroom and down the stairs. They walked along the hall and into the kitchen. A painted wooden door with a rickety handle squeaked out of its frame as Fry turned the key and pulled. Light flooded into the entrance, but darkness lay beyond. He picked up a lantern and flicked the switch casting illumination on their surroundings. Juliet shut the door behind them, closing the rest of the world out of their secret place.

As they descended the stone steps, Juliet could hear a continuous suffering wail. Her teeth bore in an enthralled smile, and she felt compelled to reach out and lovingly caress Fry's shoulder. They reached the bottom of the steps and creaked open a more flimsy, panelled door, bearing the rotting signs of age and damp. As it swung open, the sound became more pronounced. As the two entered the small room, Juliet let out an excited giggle and clapped her hands like a child at a surprise birthday party.

Lorelei was spread eagle against the damp plaster

of the cellar wall. Her hands and feet were tied with rope and secured to thick galvanised steel staples like the kind you would find on industrial padlocks. The staples had been secured through the plaster and to the stone beyond. She was naked and her normally perfectly styled black hair hung limply over her bowed face. She was sobbing uncontrollably. Fry had left several lanterns and candles burning which lit up the room enough to illuminate the centrepiece which was a jardinière he had brought down from the living room. Before a spider plant had decorated the antique piece of pottery, but now The Don's head stared straight towards his captive daughter. His blank eyes and protruding tongue were morbid reminders of the horrifying moment she had found out her father was no more.

Lorelei looked up, sensing the presence of someone else in the room. Strands of damp black hair stuck to her face as tears had glued them into position. Thick saliva muffled her words as she struggled to come to grips with the reality of her situation. "Daddy," she cried again like a lost child in a field of strangers.

"Daddy," Juliet mocked her and then aggressively pulled Fry around.

She grasped tight hold of the hair on the back of his head, tearing a few strands loose in her vice-like grip, then pulled his head towards her. She stuck her tongue in his mouth like an animal marking its territory and pulled his waist into her. Then she released him with the same quick impulse. She shuddered. All her senses alive at once.

"Baby, you've outdone yourself this time," she

said as she walked over to The Don's head. She bent down to look at it and gently smoothed his comb-over back into place. "I don't think I've ever seen you looking better," she said and pushed her lips up to the The Don's forehead.

Lorelei screamed. "Leave him alone!" as if further damage could be done, but that just made Juliet all the more giddy with the prospect of playing with her new toys. She stood up and placed her hand on The Don's head, brushing his thin hair again and again as if she was stroking a favourite pet.

"Oh Lorelei," said Juliet looking towards the pathetic young woman. "I'm not going to do anything to your daddy. Anything that has gone before is just water under the bridge now. Me and your daddy are going to be best friends," she said breaking into the widest grin yet.

Lorelei had done bad things in her time. Wicked things. She had lived a more debauched life than her father in some ways, but this was something else. This was an insanity she had never come across before—an evil that turned her blood stone cold. She wanted to scream and shout and threaten, but she realised, that's what these monsters wanted. They wanted to put a sound to her fear and suffering, so she put her head down and quietly sobbed.

*

"How long before we head back?" shouted Jules over the sound of the engine.

They had travelled three miles south of the city

on the A9. The pace had been slow, and Mike had frequently had to stop to make sure the bike kept within a tantalising reach of the horde of RAMs following them.

"I want to make sure we lead them well out of the city just in case our lot ran into any problems," he called back over his shoulder.

Jules had eased her grip a little as she gradually became used to the feel and movement of the bike beneath her. She dared to look back over her shoulder and then wished she hadn't. The nearest RAMs were no more than forty metres away. Their snarling faces as angry as ever, no sign of tiring, no hint that they would give up the chase. She placed her head on Mike's warm back and closed her eyes tight. She hardly knew the man she was with, but at least he was a man. Warm blood ran through his veins, a heart beat within him, and if the worst happened and they did not make it back then at least she would die with one of her own kind rather than alone at the hand of the devil's beasts.

*

"Daddy got called away on business, but I thought that would give the two of us time to really get to know each other," said Juliet as she returned to the cellar. She walked up to The Don's head and stood behind it.

Lorelei reluctantly looked up. The candles and lanterns still burned strong. She saw that Juliet had now changed into a pair of black leather trousers and a revealing low cut t-shirt. It occurred to Lorelei that she had seen them before and as the sad fuzziness began to lift, she suddenly realised from where. They were her clothes. She lurched angrily, and Juliet cocked her head back and laughed at the sight of the tied woman clumsily trying to reach her.

Lorelei fumed at first, but then something registered. Her right hand had moved forward ever so slightly. She turned and looked at her bound wrist. The knot was still tight, but the thick staple had edged out of the wall a little. She quickly turned her head back and noticed Juliet was still laughing in her self congratulatory manner.

"You like?" Juliet asked, gesturing to her clothing. "Who knew we'd be the same size?" she said, smiling viciously at her captive. "Y'know Lorelei, you have just been the biggest pain in my arse since the day I ever heard your damned name. Every time you've had the opportunity to bring my man down, you've done it and for that, I am going to make you suffer like you never even dreamed was possible you *fucking bitch*."

The smile left her face with her last two words and a snarl appeared heralding the revealing of the true face behind the mask.

"What do you think, Daddy, should we make her suffer?" Juliet asked, animatedly bending down to look at The Don's severed head. She stayed there a second and then grabbed hold of the head aggressively. "It's polite to answer when someone asks you a question," said Juliet.

She unclasped her fingers, making the head rock unsteadily on the jardinière and walked over to the old fashioned workbench. She took down a screwdriver with a long blade and walked back over to The Don. She looked up at Lorelei who stared out from behind her matted hair.

"Maybe Daddy needs his ears cleaning. What do you think?" asked Juliet, cocking her head to the side.

"Leave him alone," whispered Lorelei.

"What was that?" asked Juliet, getting an almost sexual satisfaction from knowing that she had finally drawn Lorelei into her sick little game.

"I said leave him alone, you insane, fucking bitch!" Lorelei screamed, jerking hard against her restraints and feeling her right hand gain a little more freedom.

Juliet frowned and adopted a mock indignant posture, putting one hand on her hip and pointing at Lorelei with the screwdriver. "You're a guest in this house young lady, and I won't put up with that kind of language from you." She took her hand off her hip and put it on The Don's head. "Just for that, I'm going to clean his ears out whether you like it or not," she said placing the blade of the screwdriver in The Don's right ear.

She paused for a second to make sure she had Lorelei's full attention and then began to push. Her face and eyes flashed and contorted with pleasure as the blade worked through the dead tissue in The Don's skull.

Lorelei screamed aggressively towards her, but that just made the experience more exciting, more fulfilling. She looked down to see the screwdriver advance millimetre by millimetre, then she looked up to see Lorelei writhing and crying. Once the gory blade appeared at the other side and Lorelei's cries turned to nothing more than weak sobs, Juliet heard her own breathing and realised just how sensual the whole experience had been for her. She wanted more. She had to have more.

"You sick, fucking bitch, I hope you fucking burn in Hell," croaked Lorelei, battling the tears that mourned the vile treatment of her dead father.

"Oh, Lorelei. This is Hell, darling. And you don't see me burning do you?" she bore her teeth in a cruel smile and sauntered across to the wall where her captive was held.

Lorelei had her head down again, her suffering sobs and whimpers doing nothing but fuelling Juliet's sadistic satisfaction. Juliet almost lovingly caressed Lorelei's matted hair out of her face and around the back of her ears. Then she gently brushed away the young woman's tears with the tips of her thumbs and lovingly stroked her cheeks before moving her talon-like hands down Lorelei's neck, over her shoulders and down the sides of her naked body. Juliet closed her head towards Lorelei's face and breathed deeply, consuming her scent like a wolf sniffing for prey in the cold night air. She moved her nose up to Lorelei's ear then kissed it gently before bringing her head back around to face her.

"Stop crying, sweetheart," she urged, cupping both her hands around her captive's cheeks. "I don't want you to use all your tears up before Fry gets home. We're all going to have so much fun together." Her dark eyes glimmered in the flickering light of the candles, flashing menacingly.

She had broken the girl in a matter of minutes. Sometimes the fun was in the breaking, sometimes the fun was in what came after. Juliet sensed there was a lot more fun to be had with this one. She closed her eyes and pushed her lips against Lorelei's.

Lorelei could feel the smile breaking on Juliet's face as her captor's kiss of celebration stabbed her senses. She knew it was now or never. Lorelei tugged her arm with all her strength and with a scraping charge, her restraint came loose. She grabbed a fistful of Juliet's hair whose surprise rendered her frozen for a split second. Lorelei used the time to summon every last ounce of primal, survival instinct she had and opened her mouth wide before lunging at Juliet's cheek, sinking her teeth hard into the soft skin. She bit down with all the force she could muster and immediately fresh screams filled the air, but this time, they did not belong to Lorelei.

Lorelei whipped her head back spitefully taking with it Juliet's cheek. She relaxed her hand and Juliet staggered back, disbelievingly. Her scream sounded funny as the sound escaped not only her mouth, but the hole in the side of her face. She saw the huge chunk of flesh hanging out of Lorelei's bloody smiling mouth, but still could not believe it, and she reached up to touch where her cheek was only to feel her own teeth. She continued to scream, but now the scream brought forth tears as well. Lorelei spat hard and the lump of flesh slapped into Juliet's face, the symbolism more than the weight of it knocking her off her feet.

Lorelei quickly got to work on untying her other hand and then her feet while Juliet, still in a state of agonised shock, tried holding the torn flesh up to her cheek to see if it would magically fit back into place. Her tormented cries gave Lorelei no satisfaction, she was a lot of things, but a sadist was not one of them. She finished untying her feet and skirted around Juliet whose eyes now shone with the light of a different kind of insanity. She remained on the floor while her former captive walked over to the head of her dead father. She swiftly withdrew the screwdriver, turned angrily, and remembering the suffering the bitch on the floor had subjected her to just moments before, she sunk the blade into Juliet's temple. The cries and groans ended instantly as Juliet's body collapsed.

Lorelei stood there looking down, her nakedness forgotten for the time being. This was the first person she had ever killed. It gave her no sense of pleasure, nor did she feel regret. They were two animals in a struggle; a fight to the death, one of them had to die and Lorelei was just grateful she had won. She rolled her tongue around summoning all the saliva she could and spat the bloody residue onto the floor.

There was no more time to reminisce or to justify. Fry could be back at any time. She needed to flee. If Fry had seized power, there was no one in the town she could trust. Lorelei had enjoyed privilege, she had enjoyed a string of men who had vowed their loyalty to her and her father, but she knew that was only as long as the two of them had power and position. Her only hope now was to get out of Loch Uig, get far away. She bent down and pulled off the t-shirt Juliet was wearing. It brushed against the wet blood on her face and head. Lorelei put it on, curling her nose at the warm, sticky dampness against her skin. She crouched back down and removed the leather trousers leaving Juliet lying there covered in nothing but a pair of white panties and a lot of red blood. She stood up and turned around. Her eyes fixed on the head of her father. She knew there was nothing she could do for him now. She knew it was just flesh and bone.

"Bye, Daddy," she said, sounding more like a frightened little girl than a grown woman. "I love you."

Lorelei made her way up the stairs and into the house.

9

"An engine!" someone shouted.

Emma immediately grabbed her shotgun and looked around for Lucy, but she was nowhere to be seen. The mutterings from the village and depot people came to a sudden halt in anticipation of hearing the same sound. It wasn't long before the noise reached Emma's ears, and she headed towards the front vehicle ready to confront whatever came their way. She felt a presence and noticed Lucy marching beside her, pulling her Glock out as she walked.

The noise got louder until the front of the Home and Garden Depot van could be seen trundling around the corner. Both women let out sighs of relief as they lowered their weapons. Emma glanced at Lucy again, the pair breathed out and smiled.

Before the transit had come to a full stop, Beth opened the passenger door and headed straight to Emma.

"We were getting worried," said Emma.

"It looks like the raiders took any central supplies of fuel, but some of the farm vehicles we found off the beaten track still had red diesel in their tanks. It took us a while to siphon it, but I think we've got enough to get everybody home and more besides."

Emma, still with the shotgun in one hand gave her a firm hug with the other.

"That's fantastic Beth," she said. The others dismounted from the transit and got warm greetings from the rest of their group.

Andy did not take part in the celebrations. After all, most of their present predicament was down to him. In a matter of hours, the weight of his guilt had turned him from a macho man to a humble fool.

"They're not back yet?" he said.

Emma's fury had been almost as powerful as Mike's when the incident with the rat trap had first occurred, but she felt difficulty maintaining it as Andy now stood before her like a lost child. She didn't answer for a moment, questioning whether her feeling sorry for Andy was a betrayal to her brother, then she gave way and just shook her head.

Beth rubbed Emma's upper arm and shoulder compassionately. "This is Mike we're talking about. He knows what he's doing, Emma. They might have had to take a different route back, or they might be just lying low for a while, but if anybody knows how to handle himself out there it's him."

"And Jules is tough," said Andy, feeling the guilt of Emma's pain. "Jules looked out for all of us, all this time." He swallowed hard, trying to force back tears. "She'll be back. They both will."

He turned and walked away, hoping the women hadn't noticed the quiver in his voice.

Beth and Emma looked at each other. "He will be back, Emma," said Beth again. "There isn't a doubt in my mind." Beth looked over Emma's shoulder to see jerricans of diesel being poured into the vehicles.

Emma turned slowly, looking at the assortment of scared, confused and blank faces. She looked towards the vehicles being refuelled.

"And what then," she said quietly.

"Then we go back and rebuild."

"Until it happens again?"

"What are you saying, Emma?" asked Beth, pulling her around so they faced each other.

"How long will we survive? How long can we survive like this?"

Beth looked around nervously, hoping nobody was listening. She guided Emma away to one side of the road.

"You need to stop this Emma," Beth said in a calm but firm voice. "Everybody's looking to you and Lucy. You need to be strong."

Emma let out a deep breath. "I'm sorry Beth. It's just a bit overwhelming sometimes."

"Everybody's looking to you, but that's not the same as having to do everything yourself. Look, when we get back, we'll take stock. We'll get organised and when Shaw and the others return, we'll look at drawing up defence plans."

Emma smiled bitterly, "Shaw's got quite a fan club hasn't he?"

Beth looked puzzled. "What are you talking about?"

The bitterness vanished as Emma realised she was taking out her annoyance on the wrong person.

"Nothing. Never mind," she said shaking her head. She put her hand on Beth's forearm and squeezed gently. "You're right Beth, thanks," she said, pausing a second to make sure the puzzlement lifted from her friend's face. "C'mon, let's get this show on the road."

*

It felt like some bizarre torture for Jules. She kept looking back to see the hellish faces of the undead masses behind her. All it would take was one mechanical malfunction, one hole in the road or a spilt patch of oil that Mike hadn't seen and that would be it. The pair would become a small feast for their army of pursuers.

Mike angled his head around. "Hold on Jules, I think we've taken them far enough."

Jules took tight hold of the thick fabric belt around his waist and closed her eyes. Nothing happened for a second, then she felt the powerful bike begin to accelerate, the engine throbbed and roared and the warm streams of sunlight began to run cool with the increasing wind that washed over them. She waited a short time and then looked back, desperately needing to see distance between her and the RAMs. The creatures were still in pursuit, but with each second they became smaller and smaller until the bike ran over the brow of a hill and they were out of sight.

She turned her head forward and breathed in the cold rushing air. It invigorated her, and for the first time in what seemed like hours, she allowed herself a small smile. The pair carried on for another ten minutes before Jules tugged on Mike's shoulder. He leaned his head back to listen.

"I need to pee," she shouted in his ear.

"Can't you wait a bit?" he shouted back, clearly irritated.

"I've needed to pee for the last half hour and unless you want a wet bum, I think we should stop."

Mike immediately slowed the bike down to a stop and pushed down the kickstand. "Do you want me to come with you?"

"No thanks, I know how to take a piss."

"I meant to stand guard," replied Mike.

Jules smiled, "I'll be fine." She jogged to the side of the road, undoing her belt as she went. A second later she was out of sight, down the side of an embankment.

Mike stood on the deserted highway looking one way then the other. He realised up until this point he hadn't actually thought about the next step, all he had concentrated on was getting the RAMs as far out of the town as possible. His gaze slowly turned to the spectacular Highland landscape and for a short while he allowed his thoughts to be lost in it before they turned to Emma and Lucy. He knew the pair of them were more than capable of getting everybody back to Lonbaig, and some of Jules's people seemed quite able, but what then? Forgetting the long term, forgetting the big picture of how to plan to avert this kind of disaster again, what about the short term?

He looked towards the embankment where Jules had disappeared and realised it had actually been a few minutes since she had gone.

"Jules?" he called. There was no reply. "Jules?" he shouted a little louder this time, but still with no response.

Mike looked towards the bike and then slowly headed towards the spot where she had disappeared. He reached around, pulling the shotgun from his rucksack and aimed it ahead of him as he descended the grassy bank.

Jules quickly stepped out from behind a clump of bushes, making Mike's heart jump.

"Fuck me!" he said taking in a sharp breath and lowering the shotgun simultaneously.

"It's sweet of you to offer, but you're not really my type," she said smiling.

"What took you so long, I was getting worried?"

"I'm sorry if I don't piss fast enough for you. Fuckin' hell, I bet you're a joy to live with," she said, readjusting her belt and heading back to the bike.

Mike muttered something under his breath and shook his head as he followed her back to the road.

"So what's the next part of the plan?" she asked as the pair shared a small bottle of water from Mike's rucksack.

"I think we should keep heading south until we find a turn that can get us onto a route which will get us back in the direction we need to be going without running into the RAMs again."

"Genius plan, you've really thought this through haven't you? Any idea which route or shall we just play eeny meeny miny moe?"

"Hey look, I'm sorry. If some complete fuckwit hadn't blown a hole in the front of your shop, we wouldn't be in this mess would we?" He fired the words with venom, and then immediately backed off realising that she was probably scared and had just as much to lose as he did. "Look. We've done what needed to be done. We gave our people a fighting chance. I didn't really have time to think about the next step, but I'll figure it out, okay?"

Jules handed the bottle to Mike and moved a step closer to him. "I've got a mouth on me, and sometimes I take my problems out on the wrong people. What you did was the right move. Like you said, it gave our people a chance."

"Come on then, we've got a way to go yet."

The pair climbed on and Mike started the engine. The wheels screeched as it set off, and in no time the place they had stopped was just a spot in the distance.

*

The convoy had passed through a number of villages but hadn't slowed down. There had been no need. Although the raid from the previous day had begun on the coast, it was clear that the villages they now travelled through had been attacked, maybe two days before at the most. If there were any survivors they would be in hiding at the sound of engines, fearing the prospect of further horror, further devastation.

Sarah shivered as she saw four crows picking at the face of a dead body up ahead. The birds launched into the air as the sound the engines approached, a temporary interruption to their feast. As the transit moved past the dead man, Sarah looked down and felt sick to her stomach as she saw dark crimson hollows where the man's eyes used to be. One of the crows stood on a gate watching her as she went past. She looked up at it to see a gooey strand of something red hanging from its beak before she looked away and began to shake.

Emma had been concentrating on the road, knowing she would see nothing good if she looked elsewhere. She glanced across at Sarah and extended her hand. Sarah grasped it and wrapped her other hand around it too. "It probably makes sense to keep your eyes shut when we're going through the villages, at least until you get used to this sort of stuff."

Sarah's hands continued to shake as she looked across towards Emma. "I really hope I never get used to this," she replied, her voice quaking, tears forming in her eyes.

"I hope one day all of this will be just a nightmarish memory for us, a snapshot from the end of what we remembered as life." Emma retracted her hand as she took hold of the wheel to steer around a sharp bend.

"I don't want to be weak. I don't want to be scared, and I didn't think I was, but..."

"Sarah!" Emma cut her off. "Don't you dare say you're weak. Nobody else would have saved the kids from your school. Yesterday, when the raiders came, you could have hidden, you could be back home with them right now, but you did the brave thing and you came to help us. There is a big difference between being weak and being scared. Bravery is doing something in spite of your fear, weakness is letting your fear rule you. A few weeks ago, I was letting my fear govern my actions, so I know what I'm talking about here. You've got real guts, so don't put yourself down." She took her eyes off the road to look across at her passenger. A smile passed between them.

"So how did you become like you are now?"

"Being thrown into the lion's den," she replied. "When choice is taken out of the matter, you either survive or you die." She thought for a couple of moments before continuing. "That and watching Mike. If it wasn't for him, we wouldn't be here, not just because of what he did, but what he showed us and what he stood for...stands for. My brother's got some serious issues, I know that, but he's also the best person I know."

*

"Juliet?" yelled Fry as he slammed the front door behind him. He stopped in the hallway waiting for a response, but none came. "Juliet?" he shouted again as he began to march up the stairs.

The property was decorated in a manner that suggested old people had lived there before. The red floral patterned carpet that led up the staircase was clearly good quality (if not a little garish), but he would get it changed soon enough. He would make this place a palace for his beloved queen. He burst through the bedroom door expecting to see her waiting for him. She had a voracious sexual appetite and it was not unusual for him to come home to find her lying naked in bed waiting for his arrival.

The room was empty. He turned to leave but paused as he noticed the wardrobe door slightly ajar and a drawer from the bedside cabinet open. He walked across and looked inside the wardrobe, then in the drawer. Nothing seemed amiss, but it was unusual for Juliet who was so fastidious with regards to tidiness.

"Juliet?" he shouted again as he left the bedroom. He started down the stairs. "I hope you haven't broken the present I got you already?"

He flashed his yellow teeth and brushed his wet pink tongue over his lips in twisted anticipation of what sight he might find down in the cellar. His feet thudded across the kitchen floor and to the cellar door. He turned the handle and found no lantern on the hook, a sure sign that his beloved was downstairs playing. He took out the lighter from his pocket and flicked it on so he could see just enough to make it to the bottom of the staircase without stumbling.

"Can't you hear me down h..." he began as he opened the second cellar door.

His heart turned to stone as he entered.

The candles flickered wildly as they approached the end of their wicks, but the lanterns threw out enough light to illuminate the gory scene. He went across to the collapsed figure on the floor and knelt down, pulling Juliet's still, warm body to him. She had been stripped of everything but her panties, a final humiliation. He looked down at her once beautiful black face to see a hole and teeth where there had once been skin. He moved his hand up to touch it and then higher to the screwdriver handle that still protruded from her temple.

No tears came to his eyes because Fry couldn't feel pain in that way—but a boiling, bubbling mass churned in his stomach.

He placed Juliet back down on the stone floor and stood up. He walked to the empty restraints and turned, resting his back against the cellar wall. In the space of a few seconds, all his plans had been turned on their head.

His body began trembling, then the tremble became a shake, and finally a convulsion, "Y'FUCKIN' BITCH!!!! I'M GONNA FIND YOU. YOU THINK YOU'VE GOT AWAY. YOU'LL NEVER FUCKING GET AWAY!!!!!"

His shouts echoed back at him, the volume and aggression of his words made him lose his voice temporarily and for a while, his ears rang. His face and eyes twitched. He had never felt loss like this, he had never felt anger so powerful. Nothing else mattered to him.

Then he heard it. The quietest of floorboard creaks from above. He sprinted to the bottom of the cellar stairs before pounding up them three at a time. The darkness was no obstacle, and whoever had made that fateful sound was now running along the hallway towards the door. Fry burst through the cellar door, into the hall and like a bullet, headed for Lorelei who was fumbling it open.

A crack of daylight widened, and she could smell freedom before feeling her head and body smash into the thick wood as Fry tackled her. All her breath left her, and she let out a desperate scream. Fry punched her in the stomach and Lorelei collapsed to her knees. Then with no more compassion than he would have for a sack of coal, he dragged her by her hair through the house and back down to the cellar. Her legs and arms flailed as she tried to make a break for freedom, but she was a pathetic fly in the web of a venomous spider. As the tears rolled down her face, she knew her fate had been sealed.

*

There were two ways into Lonbaig; "Dead Man's Pass", which was a long snaking road up an alarmingly steep hillside and was completely impassable in icy conditions. The other way was the long way round which would add forty miles onto their journey. Emma had decided to take the more direct route. Before they had begun the ascent, she had halted the convoy and explained the perils of taking the pass, but the drivers were spurred on by the fact that an end to their journey was at hand.

Sarah remained silent as the engine whirred and whined up the tarmac incline. She glanced to the side and quickly turned back to the front when she saw the sheer drop down a rocky face. She knew her fear would do nothing but distract Emma from her concentration, so she remained silent. She looked in the mirror several times to see one of the vehicles behind going perilously close to the edge and she wondered how near their own wheels were to the crumbling verge.

Emma steered the van around another corner and was glad there was only Sarah in the vehicle to hear her small whimper of concern as she jammed on the brakes. The other vehicles all came to a halt too. Most had remained in either first or second gear for the majority of the journey so far, but at least there had been some momentum. Now, though, the occupants were jolted still, the scenic beauty of the panorama below lost on them.

"Get out this side," said Emma, climbing out of the driver's side.

A question hovered on Sarah's lips, but Emma had vanished before she could ask it. She did as she was told and climbed across to the driver's seat and out. As she hit the ground, she saw Emma talking to Andy who had already got out of the vehicle behind. Andy and George, the older man who had helped Jules earlier on walked with Emma to the corner. George rubbed his fingers across his whiskered chin.

"I've only ever come up here in a car before. The larger lorries have to go the long way round, but the owners of the pub have a box van, and they manage it," said Emma.

"We can't go back. There's nowhere to turn and reversing would be suicide," said Andy, not handling the stress as well as his companion.

"There's no need to panic," George assured all of them. He was a man in his mid-sixties and had a weathered face like he had worked outside most of his life. His eyes were warm and there was wisdom behind them. "This is doable, it's just a bit tricky that's all."

Before anyone else could speak, George went to Emma's van and jumped in the driver's seat. He started the engine and Andy, Emma and Sarah shot nervous glances towards one another. The way they saw it, there was no way for anything bigger than a mini to make this bend in one piece. George gestured for them to get out of the way and they headed back to Andy's van and stood there with their arms folded, trying to suppress the butterflies in their stomach.

The van was just a few inches from the rock face. Emma had manoeuvred it as best she could to get around the bend, but had fallen short. George reversed, all the time shifting the steering wheel to the left. There was a gap of just a few feet behind and to the side of the van as the audience of three held their breath as the tyres went within centimetres of the crumbling edge. Andy signalled wildly with his hands, but George did not see him, his concentration was aimed elsewhere. Just when it looked like the van would roll over the edge, it started moving forward again, this time, George heaved the steering wheel to the right. This continued for over a minute until the van was around the tight bend and on a straight piece of road heading up the hill.

George pulled on the handbrake, climbed out and walked back down to the three figures who were stood in awe. "It's probably best if I hang back to make sure everybody can get around the corner," he said matter-of-factly.

"That was amazing," said Emma, who was still

trying to get her heartbeat back to normal.

George ignored the compliment. He was more interested in just getting the job done. "I'll hop onboard the last vehicle. If you come to any more corners like this, don't try and take them, just get word back to me and I'll do it."

With that, he climbed into the van he and Andy had been travelling in and began to negotiate the same bend.

Half an hour later, the convoy had crossed over the high peak and had begun to descend the other side, which was much straighter and less treacherous. Although they hadn't encountered another bend as dangerous as that sheer one, there had been some tricky corners and both Emma and Sarah breathed a huge sigh of relief as they began their descent.

The relief was short-lived though as they drove past the first house on the outskirts to the village. The outbuilding next to it had been burnt to cinders. How the house had avoided a similar fate was baffling to them. Emma brought the van to a stop and pulled on the handbrake. She was about to get out when Sarah grabbed her arm.

"I think we should get people settled first, don't you? We can take stock later."

The words danced in the air for a moment. Emma knew what Sarah meant. Take stock...take stock of the dead. Take stock of just how brutal mankind could still be despite everything it had suffered through together as a species. Emma didn't say anything, she just gave a nod and released the handbrake so they could continue their journey down to Lonbaig village.

As they entered, Lonbaig possessed the same ransacked look as the other villages they had driven through. Doors were left ajar, windows were broken, belongings were strewn along pathways and verges. A body laid battered and bloody against a painted garden gate. They both recognised it as Douglas Mackinnon, the owner of the post office. Emma remembered Isobel, his wife had been in the Home and Garden Depot with them. She didn't know if she was already aware of her husband's demise, but if she wasn't, she would be soon.

"Oh God!" said Sarah as she tore her eyes away from the motionless body.

"I don't think God's been listening for some time," Emma replied as the trailing path of devastation continued. They passed more bodies lying at the side of the road. "This is going to be hard for us, but it's going to be even harder for the people who've lost someone."

The familiar sign for the caravan park came into view, and Emma turned the van onto the tree-bordered drive. The road opened out into an expansive area containing static and mobile caravans. The devastation here was not as prolific. There were no bodies and no belongings strewn everywhere. The raiders had clearly been here as the odd broken window and smashed door testified, but...it was almost as if someone had begun to tidy up.

She pulled up and got out, heading straight for one of the statics while the rest of the vehicles pulled in. Sarah got out and followed her into the nicely decorated mobile home. Emma headed straight back out sweeping past Sarah.

"Hello!" she yelled over the sound of the other approaching engines. "It's Emma. Emma Fletcher, Sue's granddaughter." No one shouted a reply, and no one materialised. "It's safe to come out. The raiders have gone. They're not coming back."

Emma knew this was only a half-truth and regretted it almost as soon as she said it.

"Emma?" a voice shouted from the trees.

"Yes. Yes, it's me!" she replied to the male voice.

"It's Richard," he replied, waving some bushes to the side as he emerged.

Emma never thought she would be so happy to see the nerdy librarian again. She ran across and flung her arms around him, kissing him on the cheek. "Oh God Richard, are you okay?" she asked pulling back.

"Yes...yes, I'm fine," he replied, taken aback by the warm greeting. "There were some survivors," he said signalling back to the bushes from where he had emerged.

Figures began to emerge from the greenery. There were old and young alike. Emma recognised some of the faces.

"Who are all these people?" asked Richard as the vehicles came to a stop and a host of strangers began to appear.

"It's a long story. But they're like us. They're survivors."

"Are the children okay?" interrupted Sarah.

"Yes. Yes, they're fine. Ruth and David took them back up to Emma's house. Sarah's frame visibly relaxed at the news.

"How's Jake? Is Sammy alright?" asked Emma.

"Sammy is fine," replied Richard. "Jake is still in shock, but he's being well looked after."

Emma let out a breath and turned as the last of the vehicles drove through the gate and ground to a halt. Many people had already disembarked. Some were crying, while some looked numb with fear and bewilderment. She saw Andy trying to comfort his youngest brother, Jon, who was battling with his emotions. Jon was no more than fifteen, and although he was tall like his other brothers, there was a giveaway youthfulness to his face which betrayed his years. Emma went across to them. As she approached, tears began to run down Jon's face.

"Listen to me!" All three of them lifted their heads to look at her. "Jules is tough and she's smart, but even if she wasn't, she's with my brother. There is nobody better to be with out there. They'll both be back, but in the meantime, you need to stay strong. Your people will be looking to you. You need to help them. You need to do what Jules would do." She was about to carry on when she saw Lucy helping a man with a makeshift splint on his leg out of a box van. "Now is the time they will need you the most," she said, giving one final look at the three brothers before heading towards Lucy. As she arrived, the man stumbled. She took his other arm, put it around her shoulder and helped Lucy with him into one of the large static caravans.

They placed him down on an old fashioned sofa, and he let out a yelp of pain, but neither offered too much sympathy—he was one of the lucky ones. A man with bloody rags around his neck and scraps of cloth over his eye was led to a seat by the nurse who had been in the mobile infirmary with Lucy.

"George is organising help to get the others in," Lucy said, giving the other two women a glance before heading back out of the door.

"We're heading up to the house. Are you coming?" asked Emma.

"I've got my work cut out here," she said, nodding to the door as more injured from the explosion at the warehouse were carried in. "I'd appreciate it if you could send my medical bag down along with some of my things," she said as she headed back out to the car park.

"What about Sammy and Jake? Don't you want to see them?" asked Emma.

Lucy dropped her head. "Give them my love.

Tell them I'll try and get up to see them later."

Lucy closed her eyes for a second. People needed her. People were relying on her. She had to put everything else to the back of her mind and do what she was trained to do.

"C'mon, we're leaving," said Emma to Sarah as she walked through the crowded car park.

The pair walked up to George and Andy who were both stood talking to Beth.

"Listen. Lucy's setting up an infirmary in there," Emma said, pointing to one of the static caravans. "We're heading to my place," she said nodding to Beth, who immediately went across to stand by the side of Sarah, "I'm sending Lucy's medical supplies down, and I'll be back later on. That guy over there," she said pointing to her librarian friend, "his name's Richard, you need anything, you see him."

"Emma," called Andy, chasing to catch up to her. "Thanks!"

Emma nodded and returned to her van with Sarah. She took one look back across to the makeshift infirmary and saw Lucy in the doorway, ushering in the wounded.

Driving out of the village in the other direction, a familiar scene unfolded. The raiders had been thorough and merciless. Lonbaig would take a lot of rebuilding, not just the homes, but the place, the people. The three of them travelled in silence and Emma put her foot down on the accelerator, but seven miles had never seemed such a great distance. Just a couple of weeks ago, her gran had held a small get together, "girls only" at the house, where they had bathed in the warm afternoon sun, eaten Sue's homemade pizza, drunk what seemed like gallons of wine and talked and laughed into the early hours. That had been the best day Emma could remember in a long, long time.

And now...now this.

Emma guided the van around the tight bend. The property and outbuildings were almost invisible from the road, but as they headed down the hill, the familiar layout gave each of them a small breath of comfort. The warm feeling they experienced slowly turned cold as they noticed no sign of life in or around the house. Emma pulled on the handbrake and looked at the other two women.

"They mustn't have heard us," said Beth, refusing to believe that anything bad could have happened.

Together the three of them entered the house.

"Hello!" called Emma.

"Hello!" repeated Sarah and Beth in unison, but there was no response.

The three women looked at each other again before beginning a search of the downstairs rooms. On finding them all empty, Emma started upstairs but stopped as she heard Sarah call out.

"Down there, look!" she said as she peered

through the large bay window of the living room. There was a dinghy out on the water and a figure was waving, but not to them, to someone on the beach below.

The three of them sprinted out of the house and down the green hillside towards the beach. As wispy grass turned to sand, their anxiety lifted. At the far end of the small beach was Ruth surrounded by a number of children, all of them collecting mussels from the black rocks and putting them into buckets.

"Ruth!" yelled Emma as she ran towards them. Ruth and the children all had their backs to the three women, but as soon as Emma shouted, a stampede began. Beth made a beeline for Annie, but couldn't see John. Likewise, Emma ran towards Sammy, but there was no sign of Jake.

"Where's John?" asked Beth frantically as Annie dived into her arms.

"He's out on the boat," replied Annie, squeezing her sister harder than she had ever done. The tension evaporated, and Beth bathed in the adoration of her younger sibling, blocking out all that was wrong with the world. She edged round to look out towards the dinghy on the shimmering water.

Emma and Sammy both sobbed as they held onto one another.

"Where's Jake?" asked Emma.

It took a moment for Sammy to respond, but

eventually, she brought her tears under control. "Jake's at the house. He's not well. Ruth says seeing you again might help."

Emma pulled away from her younger sister. "What do you mean, not well? We were just at the house, there was no one there."

Ruth walked up behind them. "I think Jake's still in shock."

Emma remembered back to Mike talking about finding Jake on the hillside, but she had underestimated the severity of his condition. She stood up, taking Sammy by the hand and started walking back to the house. She looked across at Sarah who was surrounded by her joyful looking pupils as they threw warm and loving arms around her.

Emma and Sammy hurried off the sands and went back up the hillside towards their home.

"You left him by himself?" asked Emma.

"No, Dora's with him," she replied and suddenly, things made a little more sense.

The pair burst into the house and ran up the stairs. Dora jumped when they darted into the room, but her panic was replaced by happiness when Emma mouthed that Sarah was back and down at the beach. Dora ran out to greet the woman who had become like her sister.

Emma sat down on the bed next to her brother.

He was sitting upright, staring past the window into nothingness.

"Jake," she said softly. "Jakey, it's Emma."

He was unresponsive.

"Where are Mike and Lucy?" Sammy blurted, realising amid all the excitement she had seen no sign of them.

Unable to handle telling her the truth for the time being, Emma opted for the partial truth. "We brought some people back who needed our help. They'll be along later." This placated Sammy for the time being and she climbed onto the bed next to Jake, taking hold of his hand, but eliciting no response.

Emma shuffled around and squeezed in next to Jake. She took hold of his other hand and began to stroke it.

"Everything's going to be fine Jake. You'll see. Everything's going to be fine."

She didn't know if Jake could even hear her, but she hoped he could not, because she hated lying to her siblings.

10

Fry was propped up with his back against one of the walls. He had been cradling Juliet's cold body ever since he had found it. The candles had long since extinguished and all but one of the lanterns had finally choked on their last drops of paraffin. He could just make out the silhouette of The Don's head. The thought of his eyes daring to look in the direction of himself and Juliet infuriated him.

"You think this is funny? This doesn't change anything. This doesn't change anything." There was no frailty in his voice, only resolve. "It doesn't change anything, does it sweetheart?" he asked looking down at his beloved Juliet.

He lifted her head and kissed her mouth, ignoring the lifeless frigidity that greeted his lips, ignoring the sticky trails of blood that streaked her face, ignoring the gory hole where her soft, supple cheek had once been. He pulled back and held her head between his hands.

"This doesn't change anything." He looked across the cellar floor and noticed the chunk of flesh that had been torn from Juliet's cheek before looking back down at her and gently stroking away an errant hair. He shuffled to his knees and carefully laid her body down on the ground before walking across to the workbench. He pulled the drawer open and grabbed a handful of candles. Fry lit them one by one, letting the melting wax drip onto a saucer and then he pushed the candle ends onto the molten wax, glueing each one into place. He carried them across to where Juliet lay and placed them around her in a wide semi-circle before returning to the workbench. He opened the bottom drawer and removed a purple sewing pouch, unzipping the rusty fastener to reveal a hotchpotch assortment of needles, and threads. Fry removed a bobbin still full with black cotton and a needle that glistened in the flickering light before picking up the fleshy remains of Juliet's cheek.

"Well darlin'," he said lifting her head onto his lap as he spread his long legs out in front of him and rested his back against the wall. "This might sting a bit, and you're probably going to have a bit of a scar. But as a young friend of mine once said, we've all got scars."

Fry unwound a long strand of black cotton from the bobbin and doubled it over before threading it through the eye of the needle. His actions were those of a man who was about to darn a pair of old socks, somebody who was just engaging in another part of his working day. When the needle was threaded, he put it in his mouth and carefully lifted the torn flesh up to the hole in Juliet's face. He pressed it into position, squeezing misshapen edges into place where he could and then skilfully pushed the needle into the necrotic tissue of the torn cheek and weaved it back up forming his first stitch.

When Fry was a boy, his family had been poor, but Christmas had always been special. They wanted for nothing at Christmas, and one of his cherished childhood memories was of him sitting in the kitchen with his mother. A batch of jam and lemon curd tarts had just come out of the oven, and a fresh tray of coconut tarts had been put in. The warm air was filled with the fragrance of plenty. He made coloured paper chains while his mother happily sewed the seam of a red felt Christmas stocking that would hang by the fireside on Christmas Eve. The crackly old radio in the corner was turned up much higher than usual and an old crooner was belting out "Santa Claus is Coming to Town". His mother had begun whistling it and he had joined in. That memory had stuck with him through all the good and bad times he had been through. It was a memory of pure happiness, one that would never be repeated in his life.

But now, as he sat, sewing his dead girlfriend back together, his subconscious had prompted him to whistle, and despite it being mid-summer, the notes that were coming through his lips were those of "Santa Claus is coming to town."

When Fry had finished sewing, he moved his mouth up to Juliet's cheek and cut the thread with his teeth before tying another knot. He pulled her body close to him, squeezing it, but now, it was less flexible, less human. Rigor Mortis had begun to set in, and although a big part of Fry needed more time to hold her, more time to clutch her, there was a part of him that was still rational and knew that if he didn't get the body settled into position, it would become almost impossible.

"C'mon darlin' there'll be plenty of time for this later," he said as he hoisted her frame into his arms. He carried her out of the cellar and up the stairs as if she were no heavier than a pillow. He walked through the hall and up to the bedroom where he placed her into a flowery armchair in the corner, overlooking their bed. He stood back to admire his handy work and smiled.

He moved in to kiss her, and he closed his eyes as their lips met. It was the most natural thing in the world, a man kissing his woman; it made him feel alive. A thunderous knocking disturbed his intimate moment, and he frowned in annoyance as he marched out of the bedroom, making sure to close the door behind him.

"I'll be home late tonight darlin' don't wait up," he said as the latch clicked behind him.

He thudded down the stairs and wrenched the door open to reveal TJ.

"Everything okay boss?" he asked.

"Why wouldn't it be?"

TJ nodded towards Fry's clothing, which was covered in blood.

"Och!" said Fry. "I was moving stuff around in the cellar and cut my hand," he said, hiding it from view.

"Blood everywhere. I'll go change," he said, leaving TJ at the front door and heading back into the house.

"I can give you a hand in the cellar," called TJ after him.

"All done now," replied Fry.

As he walked back through the house, he closed the door to the kitchen and TJ got a smell of something familiar. Like the smell of a butcher's shop.

*

Darkness had fallen by the time Mike and Jules had navigated their way through back roads and farmers' fields to avoid the hordes of RAMs on the A9 and Inverness centre. They had driven at speed through small villages that had fallen victim to the ravages of the raiders. How many people had lost their fathers, their mothers, their brothers, and their sisters, because of those men?

Mike brought the bike to a sudden stop, almost missing the junction at the end of the narrow country lane. There was a sign that read A835 Ullapool.

"Thank fuck for that," he hissed.

"Are we nearly there?" asked Jules

"No. But at least we're on the right road now," Mike replied.

*

"There's a dinghy heading in to the dock," said Andy as he burst into one of the two static caravans that had become makeshift infirmaries.

"Lisa," said Lucy to the nurse who had been helping her all day. "Make sure Mr Fingle's leg is kept elevated and this arm needs a fresh dressing," she said giving a half-hearted smile to her female patient whose name she had already forgotten.

Lucy almost ran out of the caravan and through the car park with Andy. She removed her Glock from the back of her jeans, and Andy un-slung his rifle. George and Rob were already in concealed positions on the dock as the small dinghy got closer. Lucy looked at the approaching vessel and then across the moonlit bay to the familiar outline of the yacht. She could see silhouettes moving around on deck.

"Oh thank God," she said, slowing to a jog and then a walk. "It's them, they're back. Put your guns away, these are our people," she said walking to the edge of the dock just as the dinghy cut its motor and drifted in.

Five figures hurried up the rickety wooden steps and Lucy wasted no time in throwing her arms around the first one, Mike's gran, Sue. It was then that everything hit her. She had been in doctor mode up until now, but her emotions had rarely been in so much turmoil. She began to cry, and Sue soon realised that the tears were not down to the fact she had missed her friend, but that something was wrong.

"We were attacked," she said, trying to get her

voice back under control.

The questions then came thick and fast. The group talked for more than ten minutes before even realising there were unfamiliar faces present. When Sue found out Mike was still missing, her usual stoic demeanour began to falter.

"I need to go home. I need to see Emma and the munchkins," she said as she began to tremble. Jenny wrapped a comforting arm around her.

"Come on love, we'll both go," Jenny said, looking towards the soldiers.

"I'll take you," said Barnes, needing to see Beth. He wasn't sure if it was love. But it *was* hope.

"You should come too," said Sue.

Lucy shook her head. "There's too much to do here, and look, I don't mean to be the bringer of doom, but those raiders plundered virtually all our food. We've got children and old people. We brought some food from the warehouse, but not much"

"Well, that's something we've got a short term answer to anyway," said Sue as she looked towards Hughes and Shaw.

Lucy looked at the three of them a little confused.

"The trip went a lot better than we'd hoped. The yacht's full of supplies," said Hughes. "I'll make a start ferrying everything in," he said heading back to the dinghy.

"Look," said Lucy taking hold of Sue's arm, "I'll try and get back to the house later, but right now, they need me here."

The van moved off, it was only seconds before Sue lost sight of Lucy and Shaw in the darkness. Her eyes followed the headlight beams as they cut through the night.

Lucy headed up the three steps of a vacant static caravan and turned on a small lantern which despite its size lit up most of the interior. A few seconds later Shaw walked through the same door. The pair embraced, but it was not the embrace of two lovers. It was that of two friends who shared a powerful secret.

Tears began to trickle down Lucy's face. "Up to this moment, I haven't even thought about the possibility he might not come back." She burst out crying, "but if he doesn't it's all my fault. I pushed him to do something because I knew he was the only one who could. I put the welfare of strangers above the welfare of family." She fell down on her knees in a fit of grief. "I was horrible to him as well. I said horrible things. If he doesn't come back, I don't know what I'll do."

Shaw edged off the sofa and knelt in front of her, pulling her shaking body towards him. "Listen to me," he said, squeezing harder. "If he's not back tonight, me and Hughes will head out first thing tomorrow. We'll find him," he said over the sound of her cries. "Jesus, Lucy, this is Mike we're talking about. You said he successfully led the RAMs away from the store. If he managed that, then they didn't get him. If he got to the van, which he must have done, he would have led them out of the city. He'll either be holed up somewhere for the night or on his way back."

Lucy slowly began to take control of her emotions once again and sniffed loudly before wiping her nose on her sleeve.

"Sorry," she said, repeating the action.

"It's not like we've got boxes of Kleenex kicking about, I think I can forgive you," he said.

"No... I mean for breaking down like that."

"If anybody deserves to lose it, it's you. But I mean what I said. Mike can look after himself."

*

The huge crowd had been assembled at the football fields for over two hours. The PA system was still being set up, but the promise of a big announcement kept the mood upbeat. Rumours were flowing faster than a running tap and the lack of senior figures led to further wild speculation.

Fry was in the same room of the hotel where he had beheaded The Don earlier that day. He was with TJ, the enforcement squad and the fifteen loyal captains that had been recruited for the coup. These men were the only ones privy to the master plan, the grand design for the future that Fry had announced.

Fry held a glass of champagne up to toast. The other men in the room did the same.

"This will be a night no one will forget," he said grinning. "To the future," he said.

The men repeated the words like a mantra before all taking a drink.

"Now, in a few minutes, I'm going to be walking out in front of those men, and I want everyone here on that stage with me." He waited a moment for the words to sink in. This really was a bright new day. The Don had always showboated when he had made announcements, no matter how big or small, but this promise of a better future for all suddenly gained weight with everyone present. "We are in this together, and it's important that everyone in that crowd sees that we start in the way we intend to carry on." He raised his glass again. "When the PA system is all set up, they're going to let me know, but for a few moments, enjoy the food and drink. There'll be more celebrations later, but tomorrow, the hard work starts." He raised his glass even higher. "Slainte."

"Slainte." They all repeated before sipping the sparkling nectar.

"Where did you get to today?" asked TJ as the other men made their way to the banqueting table.

"Y'know, TJ, things to do, people to see," he said with an unnerving sparkle in his eye. TJ looked at him suspiciously and Fry looked towards the men, then leaned into TJ. "Let's just say Juliet wanted to celebrate...over and over again," he said smirking.

A look of understanding washed over TJ's face. That explained Fry's irritation when he had gone to the house earlier in the day, it also explained why he had been unreachable. TJ smiled, "You sure you're okay to give this speech?" he asked nodding towards Fry's groin and smirking.

"Wild horses couldn't keep me off that stage, TJ."

"Where is Juliet? Isn't she coming?"

"She's going to meet me there. I said I wanted to spend some time with my men."

TJ gave an understanding nod and clinked glasses with Fry before making his way to the table of food. Fry sat down in the stately armchair. He surveyed the room like a king looking out over his domain. A distant smile remained on his face as he gazed towards the table.

Earlier on that same day he had told the men now assembled before him of his plan, his vision for the future. His vision had included having Juliet by his side, his confidant, his co-conspirator. She was the only person he had ever known who fully understood him. She was the only one who had been able to kindle his true nature. It wasn't love. Two creatures like them couldn't love, but it was a bond more powerful, a bond far more dangerous and passionate. Now, that fiery passion had been doused. Something had been taken away from him and it hurt, and there was only one thing that was going to make him feel better. He still had the physical Juliet, he would always have that, that sweet, beautiful black body in his bedroom. And he still had the Juliet in his head, she still answered him in the same cocky manner, she still whispered advice into his inner ear. But there was a part of her he didn't have.

He looked around the optimistic faces of the men in the room and wondered how loyal they were. Would they understand this burning need for revenge?

"No," whispered a raspy voice in his head.

Being a leader meant making hard decisions though, tough decisions, foregoing personal inclinations and acting with your head, not your heart. The double doors to the large room opened and a man with long curly hair put his head around the corner and nodded towards Fry. For a moment, Fry just looked, still trapped in a world somewhere between reality and dreamland, then he stood up.

"Men, our stage awaits!" he shouted out like he was auditioning for a part in Henry V.

All the men laughed, it was unusual to see Fry in a state that was bordering on good-humoured.

As Fry led the men onto the well-lit stage, silence swept over the audience. The only sound was the generators working to keep the lights and the PA system working. A nervousness fell across the crowd, and they didn't know if they should cheer or clap, but in the end, they did nothing.

The microphone shrieked briefly as Fry took hold of it. The lights shone into the faces of all the men on stage, blinding them to the two thousand plus assembled in the crowd. TJ couldn't give an exact figure, but the estimate was over five hundred dead in Inverness. It was a dwindling army, but enough for what Fry needed. The newly anointed leader held his hand up to cover his eyes so he could see into the crowd.

"The Don is no more. Today I took control back for us. He had run this army into the ground. He didn't care about you or me, only himself. How many men did we lose while he was drunk on his own power? And for what? An ever-shrinking kingdom, that's what." Fry's words were greeted with silence. "So where are we now? A bunch of fucking whores beat us back in Inverness. What message does that send out? The Don was asleep at the wheel and we lost face, we lost resources and we lost ground. It's time we gain that ground back. *It's time the world hears us roar*," he shouted the last words and got yells of support. "Tomorrow we prepare, and the day after we head back north. We send a message. You cross us, you cross into Hell!"

There were more cheers and applause began to ripple.

"The day after tomorrow, we sound a battle cry. From then on, all we will need to do is show up and our enemies will submit. The day after tomorrow, we send a message that everyone will understand. Those women will have headed back to their villages on the coast. Well...their villages are going to get razed to the ground. Those women will pray for death by the time we're finished because we're going to tell the world that no one crosses us and prospers. This is a new world and only the strong survive." The clapping continued and increased in volume. "I pledge to you, from this day, *we will be the strongest!*" He shouted as the cheers became deafening. Then he stood back from the microphone and allowed himself to bathe in the applause of the fools he despised so much. They were like children, so easy to manipulate, so easy to use. All Fry wanted was absolute power for himself and his queen.

*

Mike was grateful for the dark. The headlight could only capture a small handful of the horrors that sunlight displayed so openly. These men were both brutal and thorough. There had been countless bodies strewn around the villages they had driven through. They must have been doing these raids over the space of a few days. Now, this stretch of coastline, his stretch of coastline, had fallen victim to them. How many had survived? Not enough for an army. Not enough to take the war to them. War? Yes. That's what it was. They were at war, and he had seen it coming. He had said they needed to prepare, but no one had listened. They'd have to listen now. They'd have to prepare. He brought the bike to a stop as a group of deer crossed the road up ahead.

The reflection of the full moon shimmered in the bay below. Mike looked beyond it and to the small islands. He turned and looked at the brooding cliffs behind. The coast road stretched over thirty miles. It was a wide single track with passing places. Every village should have been easily defendable.

"It's beautiful isn't it?" said Jules. "You can't believe there is such horror in the world when you see something this pretty."

Mike didn't respond, and as the bike moved off again, Jules put her arms around him and rested her head on his back as sadness swept over her.

He'd lost track of how long they had been travelling. It wasn't as straightforward as the times before the infection. There were a lot more dangers than before, and one wrong turn could be disastrous. Some roads were impassable because of pile-ups, storm damage, landslides, and a whole host of things that would normally be sorted out in a matter of hours by the council. This stretch was familiar though; a Highland coast road over forty-five miles long. There had been so many accidents on it. Accelerate in the wrong place, and you'd go over the edge. The crash barriers saved some, but a lapse of concentration could easily be the difference between life and death. Mike knew every curve and incline, and within twenty minutes they had reached the road to his gran's house. As they went down the track and the cottage came into view, he could see candlelight flickering in the living room and a flood of relief swept over him. His night was far from over, but he was going to see his family again.

He parked and ran to the house bursting through the door. Emma was already in the porch. The pair flung their arms around each other and didn't let go until his gran came around the corner, followed by Sammy. All four of them embraced, kissed and held each other tight. After a few moments, Jules appeared in the doorway and the family reluctantly let go of one another.

"How's Jake?" asked Mike.

"Same," replied Emma.

Mike headed towards the stairs with Sammy tagging along while Emma and Sue welcomed Jules.

Sammy grabbed hold of Mike's hand. "He'll start getting better now we're all together," she said as they reached the landing.

Mike stopped at the top of the stairs and knelt down in front of Sammy. "I love you so much. You know that, don't you Sammy?" He said as he wrapped his arms around her.

"Of course I do silly," she replied and Mike laughed.

He kissed her cheek, stood up and led her by the hand into Jake's room. There were candles all over the house, lighting the surrounds. Mike hadn't been into any of the other rooms, but he could sense the house was full and heard lots of quiet voices. A battery-operated night light sat on the bedside table and Jake lay fast asleep. Mike sat down and gently stroked Jake's head, but the child did not stir.

"It's okay now Jakey. We're all back together. You, Sammy, Me, Em, Gran, Lucy...we're all together again." Lucy! Where was she?

He leant down, kissed Jake's head and gave Sammy another kiss before heading downstairs to find Emma and Sue.

He walked into the large crowded kitchen and recognised a few faces from the warehouse. People were taking it in turns to squeeze Jules before passing her on to the next friend. She looked overwhelmed. Mike went across to Emma and his gran who had been joined by Jenny.

"Quite a trip you've had?" Sue said, her face lighting up once again to see Mike.

"You could say that Gran... Listen. I'll tell you all about it later, but I've got a lot to do before that. Where's Lucy?"

"What do you mean, you've got a lot to do?" asked Emma.

"Em... You think those people are going to let things lie? They'll come back here. They'll finish things off this time. Now, where's Lucy?"

Emma's shoulders sagged. Couldn't she enjoy just a few moments? Was that too much to ask? Her family reunited. "She's in the village. She's working out of the campground," she said.

Without making eye contact, Emma turned and walked away.

"She's been through a lot, Mikey," said his gran, putting a hand on his arm.

"We need a meeting tomorrow morning. We need everyone there. I'll get the word around the village. I'm heading there now," he replied.

"You're going out? Now? Your family need you, Mikey. Emma, Sammy, Jake, Me. We need you."

"Listen, Gran. I need to go find Lucy. We'll be back later. I promise. I love you, Gran, but this fight isn't over. They'll be back, and this time, they won't be looking for prisoners, they'll be looking for revenge."

His gran stared into Mike's eyes. The flickering light of the candles danced in them.

"I know these men, Gran. Their souls are stained black with death and hatred. When they come back here, the revenge they'll reap will be devastating." The flames continued to reflect in Mike's eyes.

"You look just like him," said Sue.

"Like who?" asked Mike.

"Your father."

Mike's anger flared at the mere mention of the man. "I am absolutely nothing like my father," he hissed. "I never want to hear him mentioned again. That man was dead to me long before I..." he broke off.

"Long before what?" asked his gran. Then it dawned on her. The doubts, the suspicions, the small clues trailing like breadcrumbs across the years suddenly made sense. "Oh dear God Mike, tell me it's not..." she trailed off this time.

" I'll catch up with you later, Gran," he said.

"At least now I know what happened that afternoon, all those years ago." She didn't try to meet his gaze, she just walked away, forlorn.

"People shouldn't drink and swim Gran...it can get them into all sorts of trouble," his voice was soft and eerily calm.

Mike stood there for a moment. His features unchanged, the hellish flames still lashing their reflection in his eyes. Finally, he broke his stare into nothingness.

"Jules," he called. "I'm heading to the village. You want to see your brothers, meet me outside in two." Jules nodded an affirmative while still having questions fired at her by welcoming friends.

Emma was in the utility room looking out over the moonlit bay. There were no other occupants. There were no candles. Mike walked up behind her and rested his chin on her shoulder.

"This will never be over, will it?" she said. "We'll always be fighting or running."

"I know that's what it feels like, Em...but it will be over." She leant her head against his. "We're always going to have to have our wits about us, but we're never going to have to fight men like this again."

She turned to look at him. "Fight them?" She

stood back to see if his face was serious. "Fight them, Mike?" She kept his gaze, and he saw the glisten of tears in her eyes. They shimmered in the whiteness of the moon. "Oh, Mike!"

She reached up to his cheek and gently stroked it before turning to leave. More tears formed as she walked away. She climbed the stairs and passed Jake's room. The door was ajar and she looked in on her little brother. Sammy had curled up next to him and fallen fast asleep as well. Emma carried on to the next room. The large floor area was littered with sleeping bags. Sarah's was nearest the door and Emma laid down beside her.

"What time is it?" whispered Sarah, still half asleep.

"It's late, shhh. Go back to sleep," replied Emma.

11

Jules waited as the Kawasaki engine came to life, then climbed on. The bike tore up the hill and cut through the calming whoosh of the gentle waves. The noise of the machine scared any wildlife from the road long before they reached the village. As they arrived at the campsite, Jules's brothers rushed up to meet them. Andy hung back until Mike had walked away, but then flung his arms around his sister.

"I've missed you, you little pissants," she said as she squeezed each of her siblings in turn.

Mike looked across to a large static caravan with a generator rumbling away outside. He saw Lucy in the fluorescent light changing a dressing on someone's shoulder. He watched her for a moment. The last time he had seen her they had argued. They were both at fault...well...he was probably more at fault, but they had argued a lot lately. He was still crazy about her and hoped she felt the same, but something had been amiss, like she was under more stress than usual. That didn't stop him wanting to be with her more than anything though. He'd just left his gran, who he hadn't seen for weeks to come straight down here. That was love...infatuation even.

Mike walked into the makeshift infirmary just as Lucy had finished with her patient. She was about to move onto another, but then she saw him. For a second he was scared. He couldn't read her face. Then it broke into that smile he loved so much. She took the stethoscope from around her neck and walked over to him. She grabbed his hand and pulled him into the one small bedroom of the mobile home that remained unoccupied. She closed the door, took his face in her hands and pushed her lips against his. They both wanted the kiss to go on forever, but eventually, Lucy pulled away.

"I'm sorry," she said. "I was insensitive. I should never have said those things."

"I'm sorry too, Luce. All I've been thinking about all day is seeing you again," he said breaking into a warm smile. "Listen, we need to talk." The smile left his face.

"No good conversation ever starts like that," Lucy replied.

"We need to prepare to fight for when this army returns."

Lucy pulled back from him, the same way Emma had. She looked at his face trying, hoping to see humour there. There was none.

"Sweetie...tell me you know I love you." Mike nodded. "So I'm saying this in your best interests, in my best interests, in everybody's best interests...that's insane." His face didn't change. "Mike. We would be wiped out. You said so yourself."

"We *will* be wiped out if we don't ready ourselves, Luce. We can do this. I know we can."

"My God. Listen to yourself. A small handful of us against an army of god knows how many? This isn't the Seven Samurai, Mike. This isn't make-believe, this is very real."

"This is doable, Luce. We just need everyone to work together, and we need to start straight away."

Lucy took a deep breath and looked around the drab confines of the small bedroom. "I kidded myself that this day wouldn't come, but I knew it would. If you're right and that army is coming back to finish the job, then we need to get the hell out of here. To think we can fight them... Can't you see how mad that is? Please tell me you are not so detached from reality, Mikey."

"I know how it sounds, but listen to me," he took her hands. "I've got a plan, Luce. I know how to do this." Mike's face was serious. His eyes intense. At that moment, she didn't know whether to be scared, to pity him or to believe him.

"Oh, Mike. Listen to yourself, please sweetie. Look at least talk to someone with military experience. Talk to Shaw or..."

"For fuck's sake, Lucy!" He immediately let go of her hands and feral Mike was back. The scary uncontrollable one. "What the fuck is it with you and that man?"

"Don't start this again," she said, turning equally defensive. "Give me a break and stop being such a self-righteous prick!"

*

Sue sat down in her favourite armchair. It faced out towards the bay. Her living room had turned into a homeless shelter for the night much like the rest of the house. Sleeping bags with sleeping bodies were strewn over the floor, but she couldn't sleep. She had said goodnight to old and new friends in the kitchen and acted as if nothing was wrong. But something was very wrong. Up until this night, she had only had suspicions. But now she knew. She had faced her grandson. She had looked into his eyes and she had known. Right then. Right there.

*

"Have you ever done something you regretted so badly it ate you up inside?" Lucy asked.

Images flipped in Mike's mind. He was on top of that priest in the hospital, pummelling him with his fists. The man's face barely recognisable as a face by the time he had finished. Screams filled that hospital corridor as frightened patients, some young, some old, witnessed the bloody violence. Three men dragged Mike off that broken figure. He tried repeatedly to get back to him, to finish the job, but couldn't.

There was the time Mike's dad tried to lash Emma and his mum with his leather belt. Mike was just ten, but he broke a chair over his father's back. His drunken father barely noticed, but turned his attention to Mike. He threw the belt against the wall and threw Mike to the ground where he stayed, desperately trying to protect himself from his father's foot as it kicked him in the stomach, time after time after time.

Then there was that boiling sunny day when the family had been holidaying with Gran. Mike and his father had gone out swimming. His father had had a couple of beers, but nothing out of the ordinary for him. They were about sixty metres out, and then...then Mike's father had run into trouble. Thick, leathery snakes of seaweed had caught his legs and he started to struggle. He called out to Mike for help. At first, Mike just looked on, but then thought better of it as he heard, "Help me you little bastard," in-between gurgles of seawater. Mike dived down and saw his father's feet were caught well and truly. The more he kicked, the worse it got. Mike swam back to the surface and watched his father splashing and spluttering in the water. "HELP ME, YOU LITTLE SHIT". His voice almost demonic in-between coughs. Mike took a deep lungful of air and dived again. He wrapped, two more thick belts of seaweed around his father's ankles and pulled down with all his strength. For a short time, the kicking and struggling intensified, and then...nothing.

*

Sue looked out into the bay. How she used to

love this view. She had seen it and she had loved it every day and every night. This bay. This view. It was poison now. She hated what her son had done to his family, but she could never hate him. Her eyes continued to look out across the shimmering water. Her breathing gradually becoming a little more erratic with each second, each beat. She felt a tightness in her chest. Her mouth fell open, but nothing came out. Her heart pounded and pounded and pounded and then...nothing.

*

It seemed like forever, but only a few seconds had passed by.

Lucy asked again. "Well, Mike, have you? Have you ever done something you immediately regretted? Something that eats away at you? Something you'd take back a thousand times if you could?"

"No," he said and turned to leave.

He walked back out to the Kawasaki, climbed on and powered away. He was not interested in greeting his friends back from their expedition. He was only interested in being alone. Mike headed up Deadman's pass and didn't slow until he reached the peak. The chill of the night air didn't bother him as he dismounted and released the kickstand. He had no idea what time it was, other than it being late. Other than it seeming like he had been awake for ages.

He was used to people calling him mad, calling him insane, but it still hurt when it came from the lips of someone he loved. He wasn't an idiot. He wasn't blind to the situation. But he knew that 10 men or 10000 men would not stop him from fighting for his family. The shadows of the landscape looked magical. He loved this place, he always had. He had loved Leeds, but Leeds had fallen. This place had not and he was not going to give it up for anyone or anything.

*

"He wants to go head to head with them?" asked Hughes.

"Yep," replied Lucy, dimming the light to the static caravan. Most of the occupants of this makeshift infirmary had finally drifted off to sleep. She stepped out into the cool night air and took a deep breath.

Hughes, Shaw, and Barnes followed her. Shaw and Barnes lit cigarettes and each took a long drag. Shaw finally exhaled a long plume of smoke. "I'm with Mike."

"What?" the other three replied in unison.

At that moment, the sound of a bike engine cut through the quiet and while Shaw's words still hung in the air, the Kawasaki rolled back into the campground. Mike turned off the engine and the bike came to a stop. He climbed off not missing a beat.

"Let me guess, you're discussing where you can get a straightjacket for me at this late hour?" he said half smiling.

Hughes looked distant as the two men hugged.

Mike and Barnes clapped their hands together in a firm shake and Shaw and Mike nodded at each other. He and Lucy just exchanged a glance.

"Shaw just told us he thinks you're right," said Lucy, still in a state of shock.

"You do?" Mike asked, turning towards Shaw. A look of surprise swept across his face to match that of Lucy's.

"If we run what's to say they won't track us down? We would have lost the advantage we have here. This place is easily defendable..."

Suddenly, Mike was paying attention. He could never forgive Shaw for what he had done, and in truth, if it was not for Lucy, he would probably have killed him by now, but Mike wondered if there wasn't a little more to the man than he had given him credit for. After all, it had been Shaw who had saved Emma and Jenny and now he was echoing Mike's own thoughts.

"Exactly," Mike said. "I've already told Gran and Emma, we need a meeting tomorrow morning. We need everyone there."

"Listen, Mike, Shaw," began Hughes. "You're not thinking straight..."

Mike was about to interrupt, but it was Shaw who replied. "Hughes. This is our only option." He was going to continue when the thrum of an engine from one of the box vans made them all turn as it entered the campground. It skidded to a halt, and stone chips sprayed into the air.

It was Beth who jumped out and ran towards them. She started talking then stopped. She was clearly distressed. "Mike..."

"What's wrong?" asked Lucy.

"It's your gran, Mike," she replied with a sob.

"What about her?"

"She's gone."

"Gone? Gone where?" replied Mike.

"I'm so sorry Mike. She's dead."

"What... what hap... How?" he said.

"I think it was a heart attack or something."

Mike staggered back, and Lucy grabbed his arm, placing her other hand on his back. She guided him over to the infirmary and sat him down on the step. She sat down beside him, placed her arm around him and kissed the side of his head. The three soldiers stood there in stunned silence. They had just spent weeks in Sue's close company. They had all come to think the world of her, and now this.

"I need to head back. I need to see her," said Mike, trying to get back to his feet, but finding his legs had turned to jelly.

"We'll go in a second, sweetie. I promise you, I need to see her too. But just take a breath." Lucy took tight hold of his hand and began rubbing it gently.

"It's all my fault," he said to himself.

"Whatever happened, Mike, it's not your fault."

He turned to look at Lucy in the moonlight. "It is...we need to go now. I need to see her, Luce. I need to see her."

This time he did manage to get to his feet. Lucy kept tight hold of his hand. He slowly walked across to the three soldiers.

"Will you organise the meeting?" he asked. "It needs to be everyone...it needs to be first thing... I have to go now...I have to go home.

"Of course mate," said Hughes.

"I'm so sorry Mike," said Shaw patting him on the back twice. "She was a lovely, lovely woman."

"So sorry, mate," echoed Barnes.

"Thanks guys," said Lucy as she led Mike to the waiting van.

Beth climbed into the driver's seat. She clunked the gear stick into first, and they pulled away.

"Fuck!" said Hughes as the van disappeared into the night.

"It's shit, but it doesn't change anything. We have to have that meeting tomorrow," said Shaw as he walked up to one of the crowded residential caravans and knocked on the door.

*

Mike could hear Emma crying as he walked through the door. The candles were still lit. Lanterns were hanging in places and there was enough light to see the morose looks on people's faces. He walked past the sea of strangers and up to his sister who was kneeling beside their gran's chair. Sarah was cradling Emma and they were both sobbing.

"Em?" said Mike.

She looked up and outstretched her arms like a child begging to be held by a parent. He fell to his knees, breaking his hand away from Lucy's, and wrapped both his arms around her. He kissed her head and held her tightly.

Lucy knelt down beside him and placed her cheek on his back for a moment before kissing him and then turning her attention to Sue. She looked at her...still untouched. Her mouth and eyes still open. She checked for a pulse, but there was little danger of finding one, the body was stone cold. Whatever happened was sudden. Without a proper medical examination, Lucy's best guess was a heart attack. She gently closed Sue's eyes. *Time to rest now. You got to see your family again before bowing out one last time. I'm so sorry Sue.*

"It was probably a heart attack," she said to Mike

and Emma. "It would all have been over in a flash. No pain, no suffering."

Mike broke away from Emma and turned towards Lucy. Fresh tears were in his eyes. "She was fit, healthy, she looked after herself...I don't understand," he said with a childlike innocence.

"Sometimes it's just time. There's no rhyme or reason. Sometimes it's just your time to go." She leant forward, kissed him, and then cradled his head into her.

"She'd want to be buried here," said Emma. "She loved this place since the first day she saw it. She'd want to be buried here"

"Don't think about any of that now," said Lucy. We'll get her moved up to her bedroom and we can take care of that in due time. She kissed the top of Mike's head as she got to her feet and took Beth to one side. "Could you take care of moving the body upstairs? I don't want Mike or Emma to have to do this," she whispered.

"Course I can," replied Beth. "Don't worry about anything. Sammy was heartbroken. She said her goodbyes, but she's fast asleep now though. All this has been too much for her."

Lucy looked back at the grieving siblings as she left the room. She quietly climbed the stairs and tiptoed along the hallway to her and Mike's bedroom. The house was crowded with strangers but their room had been left unoccupied. She knelt down and felt under the bed. No... no... there! The tape made a noisy rip as it peeled away from the underside of the bed. She pulled the pill bottle free and held it in front of her. Lucy sat down on the bed. The bottle there in her hand trying to seduce her... trying to suck her back in, but no. Shaw had helped her kick this habit. He had been through the same thing. He had seen the signs in her. He had made her strong. There was no way she was going to get dragged back in. She opened the lid and popped one into her hand, then replaced the bottle under the bed before going back downstairs.

"Emma...sweetie...we need to get you to bed."

Emma rose to her feet.

"Take this," said Lucy, putting the small tablet in her hand. It will help you sleep. Emma didn't even ask what it was, she just put it on her tongue and swallowed.

Emma bent down and kissed Mike on the top of his head. "I love you, Mike." she said before walking out of the room hand in hand with Sarah.

Lucy saw that Beth had got a couple of blankets and had recruited a helper to move the body. She nodded and Lucy bent down to where Mike was still knelt. "How about you and I go for a walk?" She knew sleep would be impossible. She knew neither of them wanted to be in a house full of strangers when something so personal had just happened. He didn't say anything, but got to his feet and let himself be led out into the night.

"What time is it?" he asked.

"I have no idea," Lucy replied. "Late...early...it

doesn't matter. Let's just walk."

The pair held hands like lost children in a wood. They meandered down to the private cove where they had spent so many afternoons. Just being away from the house, being away from that scene relieved them.

"Thanks, Luce," said Mike as they both sat down on the cold sand. "For everything."

"I haven't done anything."

"You have. I know you're always looking out for me. Don't think for a second I ever take that for granted."

Lucy took hold of his hand and gently caressed the back of it with her thumb as they looked out at the calming waves.

"It was my fault, Luce," he said softly.

"Mike..."

"I killed my father." Her thumb stopped. "We were swimming in this bay, he got into trouble and rather than helping him, I pulled him down further. I murdered him. And today...today, Gran finally figured it out."

He pulled his hand away and wrapped his arms around his legs pulling them to his chest. He started sobbing uncontrollably.

Lucy looked across at him, then out to the silhouettes of the small islands in the distance. She finally broke her silence. "This is the drunk who beat his wife and children? This is the drunk who used to get loaded then drive down to the store to get more liquor? D'you think I don't know what's inside of you, Mike? D'you think I don't know what you wouldn't do to save your family? To save the ones you love? It's who you are. It's what makes me love you. This wasn't some innocent. This was a man who cared about no one but himself. This was a man who could have ended up killing you, or your sister, or your mom...or another little girl like my daughter." Lucy's voice broke and she began to cry.

Mike looked across at her. "Luce, I..."

"I miss her so much," she said in between baying sobs. Mike immediately sidled up to Lucy, drawing her close. "I miss my little girl so much. I'd do anything to see her again just one more time. It was a drunk just like your father who killed her." Tears dripped off her face as she buried her head into Mike. She clawed her fingers into his chest with a vice-like strength, making him grimace. "You didn't do anything wrong," she whispered when her cries eventually died.

Mike kissed Lucy's head and angled her face up towards him. "You have no idea how much I love you, Luce." He kissed her lips and wiped away her tears with his fingertips. "You are the best thing that has ever happened to me, and you are my best reason for carrying on."

Her fluttering breaths calmed, and she moved her hand up to his cheek. "I feel the same," she said, her voice breaking a little, "but it's so good to hear it from you." She moved her lips up to meet his and withdrew. Her hand caressed his face then gently moved to the back of his head and pulled his mouth towards hers once again. They stayed like that frozen in time. They finally withdrew and gazed at each other in the moonlight. It was kind to them. It didn't show the stress lines or the grief, it just showed the two faces that fell in love with each other at the beginning of this journey.

"I love you," he said.

"I love you too."

12

The village hall was packed as the sun began to warm the morning air. There were faces both strange and familiar. Jules's people had joined the ranks of the locals, for after all, they were locals too now. The previous village meetings had been chaired by Sue and a small elected committee had sat alongside her on stage. Lucy, Emma, Raj, and Shaw were all that were left now. They were joined by Mike, who opted not to sit behind the table, but perch on one end of it. His hot-headedness was the reason he had not been asked to help form the committee, but today, he insisted on having a voice.

"Okay everybody, please quieten down, and we'll bring this meeting to order," said Shaw, rising to his feet. "Before I start, some of you may already have heard the sad news that Sue Fletcher passed away last night. She was a lovely lady, and I'm sure you'll all join me in giving Mike, Emma, and the rest of Sue's family our deepest sympathy."

Shocked murmurs began as those who had not

heard wanted to learn what had happened, but they stopped again as Shaw resumed.

"Now...under normal circumstances, I'd join you in mourning the passing of our friend, but we've come together today because there is a very urgent matter that we need to discuss and a huge decision that we have to make." He looked towards Mike before continuing. "The army that raided the villages up and down this coast will be coming back. It turns out that those of us who were in Candleton have actually met them before... They are bandits, they are mercenaries, and they are maniacs...and we have a choice to make. We have to decide whether we are going to fight or whether we are going to flee."

"We need to go now...why are we even discussing this?" shouted the voice of a frightened woman.

"We should head to the islands," shouted another, "while there's still time."

"Has anybody even tried to negotiate with any of these people?" asked one of the older men from Jules's group.

"We should run while we have the chance. When are they coming?" Another terrified voice yelled.

Mike remained seated on the table with his arms folded turning his head from voice to voice as the comments came out. A smirk appeared on his face.

"I grew up here, but it's only land... it's not worth dying for," another voice said, and a mutter of approval went around the hall.

Mike stood up and Emma started to get to her feet in fear that he was going to lose it, but Lucy grabbed her arm and pulled her. "Trust him, sweetie," she said under her breath.

He walked to the centre of the stage and waited for people to stop calling out. "You're all scared. I understand that. I've been scared before. It's not a nice feeling. It eats away at you. It spreads through you. It takes a hold of you and before long it's not one thing you're scared of, it's everything and everybody. These men...this army that's coming here...it's a big army...these are bad men...bad, bad men. They're bullies. They're cowards. They hide behind numbers and the unspeakable acts they do. They hide behind bigger bullies, crueller bullies." Mike stepped a little closer to the edge of the stage. "This man who they all follow...this man Fry. I've met him before, many, many times. He's the one who picked on the defenceless kid in the school playground with all his pals. He's the one who mugs the ninety-year-old woman who's just collected her pension. He's the one I came face to face with in Candleton after he'd dropped mortar shells on us, killing my friend and nearly killing my sister. He's the one who's coming here now to do the same, only this time he won't rest until he's won."

"All the more reason to get out now while we can," shouted one of the voices from before.

"If we flee, he will come after us. Wherever we hide, he will track us down. It might be in a day, a month or a year, but he'll find us, and all we'd have done is lived a little while longer in fear...lived a little while longer wondering if today is our last day." Mike paused and looked around at the faces. Most of them were female villagers from up and down the coast, but he saw Jules's face and her people too, then he saw Beth and Talikha. Their eyes were locked on him, listening to every word. "If we run, we've already lost. But if we stand and fight, I know we can win. Like I said, these men are cowards. We don't need to wipe them out, all we need to do is make winning so costly for them that they give up."

"How? How can we do that, Mike?" It was George who broke the silence of the crowd.

"This place is our home. We know it better than anyone. We know its strengths and its weaknesses. We know what a nightmare it is to drive up Deadman's pass in anything bigger than a Volvo Estate." A small chuckle rippled around the hall easing the tension. "We know how vulnerable the coast road can be to rock slides. We know everything about this place and that's our biggest weapon. That and us. You and me. Everyone in this room. I've been coming up here all my life. I know how proud you are of this land, and I know how proud you are as a people. Every last one of us in this room needs to remember who we are and what we've lost and ask ourselves, are we prepared to lose more? Are we prepared to carry on losing just to carry on living?" He stopped talking as Jules, Sarah, and Beth pushed to the front of the crowded room. People stepped aside clearing a path for them and they all climbed onto the stage.

"Mike's right!" said Jules. Her Belfast accent

echoing around the hall. Unfamiliar to many assembled, but honest and clear. "I don't know about you, but I'm sick of hiding and I'm sick of being afraid. Now, I don't know this place, I don't know many of you people. But I know what the last forty-eight hours has been like...and I know that my family wouldn't be here, many of you wouldn't be here and I wouldn't be here if it wasn't for this man and these two women," she said putting a hand on Mike's shoulder and then nodding her head towards Lucy and Emma. "To be honest... At first... I thought he was a fucking whack job," she said to a small ripple of laughter. "But he's the bravest and most selfless man I've known. And I know if he says we should do something it's because it's in our best interests, and we should listen to him."

Beth continued. "Many of you know Mike, Emma, and Lucy saved my life and my family's lives. There isn't anywhere I wouldn't follow them. If Mike thinks we can do this, I know we can do this."

Sarah said nothing, but stood by Mike and shot a glance towards Emma who returned it with a half-smile.

Jules's brothers marched to the front, climbed up on the stage and stood behind her. Then Hughes and Barnes did the same. George joined them and before long the crowd realised that everyone they looked to for guidance—everyone they depended on—was stood on the stage. Now, fleeing looked like less of an option. Who would bring order to their lives if they fled? Who would bring food to the table? Who would organise them? Who would defend them?

Raj stood up from behind the table and walked

to stand by Mike as murmurs rippled around the hall. "We have all lost much in these last months. But there is no greater tragedy than losing oneself. If we can no longer look ourselves in the mirror because we are ashamed of what we have become, then we have to ask what is the very point to our existence? I for one, and my wife, Talikha, will be staying here. A man's strength can be judged by those he calls his friends, and looking around this stage at the people I proudly name my friends, I can indeed be judged a man of strength."

"Thanks, Raj," said Mike as he hugged his friend.

"Okay...before we need to get the Kleenex out, can we have a show of hands," said Shaw. "All those in favour of leaving, raise your right hand." There was silence and lots of sheepish heads looking from side to side, but no one put their hand up. "And those in favour of staying." Every hand went up. "Right then. We stand and fight," said Shaw. "When this meeting is over, remain here to be assigned a duty. We have to act fast and work hard, but we can do this, we can win."

*

The crowd formed lines as they were allotted working groups by Barnes, Hughes, and Shaw. Jules and her brothers climbed down off the stage to rally their people.

"I shall go find Talikha, and then I will meet you back here," said Raj climbing down from the stage.

Mike walked back to the table where Lucy and

Emma were sitting. Beth and Sarah were standing with them. Sarah had her arms folded and a smirk on her face.

"What?" he asked.

"You could feel the mood in the room change," said Sarah. "It was...incredible. It was like you just won them over with your words. I've never seen anything like it in my life."

"My brother can be very convincing when he needs to be," said Emma.

Mike smiled and walked around the table to take a seat next to Lucy.

"So," he said leaning forward on his elbows and clasping his hands. "We're in it now aren't we?"

*

"Day after tomorrow," said TJ as he rolled the maps back up and replaced them in the tube. "We could head out sooner, but it makes more sense to go prepared, not rush things." Fry sat back and took another long puff on his cigar. "Is Juliet going to be coming with us?"

"Juliet will be keeping an eye on things here for me. I'll have my best men with me. I need someone I can trust," he said. "I don't want that fucking bitch Lorelei heading back this way and trying to fuck things up. I still can't believe she managed to give us the slip." Fry observed TJ out of the corner of his eye as the blue smoke weaved its way into the air. No alarm bells. That was good. He'd hate to have to kill TJ after all this time.

Fry stood up and plunged the thick cigar into the ashtray. It was only half-smoked, but he could afford this kind of decadence now that he was in charge.

"I'm going home for a few hours. You know where I am if you need me, but only if you need me. I need to spend some time with my woman."

TJ nodded and smiled. "Okay, boss, have fun."

A grin adorned Fry's face as he left their headquarters in the hotel which had previously been The Don's pleasure palace. He got respectful nods from all of the men he passed, which he returned as he walked through the streets and to his house. The place was a hive of activity. He could hear the sounds of sheet metal clanging as they were pushed against the side of buses for welding to create makeshift armoured cars. He could hear the clunks and thuds of supply trucks being loaded with boxes of munitions. All was as it should be. He walked up the garden path to his front door and entered.

"Honey, I'm home," he shouted as he took off his thick woollen jacket and hooked it on the coat rack.

He trudged up the stairs and burst through the door. The smell of decay engulfed the bedroom, but Fry's psychosis had rendered him immune. He walked over to the chair where Juliet's slowly rotting corpse sat, bent down and kissed her on the mouth.

"I missed you," he said before going to the bed and lying down. He weaved his fingers together behind his head and laid looking at her and smiling. "Day after tomorrow. That's when we're setting off. TJ's got everything in hand. All our plans are coming together, my darling...everything we've worked for...and that BITCH!"

His calm demeanour disappeared, and he shot up to sit on the edge of the bed. His intense eyes pierced through the veil of this world and into the next, searching for his beloved Juliet.

"That bitch," he said more quietly this time. "She won't be bothering us again."

He lay back onto the bed and rested his head on the pillows once again, gazing at his Juliet as he drifted into sleep.

*

Shaw brought the van to a stop. He and Mike had discussed their plan once, then sat in virtual silence for the rest of the journey. They had parked on the outskirts of a medium-sized village along the A835. It had a school, a doctor's surgery, a few shops and amenities. There was nothing remarkable about it, but Mike had seen a RAM as he had sped through on the bike with Jules. He guessed that where there was one, there would be more.

The pair of them looked and waited for several minutes before Mike reached across and smashed his fist against the horn, holding it there.

"Nice...subtle," said Shaw.

Mike just glanced at him before removing his hand from the horn. Nothing.

"Let's head to the school."

"Why the school?" asked Shaw.

"Good a place as any. Plus, who knows, the kitchens might not have been cleaned out. There might be some canned or dried stuff we can take back."

"We're not scavenging, Mike. We've got a specific goal. When you start deviating from a plan, things get fucked up."

"So how's the plan going at the moment?"

"Are you sure this was the village? Are you sure you saw one?"

Mike just looked at him again. Shaw released the handbrake and followed the signs for the school. It was a short drive along a quiet road with well-kept houses. The place looked serene and untouched by the devastation that had steamrolled over the rest of the country. He brought the van to a stop at the gates of a building that was about the size of half a football field. There was also a sign for the village sports centre and swimming pool.

"Big place for such a small village," said Shaw.

"Drive up to the staff car park," said Mike. "These schools tend to service a few villages, not just one."

"So what's the pla—" Shaw began to ask but was interrupted by Mike banging his fist hard on the horn once again. They sat in silence for a moment and then Mike climbed out, retrieving his rucksack from the footwell and throwing it over his shoulder. Before Shaw even had chance to pull on the brake and turn the engine off, Mike had swung the two glass panelled doors wide open and begun to walk down the dim, echoey corridor. He had noticed a small poster on the side window saying emergency meeting tonight in the William Wallace School Gymnasium 8 pm. There was a larger poster, on a wall above a row of lockers. One corner had started to peel, and Mike thought back to being trapped in the house back in Skelton. He had seen a flyer for a village meeting there. All these small places, having all their meetings; meetings that solved nothing.

He heard the door behind him open again and footsteps jogging to catch up. Shaw grabbed Mike's shoulder and pulled him around so they faced each other. His face was more bewildered than angry.

"This has to stop, Mike." When Mike just looked at him, Shaw continued. "It's madness. I get it. You don't like me...hate me even. But we live in a small community. We both have important parts to play. We can't walk around like any second a war will break out between us. People are looking to us."

Mike raised an eyebrow, shuffled his shoulder free, and turned to carry on down the corridor. Shaw went after him and pulled him around more vigorously this time. Mike dropped his rucksack and faced up to Shaw. They were roughly the same height and there was just a matter of centimetres between them as they stood face to face.

"You want to do this again? Now? While we're

out here? Fine. Let's do this, Shaw," said Mike backing away and getting into a fighting stance.

"I don't want to fight you, you fucking idiot. I want to bury this shit between us."

"What shit, Shaw? You coshing me when I trusted you, and leaving me and my fucking family for dead while kidnapping my girlfriend? Is that the shit you're talking about burying? There are two reasons you're not dead already. You saved Emma, and I made a promise to Lucy."

"Fuck Mike...under the thumb already are you?" Mike took a step towards Shaw, holding his fist tight by his side.

"I swear Shaw, don't push me."

"I can only apologise so many times. It was a split-second decision that I'm going to regret for the rest of my life. Jesus Christ, Mike, Lucy forgave me, why the hell can't you?"

Just then, Mike unleashed a punch that sent Shaw cascading into a wall of lockers. Mike felt the lip burst against his knuckles and before he knew it he was on top of Shaw, punching his face again and again. Shaw didn't retaliate. He looked almost grateful with each strike that bruised and bloodied him. After a few seconds, Mike paused, released Shaw and stood up. He turned his back on the downed figure, trying to bring his anger back under control.

Shaw clambered up the lockers and gathered himself. "Feel bether now?" Shaw's lip was bloody, he had bitten his tongue, and as Mike turned to look at him, he saw the damage he had done.

Mike quickly turned away with a small tear forming in his eye. "Why did you do it? I trusted you. You saved my sister. Do you have any idea how fucking angry that makes me? You saved a member of my family, I desperately want to be grateful to you, but you did that other thing too. How the fuck can I trust you ever again?"

When Shaw replied it was hard to understand him with his fresh speech impediments, but Mike listened hard. "You're right not to trust me. Trust is something that you earn. I need to win it back. I am sorry Mike." As Shaw spoke, Mike heard the lisp less and the words more. "Whether you believe me or not. I will never put any of you in harm's way again. Lucy is one of my best friends. She loves you, Mike—you make her happy. That's all I want for her. She forgave me for what I did. She understood."

"Understood what?"

"I was overcompensating. I was trying desperately to be someone I wasn't. You think it's easy being gay in the army, Mike? You think people don't scrutinise you a thousand times more? Question your decisions a thousand times more? I fucked up. I fucked up monumentally, and now I need to do whatever I can to make it right."

"You're gay?"

"Fuckin' hell your quick aren't you? Yes... I'm gay. Anything you want to say?"

"Like what?"

"You want to make a few queer jokes at my expense?"

"Why would I do that?"

"You're not going to take the piss?"

"I'm a lot of things, Shaw, but I'm not an idiot and I'm not a homophobe. I couldn't give a fuck if you're gay or straight. I judge a man on his actions...on whether he'll stand up and do the right thing when it counts."

"Are we going to start fresh you and me?"

*

Hughes turned off the engine, took a final long drag on his cigarette and threw it down to the soil, carefully stamping on it as he climbed out of the digger to ensure there was no danger of it starting a fire. The weather had been consistently dry and hot for the last two weeks and the whole area could go up like a tinder box. He reached around the back of the seat and removed a bottle. He unscrewed the top and took a couple of gulps as he heard the sound of an engine.

"Hi," said Emma as she brought the Kawasaki to a stop and climbed off.

"Alright, love," said Hughes wiping his brow.

"How's it going?"

"Nearly done," replied Hughes. "The other three roadblocks are in place, I'm just putting the final touches to this one," he said looking at the piles of earth and rocks he had dumped behind the felled pine tree. "Most of the ground along this road is way too marshy to get a vehicle on, so if they want to come this way, they've got no options but to know the shortcuts, or move the roadblock." Emma nodded appreciatively. "How's it going with everything else?"

"Mike and Shaw are away. George has a big team putting together the...erm...whatever you want to call them. Barnes is still working his way down the coast road. We've got foragers on the beach and in the woods. We've got a team of people making hand weapons...at least nobody has any time to think about what's coming."

"And how are you feeling, love?"

It hit Emma that with everything going on, she had almost forgotten about the pain. "Numb. I can't focus on anything other than this. My gran died, my little brother is catatonic, Mike is heading straight into the mouth of the beast...again. It's like there is so much shit swirling around me that I can't think about any of it." She paused and added, "Honestly, what do you think our chances are?"

Hughes wiped the sweat from his brow using his forearm and took another drink from the bottle. He swiped another swarm of midges away from his face and turned towards Emma. "Honestly love...I think we're up shit creek. I've known Shaw for years. He's always had his head screwed on, but it's like he's trying to make up for what he did. He fucked up big time when he did what he did to Mike and Lucy, and now I think he wants the slate wiped clean. He wants to prove himself. He wants to win trust back. He's so desperate that I think his good sense has gone out the window." He pulled another cigarette out of his top pocket and lit it up.

"But...why didn't you say anything. Why are you going along with it?" Emma asked.

"Why are you?" he asked. "Other than running, I don't have any better ideas and our Mike might be a fucking psycho sometimes, but give him his dues, he's never a coward. And he's right. What's to say we run and in six month's time we have to run again, then again. What kind of life is that? This Fry and this army of his, they're armed, they're brutal and there are thousands of them. I don't care how well we prepare. I don't care how well we arm ourselves, we're not going to be able to keep them all out. I think this is it, love, but I'll be buggered if I'm not going to take out as many of them as I can before they get me." Emma took the cigarette off Hughes and inhaled a lung full. "I didn't know you smoked?"

"Like it matters now," she said handing it back to him and walking towards the bike. "I believed them for a while. I believed Mike and Shaw".

"As I said Em, I think Shaw is not himself right now...and Mike. I can guarantee, there isn't any doubt in Mike's head that we'll win this. If we all ran, I'm pretty certain Mike would stand and fight alone. I love the kid, but...he's fucking mental." Hughes burst out laughing.

Emma didn't laugh. She sat astride the bike looking at Hughes. "He stands up to bullies, that's all," she said under her breath.

"What did you say?"

This time she was firm, and her eyes pierced Hughes. "He stands up to bullies. He always has. He stood up to my father. He stood up to that priest. He stood up to those men who took Beth. He stood up to Shaw, and he's stood up to Fry before now. Everybody else runs scared, including me. He was my little brother, and he made sure I was okay while he got the beatings of his life. He hasn't changed. He will always stand up and do the right thing because if you're doing the right thing, you can never lose. If you're doing the right thing, the bad guys can never win. They only win if they turn you into themselves...if they turn you into cowards. Mike will never let that happen. I'd rather stand by his side, and the pair of us face this army down together than turn and run. I didn't get that before. I didn't understand. I do now." The bike growled to life and Emma sped off.

"Fuck me," said Hughes to himself. "It's fucking genetic."

*

Sammy placed a full bucket of mussels down in front of Sarah before picking up an empty one and starting back towards the rocks.

"Hey," called Sarah after her. "You should have a little break and something to drink, Sammy."

"I'm fine, thank you," the young girl replied. "When I've finished here, I'm going to head to the woods and pick some mushrooms.

"You should be careful trying to do that Sammy, some mushrooms are dangerous y'know, sweetheart."

"Nanna Fletcher used to take me when I came to visit. She taught me which ones are dangerous and which ones are good. Just like she taught me about the different seaweeds and the different plants. Did you know you can eat the roots of dandelions?" she asked proudly.

"Erm, yeah, I did hear something about that," replied Sarah.

"Well, did you also know that you can make a kind of coffee out of them? There are Alexanders growing all over this area. You can cook them and eat them like asparagus. Cow Parsley can be eaten in salads, elderflowers are delicious eaten straight off the stem and you can also make elderflower cordial and elderflower wine. There is food all around us. We just need to know where to look."

"Did you have many friends in school?" asked Sarah.

"No...I tended not to mix," said Sammy.

"Figures," replied Sarah, smiling to herself.

*

Mike reached down and picked his rucksack back up, looping one of the straps over his shoulder. "We need to get going, we've got a lot of work to do," he replied, heading down the hallway towards the sign that said dinner hall. Shaw wiped his bloody face with his shirt sleeve and followed him.

He caught up, and they entered the large dining hall together. It was frozen in time. The small orange plastic chairs were all tucked in neatly under the tables, and it catapulted both of them to childhood memories of their own school dining halls. Mike walked up to the large stainless steel serving area and leapfrogged over to stand where a hundred dinner ladies had stood before. He looked to see all the empty chairs that would never be filled again. All the large stainless steel serving trays before him that would once have been full of mashed potato, rancid baked beans, and sausages made of God only knew what, were also just hollow reflections of the past.

"Makes you think doesn't it?" said Shaw, experiencing exactly the same feelings.

Mike didn't respond but turned to explore the kitchen behind him. He pushed open the swing doors, and his shoulders sagged when he saw rows of empty shelves and empty knife racks. He walked further in and started opening cupboards to be greeted by more emptiness.

"Fuck!!! He hissed, throwing one of the empty stainless steel knife racks at the wall like it weighed no more than a cricket ball. The knife rack made an echoing clatter before it finally came to rest. "Fuck!" he said again.

Then he heard something from behind the wall he'd thrown the knife rack towards. It sounded like a shuffling, thumping, bumping sound.

"Shaw?" he called, but there was no response. "Shaw?" he shouted louder this time, but once again to no response. Mike pulled the swing doors open to find Shaw in the position he had been in previously, but looking towards the dining hall doorway. "I was calling you," said Mike.

Shaw just raised his hand to silence him as he continued to look towards the entrance. The soldier, reached around with his other hand to pull his Browning 13 from his belt. He brought it up in anticipation, as Mike began to hear a noise more like a rumble than a shuffle.

"Fuck!!!!" they both cried simultaneously as the horde of RAMs burst into the dining hall. Children, teenagers, adults, grunting, growling that familiar foul, deathly gurgle. Shaw immediately began to take aim and fire. Headshot after headshot made the beasts crumble to the floor, but there were dozens...more than dozens. Shaw took a final shot, emptying his magazine, and jumped across the serving counter to stand with Mike who took aim with the pump-action shotgun and fired wide-spreading blasts into the advancing swarm of the dead.

"Mike, come on!" yelled Shaw, grabbing him and pulling him through the kitchen doors as the first of the creatures crashed into the serving bar. Some wedged from the force of the dumb beasts behind them, some began to crawl over, but more still shuffled the long way around to get to the kitchen. Mike nearly lost his footing as Shaw dragged him through. The soldier looked around and immediately put a wooden mop through the two door handles as the first of the RAMs tried to crash through. The wood bent badly and as hands reached through the gap, began to crack.

"Here, quick," said Mike taking one end of a sturdy stainless steel prepping table. Shaw took the other and the pair struggled with it across to the door, leaving scores on the polished tiles as they dragged it. "Come on, another," said Mike and the two of them pulled, dragged and pushed another heavy table into position, resting it against the wood. Arms reached through desperately hoping to grab something living. Ghoulish faces pressed against thin panels of safety glass and the sounds of the dead sang through the air, sending chills down the spines of their captives.

13

"You know, Lucy, Mike would see this as defeat, planning an escape," said Raj as he sat on the infirmary steps. Talikha was beside him and Lucy stood with Beth.

"It's not defeat, Raj, it's sensible. We're going to put up a hell of a fight, but we have a responsibility to these people. They're not warriors, they're crofters and fishermen's wives and families. We can't expect them to do what a soldier can do. We just need options." Lucy looked at Talikha and then back to Raj. "We are the calm heads. We are the ones who have to see the bigger picture because right now, all Mike sees is red. He's taking Emma down the same path. I'm not saying we won't win Raj... I'm saying we plan to survive at all costs."

Raj took a deep breath and clasped his hands together, making a steeple of his two index fingers and pushed them up to his pursed lips. "Very well. I will assemble a small get away fleet in the bay next to the cemetery, but I beg you, not a word of this to anyone.

Mike would see this as betrayal."

"Don't worry about Mike, this is too big."

*

George was more relaxed in the huge mechanic's workshop than he was picking mussels on a beach or foraging for food in the woods. He had been designated with the task of weapons and munitions maker as well as getting several motor vehicles from various states of disrepair to full working order. Richard and David were working alongside him, and a few of the people he trusted from the Home and Garden Depot were providing the strong backs and nimble hands required. They had recruited some of the teens to scout and collect the supplies they needed. There was a makeshift production line on the benches. Molotov cocktails were being loaded into bottle crates that had been liberated from the cellar of the village pub.

"What are those?" asked David, pointing to two large plastic bins filled with some strange looking objects.

"Don't ask me," George chuckled. "One of Mike's requests. Tennis balls, a few nails through so they look a bit like the balls from a medieval ball and chain. Small hole in the top, fill it with sand, then seal it with a bit of mastic or whatever we've got. I'm guessing he's wanting to launch them at the enemy." George shook his head, "I don't tend to question Mike when he asks for something," the three men laughed. "But... I'm sorry to say, I think these are a bit pointless. The nails only stick out about an inch and a half at most. I doubt if they'll kill anyone."

David picked one of the nail balls up. "They're heavy, they'd cause damage," he said.

"Damage, anything can do," replied George, "The battle we're about to fight, we need more than damage."

George walked outside with Richard and David. They passed several vehicles which were now in full working order including three motorbikes, a Subaru Impreza, three four by fours and a few smaller economical run-arounds. Although the raiders had stolen lots of stored fuel and even siphoned some, there were enough vehicles hidden and too far off the beaten track for them to find. The locals had managed to pull together a good store of diesel and petrol which would run the vehicles and the generators for a while.

David held a heavy open book in his arm. "Do you think they'll work?" He directed the question at George who slowly walked around five boat trailers. The team had constructed mangonels; medieval siege weapons that were relatively mobile thanks to the large trailers. Although some of the components had been switched, essentially they were to the original design that Richard and David had found in one of the comprehensive library of books they had brought. Mangonels had originally been created to catapult large rocks and stones at the enemy.

"I know they'll work," he said, pulling out a pipe from his pocket. He took out a small pouch and pressed tobacco down firmly into the chamber of the pipe before lighting it with an all-weather lighter that did not even flicker in the breeze. He inhaled deeply, and a self-satisfied smile appeared at one corner of his mouth. "We really fell lucky with the supplies. Having that boatyard here was a Godsend, the materials were perfect for what we needed. We'll keep making as much as we can while we can. These weapons won't really be an even match for what they have, but the high ground will give us a big advantage. These will be devastating on high ground." He paused and looked towards his two companions. "Y'know gents. If by some miracle we get through this, we're going to have to start again." He looked back into the workshop. "We will have to think about everything from hunting and fishing to travel and communication. I think the three of us work and think well together. I think we could help build something good out of the ashes of all of this." Richard and David smiled. They had always been outcasts, never vital parts of a team and now they had been told they would be instrumental in rebuilding society. The pair of them swelled with pride.

"We brought an awful lot of books with us. Mike insisted. Starting again wouldn't be a bad thing. Society was floundering long before this. Maybe we can build something better," said Richard.

George took another long puff on his pipe and let out a big breath of blue smoke. He nodded slowly. "I do like a good project."

*

Sarah was alone in the kitchen as Emma walked in. She had been coordinating the collection of food all day, keeping an eye on youngsters and old folk alike, and she was visibly drained. She sat at the table, her head leant against one hand as she tried to get her second wind.

"I've got something for you...but don't tell anyone." Emma reached into her rucksack and brought out a small jar of coffee.

Sarah's eyes widened further. "Where the hell did you find that?" she asked.

"I have my means," Emma replied, smiling.

Sarah gave Emma a hug. "You have no idea how badly I need this. I am desperate for a coffee. This foraging and organising lark is exhausting." Footsteps came down the hallway and Sammy entered the room.

"I've organised a group of us to go up to the woods to pick mushrooms," she said.

"Erm..," said Sarah unsure of the safety aspect of a young girl leading an expedition to pick mushrooms.

"Cool," replied Emma. "Take Gran's book and remember to look out for wild strawberries too. It's been mild this year, there may be a few kicking about."

Sammy nodded, disappeared for a moment then reappeared with a procession of friends in tow including Annie, John and a number of the children from Sarah's school. They traipsed out of the door and Emma and Sarah both laughed.

"Your sister is something else," said Sarah.

"She is that," replied Emma.

This time it was Beth who came through the door. "Jake's been mumbling in his sleep. That's the first time I've heard a sound out of him since it happened. That's got to be a good sign, right?"

*

Sweat was pouring from Mike and Shaw as the pair just looked towards the doors, not quite understanding how everything had got out of hand so quickly. They turned to look around the kitchen. There was no exit, there were no windows, just a few skylights.

"That's the only way out," Mike said, trying to be heard over the sound of the RAMs.

"And how do you reckon we get up there?" asked Shaw.

Mike walked across to one of the serving tables and climbed on top. He jumped up with his hand stretched above him and was still around two feet short of reaching the skylight. "We're going to have to put something on top of here and climb up."

"Put what on top? The tables weigh a ton, we can't lift those, and the stools are too narrow and too rickety for us to get up there."

Mike jumped back down and pulled the crowbar from his rucksack. He smashed it against the tiles and plaster around one of the kitchen wall cupboards and when enough fell away, he pushed the crowbar in and began to lever the cupboard off the wall. More sweat was dripping off him by the time the heavy stainless steel cabinet crashed to the floor. The loud noise riled the horde of RAMs into a heightened state of agitation and a deafening screech sliced through the air as one of the tables against the door inched across the tiled floor.

Not needing words, Shaw and Mike heaved the hefty cupboard onto the prep table and pushed it into position under the skylight. Mike then placed a stool on top. He climbed first onto the table, then onto the cupboard and finally balanced on the stool. He heard something and looked down to find Shaw had climbed onto the table and was holding the stool in position. Mike chipped away the plaster around the screws holding the skylight brackets in place, then used his signature brute force to finish the job, bringing the crowbar up with lightning speed and sending the thick Perspex fitting somersaulting onto the roof of the school. He replaced the crowbar into his rucksack, reached up and grabbed the edges of the gap. His muscles tensed and rippled as he pulled himself up. The fresh air washed over him in a wave of freedom as he climbed out into the open. He took a deep breath, then immediately turned back and extended his hand down to help Shaw climb out.

Shaw stepped up onto the kitchen cupboard then carefully climbed onto the narrow seat of the stool and extended his hand up to Mike. For a second there was doubt in Shaw's mind as to whether Mike would help him out, but then he saw the younger man placing his other hand further along the skylight opening to get a better grip and reaching down. Just then, there was another piercing rip through the air and instincts overrode sense as Shaw twisted his head to look at the door.

"Nooo!!" Mike yelled as everything stuttered into slow motion.

Shaw turning his head down was enough to upset the balance of the stool which edged off the kitchen cupboard sending him tumbling. He landed heavily on his ankle which folded underneath him with a crack. Shaw screamed in pain and without pause, Mike edged his feet and legs into the gap to make his way back down, but this time it was Shaw who yelled, "No!"

"Mike, listen to me. I'm done for. This is it. Don't risk your life for a lost cause. Even if you get down here, how do we get back up?" Shaw pulled a fresh magazine from his bum bag and shoved it into the Browning with a satisfying click. He used his good foot to slide across to a cupboard to rest against. "These things are going to get in here eventually but right now I can buy a bit of time for you to round up a couple of stragglers. Let me do that at least. Let me pay you back for what I did to you and your family." Tears fell down Shaw's face. "Do you think we can call it even then?"

A loud high pitched scrape sounded from the doorway again as Mike looked down at Shaw, who looked up at him like a child wanting forgiveness from his father. "Yeah, Jim, we'll be even mate, don't worry about that."

Mike swivelled his legs back around and stood up breathing in the warm fresh air as the growls of the RAMs rose from below. Tears appeared in his eyes again and he gritted his teeth, aggressively running his fingers through his hair like a comb.

"Fuck!!!" he growled as frustration and rage took over. He crouched down, covering his face with his hands, blocking out the daylight, trying desperately to block out what was happening below. He removed his hands, the tears were gone and the look had returned. The look that said no, I don't accept this. Mike stood up. "No."

The bushes didn't give Mike the softest of landings as he lowered himself from the roof, but their springiness was better than him hitting hard ground. He stood up, dusted himself off and began running back around to the entrance of the school. It wouldn't be that long before the creatures broke through the door and Mike was certain that Shaw would save a bullet for himself, so he had to act quickly. He reached the school entrance where he had been just a few minutes before, although it seemed like a lifetime ago now. As he entered, he could hear the deathly dirge from the dining room. He hadn't noticed the stench before, but he did now. How he hated that smell. He reached the food hall entrance and looked inside. All the RAMs had their backs to him. They were fixated by the trapped prey in the kitchen. Mike didn't do a headcount, but he guessed there were maybe seventy or eighty.

He saw small explosions of red bursting into the air as Shaw began to take out the beasts thrusting their heads through the widening gap. Mike put his rucksack on the ground, pulled out the shotgun and reloaded it. Such was the noise of the RAMs and the firing from within the kitchen, that he went unnoticed. He took out the hand grenade he had taken from the raiders, and the two machetes he loved so dearly. He placed the rucksack back on his shoulders and crisscrossed the machetes inside ready for action.

Mike looked down at the grenade. He had no idea what a L109A1 was, but he hoped it was not just a flash-bang otherwise he was in serious trouble.

"Here goes nothing," he said pulling the pin out and throwing it into the crowd gathered at the far end of the dining room trying to make their way into the kitchen.

He ducked back behind the wall and covered his ears with little effect as the sound of the explosion filled the hall and the corridor beyond. He waited for just a moment before marching into the freshly created battle zone. It looked like a scene from Hell. Pulpy red residue painted walls. A hand had somehow glued itself to the ceiling like some weird outtake from the Addams Family. There were black and red body parts scattered everywhere. All the windows to the dining hall had shattered. Glass was still clinking as it fell to the floor. There was a lake of mashed red bodies and broken chairs and tables. The doors to the kitchen had moved even further and now the few remaining RAMs still standing were more determined than ever to squeeze through the widening gap.

Mike headed straight towards the kitchen. Some of the beasts not finished off by the blast dragged themselves along the floor to try and reach him. Their arms outstretched, their fingers hopelessly dancing in the air desperate to grab him. Mike pulled one of the machetes out of his rucksack and gave each of the would-be attackers a decisive swipe, finishing them off one by one. His sounds not enough to attract the attention of the twenty-odd surviving RAMs hammering at the kitchen doors.

More shots sounded from within the kitchen and fountains of red erupted from the back of three RAMs heads. Mike could still feel the heat from the grenade as he advanced further into the hall. The machete whooshed through the warm air before striking down another pathetic creature reaching out to him like an orphan from a Dickens novel pleading for food. The skull cracked and this time, the sound caught the attention of a handful of RAMs at the back of the crowd. Five of them turned and began to head towards him. Three walked straight into the serving bar and began to climb and shuffle across while the two to the left retraced their steps around and out into the ghoulish landscape of limbs, bones and blood created by the grenade. Mike swung the machete again, chopping through the skull of another battered body, before replacing it in his rucksack. He raised the shotgun and fired at the first RAM as it came charging at him from around the serving area. Its face disintegrated, and it flew back knocking the other off its feet. Mike took advantage of the collision and ran, skidding to a stop at the serving counter. Keeping the shotgun ready in his left hand and whipping the machete from his rucksack once again, he slashed and smashed through the skulls of the stretching, struggling beasts, reaching towards him over the stainless steel surface. With each strike, the bodies withdrew and collapsed. More creatures from the back of the crowd were aware of him now as the echo from the shotgun blast had ricocheted around the walls.

Torn between a trapped meal in the kitchen and a sitting duck in the open air, another six of the RAMs advanced towards him. Four lunged frantically struggling over their fallen brethren and the worktop.

Mike spiked through the head of the first before replacing his machete to raise the shotgun towards the second RAM who had now gathered itself once again and was running towards him. Another expansive explosion of red as the shell blew half the beasts' head clean off. Mike fired again at two more advancing creatures, the shot took the first one out, but that was it for the shotgun now. He dropped it to the floor, and as the second beast leapt at him, he struck at it in mid-air, cutting through its eye and the bridge of its nose, chopping into the brain and putting it out of its eternal misery.

Shots continued to fire from within the kitchen and more RAMs dropped. Mike swivelled, took out his second machete and hacked at the remaining creatures trying to reach him over the counter. One at the far end flopped over onto his side and began to rise while he had blades caught in the heads of two creatures. He kicked out at it hard as it advanced on him and it fell back, he tried to remove the machetes, but they were lodged, so he released the handles and let the creatures slide to the ground. He quickly pulled the rucksack from his shoulders and delved in it, retrieving his hatchet and a long screwdriver.

He replaced the rucksack on his shoulders, got into his battle stance and waited for the beast to charge at him again. More shots fired from the kitchen and Mike suddenly realised there were only five RAMs left standing.

Two at the door, one hopelessly reaching over the counter and one following the creature that was now running towards him across the blood-covered floor. Mike swiped the beast's arms away and plunged the screwdriver straight through its temple. It instantly dropped to the ground, and Mike didn't bother retrieving the weapon but ran to meet the other RAM. He leapt into the air and brought the hatchet down like Thor's hammer, splitting the monster's head in two as it collapsed to its knees and onto its face. As two more shots brought down the remaining creatures at the door, all that was left was one struggling beast with its arms outstretched over the counter; the guttural growl gurgling at the back of its throat. The grey eyes punctuated by malevolent jagged pupils flared, and for a split second, Mike thought he saw recognition of its own impending demise as he lifted the heavy serving dish and brought it down over and over again on the beasts head until it was nothing more than a reddish pulp of black hair, brain and bone. Where once overflowing baked beans or spaghetti hoops would have dripped down the side, now gory morsels clung to the stainless steel tray like glue.

Mike staggered back and dropped the dish to the ground with a ringing smash. Sweat poured from him onto the ground, washing thin salty trails into the congealed blood.

"Mike?"

"Yeah!"

Mike collected his weapons, wiping them off on a wad of paper napkins left behind. He replaced them in his rucksack then headed toward the kitchen, pulling bodies out of the way when there was no clear path.

"You do realise, if an army of RAMs couldn't shift the doors enough to get in here, there's no way you're going to?" said Shaw as Mike stood in front of the kitchen entrance.

Mike reloaded the shotgun and fired two shots at the hinges on the right-hand door, making them and the joints around them disintegrate. He booted it above the halfway point and the door swung out, pivoting over the table behind it. Mike sidestepped to avoid getting hit by the heavy wood as it clattered to the floor. Not missing a step, he climbed over the table to see Shaw still sitting where he had left him.

"You couldn't even let me go out like a hero?" asked Shaw smiling.

"That'd be okay for you. Can you imagine the fucking grief I'd get for letting the only gay in the village die?" They both laughed at the reference to the popular character from TV's *Little Britain*.

"You're a prick," said Shaw with a smile on his face.

"Yeah... I hear that a lot."

"Thanks, Mike."

"For what?" They both laughed again.

Mike walked over to where Shaw sat and crouched down by his side. He took his arm and placed it around his shoulder before the pair carefully rose, making sure Shaw's shattered ankle didn't touch the floor. It took them ten minutes to get out to the van. At one point the floor was so littered with decimated corpses that Mike had to carry Shaw over them.

When Shaw was safely back in the passenger seat of the van and as comfortable as he could be, Mike headed back to the dining room. He put on a pair of elbow-length protective gloves, a face mask, some goggles, and dragged six of the most complete corpses out into the hallway. Mike proceeded to remove four rubble sacks from his back pocket, slice open the stomachs of the RAMs, and fill each sack about two-thirds of the way up with soft, fleshy, bloody innards, before pulling the drawstrings tight and returning to the van with them.

He placed the sacks in the back of the van, stripped off the gloves, the mask and the goggles and wrapped a tarpaulin over them to make sure they wouldn't move around.

Mike climbed into the driver's seat, reached underneath and pulled out a bottle of vodka. He poured some over his hands, wiped them dry, took two big gulps, and handed the bottle to Shaw.

"You okay?" asked Shaw.

Mike burst out laughing. "Oh yeah! I'm just peachy," he said grabbing the vodka for another swig. He handed it back to Shaw and turned the key in the ignition. "Right then, let's get this show on the road," he said as the wheels began to turn.

*

Hughes raised the binoculars to survey the valley. "Well, it's just a waiting game now," he said, sweeping the lenses up the long winding road.

"We did pretty good today," said Lucy. "All of us. From the kids to the old folks. Everybody pulled their weight. Everybody did what was needed of them. The fishing boats brought back a good haul. We've got weaponry...mediaeval weaponry, but hell, it's better than nothing."

"I wonder how the lads are getting on?" asked Hughes.

"They'll be fine. They know how to handle themselves," replied Jules.

Lucy smiled. Behind the smile there was worry though. She had gone all day without seeing Mike. Darkness hadn't arrived yet, but the evening would start drawing in soon. She needed to think about something else. "So we've got the sentries posted. Everyone knows what they're doing?"

"Don't worry. I've got people I know I can rely on in place," replied Jules. "They've got flares. We've got people on the peaks ten miles from the blockades. The second they're in sight, we'll know and then it's battle stations. Andy and Jon are stopping up here for now. I've organised rotating shifts."

The group stood in silence taking in the

picturesque landscape when the radio crackled to life. "This is East Ridge...I can see the van...they're back...heading to you now...over."

Without realising it, the moment the broadcast had started, all of them had held their breath, now, they all exhaled in unison and relieved smiles warmed their faces.

14

Fry was oblivious to the reek that stuck in the air, coating everything in foulness and decay. His madness had finally taken over. From birth, it had only been a matter of time. A broken hourglass, sometimes a grain of sand would fall, sometimes more. It would all empty eventually, but there was no way of telling when until it had happened.

Fry's day of complete and total madness had finally arrived.

"Mornin' my love," he said as he leaned over to kiss Juliet's slowly rotting corpse. "Big day ahead of us today," he continued, climbing out of bed.

Fry walked to the window, naked. He stood there in the morning light; glass and a net curtain shielding him from the outside. He looked back towards the bed.

"Aye, a big day. These fucking people." A snarl

appeared on his face, his unkempt ginger beard only partially hiding his yellow teeth and red, angry skin. His voice began to rise as he continued. "These fucking people. They think they can kill my men. They think they can take what belongs to me and then go scurrying back to their holes like little rats!" He spat onto the bedroom carpet. When he carried on his voice was booming, "Who the fuck do they think they are? Who the fuck do they think they are that they can piss over me? They think they can steal from me and just go back to their little hidey-holes? Well they've got a wee surprise in store now." He stopped and looked back towards the bed.

"Yes," he continued almost whispering. "They've got a surprise in store. It's time for these people to understand who they're dealing with. I will make you so proud, Mummy. I will give you the kingdom you longed for. And these snivelling little shits are going to pay for what they've done. I'm going to reap a new kind of vengeance that will make the whole world shiver when they hear my name. No one will ever cross me again. No one will ever dare." He looked back through the lace curtains. His eyes glazed with tears he could not feel. Then he stared back towards the bed. "Mark my words, sweetheart, when this day is over, no one will ever forget my name."

Three booms resonated from below. "The canons, Mummy. The canons are firing for us."

Boom...boom...boom—there they were again.

"Fry!" shouted the familiar voice through the letterbox.

The towering Scotsman breathed in a lungful of rotting air and marched across to the window. Opening it, he called down, "Be there in a minute, my friend." Fry turned back towards Juliet. "All being well, my sweet, I will be back with you the day after next. I promise you some new trophies too...some new playthings."

Fry got dressed, tied his boots, checked his pistol and walked to the door. He threw one long loving glance back at his Juliet and left.

He stepped out into the morning air and inhaled deeply. He turned to TJ. "When this battle is over, everyone will fear our names. We will own this land. We will own every soul and everything in it. There will be no man and no army that will try to stop us." A toothy yellow grin appeared on Fry's red face and a chill trembled down TJ's spine. He suddenly realised. He was Faust, and the deal had been sealed long since.

*

Mike saw Emma, Lucy and Hughes as he turned the final bend before the barricade. The three of them had clambered over, too excited to wait any longer. Despite the pain Shaw was in, happiness fell over him like a cloak. Mike pulled on the handbrake and ran to where Emma and Lucy stood. The three of them melded together in a tight embrace. Hughes stood back for a moment and when he realised he wouldn't get to hug Mike any time soon, he walked to the van, puzzled as to why Shaw hadn't got out.

"Broke my ankle, didn't I?" he said as Hughes opened the passenger door. "And before you ask, no...it was an accident."

"Come on, then," said Hughes, putting Shaw's arm over his shoulder and swivelling him out of the seat. "Let's get you seen to."

It took several minutes to get Shaw over the barricade. Twice he nearly passed out from the pain as first Mike, then Hughes lost their grip on him and Shaw's broken ankle felt the brunt of his weight. Eventually, they made it, and Lucy and Hughes got Shaw into a car.

"I'll get him comfortable down at the infirmary, and then I'll meet you back home," Lucy said kissing Mike on the lips. She suddenly stopped and they looked at each other and smiled. 'Home'…a small word with a big meaning. Mike kissed her again.

"See you soon."

Lucy climbed into the car, and they drove away. Mike waited until they were out of sight, and then climbed into the car Emma was driving.

"I need to see Sammy and Jake," said Mike as soon as they pulled away. "And then we all need to get a few hours rest."

*

Mike didn't wait for the car to stop before he opened the door and started towards the house. He reached the garden gate and Sammy was already running up the path towards him. She leapt into the air as she approached and Mike caught her, squeezing her with all his might. She giggled and cried and squeezed back with all her strength.

"How's my Sammy Bear?" he asked.

She didn't respond, she just held her brother tight. Mike continued into the house, carrying her as if she weighed no more than a bag of flour.

Ruth came out of the kitchen, followed by two of the younger deaf children from Sarah's school. Ruth's sign language was still patchy, but she was getting better and the children loved her. When she saw Mike, her mouth fell open and in an uncharacteristic show of emotion, she burst out crying as she took hold of him in a motherly grasp. Still clutching Sammy in his left arm, he threw his right arm around Ruth and kissed her on the head. The three of them stayed like that even after Emma had entered. Finally, they broke their clench and Mike kissed Ruth on the forehead again before heading up the stairs, still without saying a word, still with Sammy holding on to him. He walked into the bedroom, set Sammy down on the floor and then sat himself, taking hold of Jake's hand.

"How's my little brother?" Jake's eyes were closed, but the lids trembled as Mike spoke. "We're together again now, Jake. You, me, Sammy, Emma, Lucy..." he broke off. He was about to say Gran, but then it hit him like a lightning bolt. He stopped and swallowed hard. Tears formed in the corner of his eyes and he held Jake's hand tighter. "I need you to come back to me, little brother. I need you to come back."

Mike dropped his head and his tears fell from his

eyes onto the dirty black denim of his jeans. Sammy placed her arm around her older brother as he sobbed.

"Come back to us Jake," he stuttered again through heavy sobs.

Mike pulled his hand away from Jake's and wiped away the tears with his palms. He had been through so much in the past few months, the past few weeks, the past day. He had lost so much, but fought so hard to get things back on track, but now...now he was faced with one tragedy he had no power to fight. He shuffled free of Sammy's embrace and stood up. He walked across to the window and looked out at the ocean through his tears. He remained frozen there, lost in thought... deaf to the world around him. Deaf to...

"Sammy?" came the croaky voice.

"Jake!" she squealed and almost dived onto him. Her hysterical giggles began again. "Jake! You're back."

As if coming out of a deep sleep, Mike blinked and turned towards the bed. He saw his little sister squeezing Jake like he was a well-stuffed teddy bear, and Mike's tears started again, but this time, they were tears of happiness.

*

"We've got about four hundred rounds for the SA80s...not many considering the numbers we're going to be facing," said Barnes as he stood on the stage with George and David. The audience consisted of Jules and her brothers, Emma, Lucy, Beth, Mike and Hughes; this was the war council. "The rifles themselves, thanks to Jules and her brothers, we've got forty-two. All told we've got about a hundred and forty able bodies, excluding kids," he continued. "There are about twenty including us who have fired weapons before, but none of Jules's lot were trained."

"We can use them well enough," said Andy.

"Shut your hole, Drainpipe," replied Jules. "He's talking about proper training."

Barnes continued, "It makes more sense to distribute the lion's share of the ammo to the people who can do the most damage with it. I just really wish to God I'd brought the L115A3 with us, but I didn't really have time when we left Morecambe."

"Who wouldn't want a sniper rifle soft lad?" said Hughes, "but we fight with what we've got. The SA80s have about a 400-metre range and you're the best bloody sniper I've ever seen. We just have to make the shots count," he said winking at Barnes. "Now, George, how are things looking on your front?"

"Actually... quite good." George smiled and looked towards David. "We've built five mangonels. Each one should have a range of about 1300 feet. I'm sorry," he said turning to Barnes, "I'm old, I still work in feet and inches."

Emma looked around at the faces to see if she was the only one who didn't understand. "Mangonels?

What are mangonels?"

"I'll be able to show you when we're done here. I was wanting to get them into position. They're an incredibly powerful catapult. They were used in medieval times."

Emma nodded and smiled, still oblivious to what they actually were.

"Doc, how is the infirmary looking?" asked Hughes.

Lucy let out a small snort of laughter. "Well, the infirmary consists of two static trailers now. I've got Talikha and Raj manning the place when...when everything starts. As far as supplies go, we're not in bad shape. We still have most of the kit we took from the ambulance and we've had a lot donated from home first aid kits, but you do understand? I'm not a surgeon, guys." She looked around at the assembled faces. "I'm a GP. I'll do the best I can do, but I can't perform miracles. I..." Tears appeared in her eyes, and Mike immediately took hold of her arm and led her out of the hall.

"I'm sorry...it's just a lot of pressure," said Lucy.

Lucy rubbed the palm of her hand across both her cheeks and swallowed. What she wouldn't give for an oxycodone tablet now—just one. "Luce, you've got this. I've seen what you can do and there is no one better equipped."

"Oh, yeah! I'm just a tower of strength."

Mike smiled and pulled her close. "Nobody is expecting miracles, Luce. We do what we can. We do the best we can." He kissed her on the forehead and gently wiped away the remaining tears with his thumb. "Come on," he said, taking her hand, let's get back in there".

As they re-entered, a discussion was going on that had everybody excited.

"So let me get this straight, George," said Hughes, "You think you could put one of the mangonels on a boat deck?"

"I'm not saying it would be easy," replied George, "but we've certainly got a couple of boats that are big enough and with enough manpower, we could get one of the mangonels hoisted on. Worst case scenario, it could go on in sections."

Hughes looked at Barnes, Mike, and the rest of them, a huge smile breaking out on his face. "Bloody 'ell, why didn't we think of this before? We've got our own navy."

*

Fry sat on a rock, alone. The convoy had come to a halt. It was not as impressive as it once was. The coaches with welded metal panels did not look as robust as they once had. He had seen what had happened in Candleton. He had seen his army defeated. Only a small handful of motorbikes remained. They still had cars and vans. They still had men, lots of men, but not as many as there had been once.

"They don't respect you."

Fry's head shot up. His eyes still looked down to the convoy from that comfortable rock on the side of the hill, but he listened. He listened to the voice.

"You need to lead them. How many have deserted? Do you think this army was as big as when The Don was running things? Do you? Really? Because to me, it looks tincy-wincy compared to then. There are still those who are too lazy to leave. Too scared to leave. But are they scared of you? I don't think so, honey. They're scared of facing life outside alone. The Don used to take the lion's share of all the spoils, but he was predictable. The men knew where they stood. With you, they don't have a clue. They're not loyal to you like they were to The Don. They will always be The Don's men. Mark my words, when an opportunity comes they will take it."

Fry turned his head, "What do you mean?" he asked, his voice broke with more than a hint of paranoia.

He was greeted with silence.

He turned around fully, searching his surroundings, but there was nobody there. He returned his gaze down to the convoy with a disconcerted frown. A figure broke away from the milling bodies and headed up to him.

"You okay?" asked TJ as he approached.

"Just getting some air," replied Fry.

TJ laughed. "We're in the middle of the fucking

241

Highlands, that's all there is here." When Fry didn't even break a smile, TJ straightened his own face. "Are you going down to get some scran? Soup's not bad."

"In a while," he replied.

There was a pause and TJ turned to leave, "I'll see you down there then."

He was almost out of earshot when Fry spoke again.

"Our army doesn't seem to be as big as it once was," said Fry.

TJ stopped in mid-stride. Was it an observation or a question? "We lost a lot of men in Inverness..." he replied.

"And?" replied Fry, sensing the evasion.

"... nothing. We lost a lot of men and a lot of resources." TJ began to walk away again before turning back once more. "You should really get something to eat," he said before continuing down the hill.

"He's hiding something from you. You think you can trust him, but you can't. He's plotting." Fry watched as TJ walked up to a group of men sat on the hard shoulder drinking their soup. They spoke for a few seconds and then all erupted into laughter. "See!" said the voice. "You need to start listening to me."

"I am listening," snapped Fry, turning his head and once again seeing nobody there. "I am listening."

"The men look up to him. The men like him. Who do you think they'd follow if he challenged you?"

Fry's head snapped round again. "TJ is my pal. He's always been loyal."

"Honey. I'm your only real friend. Your princess. Your queen. I'm the only one who knows you. I'm the only one you can trust. Don't let things get out of hand, Daddy."

Fry closed his eyes, the lids flickering like a faulty light bulb. More laughter exploded from down below, and Fry's eyes shot open again. He focussed his attention on TJ. "All this time there's been a rat in the ranks."

"Come home soon, Daddy. Your queen is waiting." A serpentine smile stretched onto Fry's face.

*

The Ford Fiesta came to a sudden stop, sending the gravel in the courtyard of the camping ground flying through the air. Emma, Lucy, Mike and Hughes were in conversation, but all stopped when they saw the car enter. Due to the limits on fuel, travel was to be kept to an absolute minimum. Sarah had been tasked with handing out the orders and directions to the remaining inhabitants on the stretch of coastline. For her to be there, something was wrong.

Before the car had come to a complete stop, Sarah opened the door and began to climb out. "It's all going to hell!" she called out. Her eyes seemed puffed as if she had been crying.

"What is it, sweetie?" asked Lucy, putting a reassuring hand on her forearm.

"I did as we said," she replied. "I spoke to everyone in the village first thing. That was fine. I headed up the coast and there were a couple of houses where no one was home, then more and more and more. They've gone. They all picked up and left in the middle of the night. We've got the people here. We've got the people in the houses between here and just past Sue's place, but that's it. There isn't another soul. I couldn't even find anyone at the lookout on the north ridge." She burst into tears again, and the soldiers broke away from the group, immediately stepping into action.

One of the static caravans next to the infirmary had been turned into an ops centre. A generator was running to keep that and the main infirmary powered. Hughes marched up to the desk and picked up a radio from its charger.

"North Ridge, this is base, over." Silence. Hughes released the speak button and tried again. "North Ridge, this is base over." Nothing. "East Ridge, this is base, over." Hughes looked at Mike, they both had worry in their eyes. The lookouts were the early warning system. Without them they were blind. The enemy could be on them with no notice.

The radio crackled, "This is East Ridge."

Both Mike and Hughes let out a deep breath.

"Thank Christ for that," said Mike.

Hughes hit the speak button, "Just a radio check," he replied. "You okay over there? Over."

"No sign of movement yet. You'll be the first to know when there is. Over."

"Ok, thanks. Over and out," replied Hughes.

"We need to get someone to the north ridge fast," said Mike.

"Jules's two brothers, what's their names?" Hughes snapped his fingers, trying to jolt his memory. "Y'know, not the dopey twat, the other two."

"I know which ones you mean," replied Mike. He picked up one of the spare radios and started to head out.

"Give them the Impreza and tell them to fall back when they see anything. We need to get this situation unfucked right now," said Hughes. Mike nodded and left.

Hughes flopped into one of the armchairs. What the hell were they doing? The "Ops room" was a bloody holiday caravan. Their vehicles were cobbled together leftovers. They were making medieval siege weapons. "Fuck me! I must have lost the plot too. Whatever you've got Mikey, it must be contagious."

Outside Sarah was still reeling. "I don't know what we're going to do. There's virtually nobody left."

"When you say virtually nobody, how many do

you think we're talking about?" asked Lucy.

"I'd say we'd be lucky if there are ninety of us left. From here up the coast."

Lucy let out an exasperated breath. Emma snapped, "Fuck 'em. We don't want cowards fighting with us anyway. Cowards turn and run when things get bad. Better they do it now than when we're in the fight." She looked towards Sarah, then at Lucy who both returned her gaze with shock. "Tell me I'm wrong. The people who are with us, by our sides, are here because they believe in what we're doing. They believe in what we stand for, they believe in what we're fighting for." She paused. "We're better with one of them than a hundred cowards."

"Emma..," Sarah began.

"I'm not an idiot, Sarah. I haven't gone mad. But all we need to do is make capturing this place too expensive for the enemy. The way we've planned this gives us the best chance of that. I know it's a roll of the dice, but it's better this than running for the rest of our lives, being chased to our deaths like wild animals in a hunt. Here, we have something to fight for. Out there, all we have is a reason to run. Do you want to do that for the rest of your life?" Emma spoke the last words softly.

"No," Sarah looked down. Her voice was barely perceptible.

15

The kitchen back at Sue's place was a hive of activity. Soups, stews, bread were all being made in batches. Sarah's girls were the backbone of the operation. There were a couple of villagers helping to prepare sandwiches too. This was the obvious place to have the food preparation. Sue had grown a lot of produce, she had also prepared a lot of food for village functions, and Daisy, the goat, was still producing milk. There was a bay below where seaweed could be harvested, as well as mussels picked off the rocks and there was still the odd small fishing boat that ventured out, even today. The troops needed to be fed.

Dora gestured to Jenny to try some soup. Jenny ladled some into a bowl and cut a doorstep slice from a cooling loaf. She dipped it in the soup and smiled as she tasted it. "Delicious," she said and Dora beamed momentarily before beginning to portion the soup out into an array of thermos flasks that had been collected from households up and down the coastline. No one knew what to expect if and when this assault came, no one knew how long it could last, but everybody was going to contribute in any way they could.

*

George, Richard, David, Barnes and Hughes were all assembled at the dock. They had one of the mangonels on a trailer and George had managed to erect a hoist to get it onto the deck of one of the fishing boats. Once it was onboard, they would bolt it down. They had tied a wooden rowing boat to the stern. This was going to be used to transport the rocks, stones, and other munitions that would be catapulted towards the enemy.

The men worked well together as a team. For George and the soldiers, this was nothing out of the ordinary, they had worked in teams all their lives. For the librarians though, they began to feel an air of self-worth they had never felt before. To be relied upon, to be valued, to be listened to—this was something they had not experienced before. It had been Mike who had brought them here. It had been Mike who told them they mattered, that they could be instrumental in building something new. As the large siege weapon thudded onto the deck, Richard and David steadied it to counter the movement of the boat on the gently rocking waves.

"Nice work lads," said Hughes looking down at the mangonel. "This wouldn't exist without you two. You have no idea, how much of a difference you've made to our chances." Hughes broke his gaze, "Now come on, let's get this bugger bolted down otherwise our navy will last all of five minutes."

Barnes jumped across with a power drill, and some other bits of hardware, and the team got to work on fixing the huge catapult to the deck.

*

Beth was already at the barricade when Jules and Andy arrived. Even though the road was open and completely passable, and even though they were a couple of hundred feet above, it was still called the barricade, because if all went as it should, that is what it would become. The plans, although hastily drawn up, were brilliant given what resources and amenities were available. The intricacies of them had been discussed time and time again as had the execution. Many people followed blindly, but some knew exactly what should happen and how it all worked.

The ridge peak was bustling with people digging, with people carrying large stones and boulders, with rocks being rolled into place to provide cover from enemy fire. The only way onto the ridge was either by an awkward rock climb or a trail that led to it from a sharp turn one hundred metres further down the road. It was unassailable to the enemy unless they actually got through the barricade, or for some reason, the barricade didn't deploy. If that happened, all bets were off and they had already lost.

Jules and Andy surveyed their surroundings. Tents had been put up. One of them had a red cross on a white background. Two smaller ones had the words

MALE and FEMALE painted on the outside. These were crude toilets which gave someone a little privacy to use a bucket, which was then to be emptied into a pre-dug ditch, and covered with soil or sand. It was all crude, it was all basic, it was all ugly, but it was all they had and all they would have until this was over.

"Where do you want us?" asked Jules, un-shouldering her SA80.

"We're just waiting for George and his...anti-tank guns," said Beth.

Jules and Andy let out a small laugh. The plan to build siege weapons had sounded mad originally, but it made perfect sense to them now. George and his helpers had worked around the clock to build them and the terrain of the coastline and the steep incline of dead man's pass was going to make them devastating.

Beth had been given precise instructions as to how the areas should be prepared. Two sections of ground had been levelled off and a mound of earth and rocks had been piled in front to make the mangonels invisible from the road. All this work had been done by the small group of people with her. There had been no mechanical diggers for this operation, but shovels and picks and blood and sweat. The tears would come later.

"Was that Rob and John I saw shooting by earlier?" asked Beth.

"You heard what happened?" asked Jules, keeping her voice low. Beth nodded. "Well, they're heading to the north ridge. They're our lookouts," she said as the drone of engines whined through the morning air. The three of them turned to see a pick-up and a Land Rover struggling and wheel spinning up the trail, both with trailers in tow. Hughes and George were driving the two vehicles, while Richard and David were in the passenger seats. They had picked Mike up on the way. Time was of the essence now, and he wanted a full debrief from George about what weaponry they had at their disposal. Mike was impressed by what George had managed to do in such a short time and felt a pang of guilt about not letting him in on the full plan.

Within twenty minutes, both weapons were in position. Richard and David would stay with them at the barricade. It was time for everyone to get to their places. George had hand-picked a crew for the boat and that had already set sail. They had no idea how long this would last. They didn't even know if Fry really would come back, but it was too much of a risk to take. Mike believed he would and that was enough for most people.

Hughes took his work gloves off and extended his hand. "This was a real achievement, fellas," he said, looking at Richard and then David. His iron grip crunched both their hands in gratitude. His gaze moved to Jules, Andy and Beth. "Right then, you're in charge now guys. You know the brief. Barnes will be coming up here shortly. He's bringing the rest of the ammo and a few more rifles..." Hughes paused and looked around at the tents, the people, then his eyes went down to the road and beyond. "I'll see you when this is all over."

Beth flung her arms around him and squeezed, then gave him a big kiss on the cheek. "Good luck Bruiser," she said, and they both shared a smile. He swallowed hard. It was difficult not to get emotional. For all the hard work, for all the bravado, these could be their last hours. None of them were oblivious to the reality of what was going on.

"Good luck to you, sweetheart," he replied, "You volunteered for the East Ridge?"

"Yeah, I'm going to head across there soon."

"Take care, Beth," he replied.

"I will. Don't worry."

Mike hugged Beth. "I'm glad it's you going to the ridge." They both smiled. "You're one of the few people I have complete faith in Beth." She didn't say anything but just kissed him on the cheek. He turned and walked back to the car, shaking hands with Richard, David, and George on the way, before giving Jules a powerful embrace. He climbed into the waiting vehicle and as soon as the door closed, Hughes started the engine and they pulled away.

Jules walked up to George and took his hand. "People said it was me who kept us alive back in Inverness, but we both know the truth."

George pulled out his pipe from his inside pocket and patted down the tobacco already in the bowl. He lit it and sucked in a deep breath. "We both had parts to play, chicken. You're a natural leader. People might listen to what I have to say, but people follow you. You give them hope. You give them a reason to carry on. You gave me a reason to carry on."

Jules sniffed and wiped her nose on her sleeve. "I love you, George."

George's eyes misted over in the wave of blue smoke that he breathed out. He cleared his throat, "Let's not get emotional, shall we? We've got a job at hand." He pulled away and walked over to the mangonels, inspecting them as if he'd forgotten to check something, but in reality, he just wanted to hide his own tears.

*

The physical barricade in place on "The Pass" was within the last one hundred metres of the road before the summit. When the attack began, no end of obstacles would be unleashed to make the ascent more treacherous than it was normally. One of the mangonels had been positioned next to the barricade, the other close to the summit. The destruction these had the potential to cause from this height would be a sight to behold. Although the encampment for this position was actually at the summit, the barricade would be the main focus when the battle commenced, so a few tents had been set up nearby. Food was being handed out by Sarah and two of her girls. Lucy and Emma were in charge of operations until Hughes or Mike returned. Boulders, rocks, and stones were piled next to the catapults. Drums with oil stood by them. Bottle crates that had once belonged to the local pub and carried nothing more than lemonade and cola, were now stacked by the roadside and filled with Molotov cocktails. They were guerrillas willing to do whatever it took, willing to use whatever they needed to repel the enemy.

Emma brought the binoculars back up to her eyes. She looked in the direction of where the warning flare should fire from, but the sky was clear. They were in regular contact by radio as well, but there was always a risk the radios might not work, so they used a secondary method too. Everything had been planned. The flares would alert the enemy to the position of the lookouts, but their escape would be down the opposite side of a hill to which they had seen the enemy. In addition, the road was already blocked by a number of tree trunks just after that point. It had been a method they had used back in Candleton with some success. It didn't stop the marauders, but it delayed them. This tactic would ensure that when the flares were used, their lookouts would be home safe by the time the attack started. The ones creating the blockades knew of cross country bypasses should they need to get round in a hurry, but for any stranger, moving the huge logs was the only option.

*

"So how long have you and Beth been a thing?" asked Jules with a mischievous smile on her face. Barnes was in mid-gulp of his soup, and he turned his eyes towards her. "Don't worry, no one else knows. I'm just good at picking these things up."

Barnes placed the mug back down on the edge of the rock where he sat. He looked around at the others, but they were all involved in their own conversations, their own thoughts. "We've tried to be discreet. I mean, her husband died not so long back. It's...complicated."

"Listen. Nobody knows when their time is up. We all need to find the small pleasures and comforts where we can. No one would judge either of you. Jesus! They'd be happy for you if anything," replied Jules.

"Well, it's probably going to be a moot point after today anyway, isn't it?"

"Oh ye of little faith," she said, smiling, before taking another sip of her soup and casting her eyes out to the rippling bay.

*

The farm had long since been abandoned. On the army's last trip north, they had used it for a few days to store the treasures they had pillaged from the surrounding villages, but now it served as a rest stop. The trip north had taken more time than expected. Blocked roads and roaming hordes of RAMs had slowed them down and the troops were tired. Fry's increasingly erratic behaviour concerned his lieutenants and the unease rippled around the encampment. Tents were hastily erected and two chow wagons had started dishing up food before the army bedded down for the night.

Fry sat in an old, but well-constructed red leather armchair. His feet stretched out onto a mahogany coffee table and he blew smoke rings into the air as he puffed away on one of The Don's fat cigars. Next to the chair he had placed a holdall, which he carried around with him everywhere. Speculation was rife around the camp as to what was in the bag, but no one really knew. The radio next to his boots hissed and an American woman had a short conversation with another woman about changing the watch. The other woman, whose voice Fry felt sure he had heard before, said she was fine and the conversation ended.

He grinned, a big, yellow-toothed grin, holding the cigar in his teeth, he scratched his mottled red beard, and reached down, gently patting the holdall like he was rewarding a good dog. Fry sucked on the cigar, removed it from his mouth, leaned back his head and breathed another stream of smoke into the damp air of the old fashioned living room.

That voice. Where did he know that voice from? It was a little scratchy over the airwaves, but he knew it from somewhere. Well, it didn't matter, he would find out soon enough.

"That bag is starting to smell a little ripe, lover," said Juliet's voice.

The grin faded a little from Fry's mouth. His eyes narrowed. "We've had this discussion, sweetheart. It's something I need to do." He swung his feet off the coffee table and sat up, leaning towards the armchair across from him. His piercing eyes focussed on nothing—thin air—but that's not what they saw. Nothing wasn't what his ears heard. Nothing was not the fragrance his nose smelled.

"They have to see. They have to see," he leaned back in the chair and put his feet on the table once more, all the time staring towards the other chair.

"I told you, I think it's a mistake, but you do what you want to do, Daddy."

"You have a lot to learn about being a leader, my queen. They need to fear you. They need to believe you are the only one who offers an answer, the only one worth following." Fry's eyes flared as he spoke.

"And are you worth following, Daddy?" she giggled, mocking him.

Fry jumped to his feet. He flung the cigar to the floor, and it disintegrated in a small explosion of fiery embers. He marched across the room and leant over the chair, his hands grasped the arms of it, his fingers curled around almost tearing the fabric. He spoke quietly, but with menace. "Remember your place, my love. Remember where we met. Remember who I am,"

He straightened up, still staring down at the chair, just as TJ walked into the room.

"Erm, are you ok?" There was no response. TJ moved closer. "Boss. Is everything alright?"

Fry looked towards TJ. He looked confused for a moment, but then the gears engaged. "Everything's fine, I...I thought I heard something, that's all."

TJ looked around the large open-plan room. It had been deserted for some time. The smell of damp suggested it had been months at least since it was properly lived in.

"Could be mice, rats, anything."

"Yeah... rats," replied Fry.

TJ pulled out a map from his pocket and unfolded it. "We've established the two most likely places for a look-out team, he said pointing on the map. Fry looked, but there was no register of recognition on his face. "I've prepped the reccy squads. I'm sending a few of our best lads. I've told the other garrison to stay put. There'll be a watch in place for them too, but if we can capture at least one of the look-outs, we should be able to get the info we need to find the other." TJ spoke without feeling. There was no joy in the prospect of capturing and torturing someone for him, it was merely a means to an end. It was a means to bring this battle to a decisive close with a minimal amount of loss for his men. But the smile that crept onto Fry's face and into his eyes, sent a nervous shiver down TJ's spine.

"Good work. Keep me informed."

"They're dishing up outside, do you want me to get something brought into you?" asked TJ.

"I'm fine as I am," replied Fry, looking back towards the armchair in the corner of the room.

"Okay then, I'll let you know when there's something worth reporting," said TJ, keen to get out. As he walked down the hall, he heard Fry whispering, and an uneasy feeling came over TJ once again.

*

"I think Shaw's ankle is going to be fine. Raj is going to operate on him; he's got so much surgical experience, he makes most doctors look like amateurs. We've got Shaw doped up with painkillers at the moment so he's not feeling much. He told me what happened though, he told me how you saved his life."

"Meh," replied Mike who put his arm around Lucy to help fend off the night's chill.

Lucy smiled. "You can't kid a kidder, Mike. I know who you are deep down, remember."

They both sat on a rock, a few metres up from the blockade, looking out at the starlit landscape. She leaned her head onto his shoulder, and he kissed her. "When I was stuck in that kitchen, it was the thought of you that saved me. You and Em, and Sammy, and Jake. It feels like I've known you all my life, Luce. It feels like we were meant to be together."

Lucy leaned up and kissed him back. "Careful, Mikey, you're not becoming a fatalist on me, are you?" She pulled away and smiled at him, gently stroking his cheek.

"I'm not doing a good job at explaining..."

"It feels right," interrupted Lucy. "We're from different countries, different backgrounds, almost different generations, but this...you and me...it feels right. It feels good. The thing is, sweetie, you never know who you're going to fall in love with. You never know when it will happen, and when it does, you never have any control over it. You let it take you on a journey. We're just passengers,

259

you and I, but there is no one else I would rather be sitting next to on this rollercoaster."

She edged closer and moved her lips to his. Their kiss lingered, and Mike closed his eyes, allowing himself just a moment of pleasure.

"Ahem," coughed Emma, "Budge up," she said to her brother, squeezing onto the rock next to him and breaking the romance in a split second.

"Why don't you join us? It's not like we were doing anything," he said.

"Okay then," she chuckled. Mike took hold of her hand, Lucy took hold of Mike's and the three of them sat in silence, looking out into the cold night.

16

Beth finished peeing and pulled up her jeans. She was annoyed at first that her companion had insisted on the campfire, but it was a cold night, and it was small and well covered, and grudgingly she had to admit, it made things a little more comfortable. As Beth stepped out of the thicket, she could tell something was wrong. The other lookout had vanished, and the rocks surrounding the flames had collapsed. She ran for her rifle, only to feel the wind knocked out of her by a hammer blow to the stomach. She doubled over and fell to her knees in pain. She saw feet kick earth and rubble over what remained of the fire, and felt her shoulders almost dislocate as two powerful figures dragged her to her feet. Beth tried to kick and struggle free but to no avail. With one last burst of effort, she pulled her arm around, clutched the handset out of her breast pocket and squeezed the speak button.

"Let go of me, let go of me. Help, someone..."

One of the guards snatched the handset from her

and pulled her fingers back making her squeal with pain.

"Try any more fucking tricks, and I'll snap them," he shouted.

They began to descend the steep hill. Beth was angry with herself, how had she let them get the upper hand? How had she not seen anything? The goggles. They were wearing army uniforms, they were wearing night-vision goggles. These guys were pros. *Shit*, I've just killed us all, she said to herself.

Her feet occasionally hit the ground, but Beth was being carried by the two men like a feather in the wind. She kept catching glimpses of the other look-out. There was only the natural light of the stars to see by, but he looked unconscious. He was a burly figure and the men at either side of him seemed to be dragging him down the hill.

They eventually reached the road and one of the men brought out a small but powerful torch. Beth didn't know the specifics of Morse code, but it looked like that was what he used. A minute later, she heard an engine and a minibus came to a halt in front of them. They piled in and that's when the real enormity of what was going on hit her. She was never going to see Annie or John again. She would never see Barnes, or Emma, or Mike, or Lucy again. She was in a minibus travelling to...Hell. She had been saved from a nightmarish torture when she was imprisoned in that garage back in Leeds. She had been used time and time again by scum. It made her feel sick, it made her feel dead inside. Despite everything, things were starting to feel normal again, but now... *Oh God please, no.*

The journey seemed to take forever, but that was the nature of the roads in this part of the country. Highland roads were rarely straight. They followed the best paths nature would allow which usually meant twisty turns and turny twists. It's why Dead Man's pass was such a huge tactical advantage to the group. Without a helicopter, there was no way to ascend that road quickly, but some of that advantage would be lost if the enemy could make a surprise attack.

The minibus turned onto a farm track and immediately, Beth could see lights and campfires stretching some distance. This was a huge army; hundreds, maybe thousands. Buses and lorries, trucks and bikes lined the tracks. As the headlights wound up the road, she could see metal panels welded onto vehicles for protection against attack, just like she'd seen in Candleton. The minibus pulled up outside the large farmhouse. The guards she had been sat between, manhandled her to her feet and dragged her out. Just one guard pulled her unconscious companion out. He let go and the body thudded to the floor. In the subdued light she saw something shiny and black streaming down his temple. *Was he dead?*

She stood there, surrounded by threatening figures, all glaring towards her. *Please let me die, God.* Fear welled inside her. Death would be a better alternative than what she knew awaited her. The guards marched her towards the house. There was a generator chugging away by the front door and lights lit up the hallway and living room as they went inside. There was a smell of damp, but something else too. Death...decay...something. It felt unnatural, it felt...evil. What was it? The guards threw her down onto the sofa.

A man came in. "Where's the other one?" he asked.

"Didn't make it, TJ. He struggled too much, we didn't want him to give the game away and let her escape."

TJ nodded, "Fair enough. Fry will be down in a minute. You've done well lads. I'll make sure he knows."

Beth became light-headed. *Fry, Fry, Fry.*

The heavy footsteps moved across the landing and with each tread on the stairs, Beth felt a little sicker inside. She had met Fry once before. She knew then what kind of man he was. He chilled her very bones. Before, Mike had been there to save her, but now she was alone. She had never been more alone in her life, and as that same black-souled monster entered the room her knees trembled, and she began to stumble forward, only for the two guards to grab her and pull her back upright.

A booming laugh came from Fry's belly as he laid eyes on his new captive.

"Beth!" he yawped like greeting a long lost friend. "Beth, darling!" He was carrying a half-full bottle of whisky, he went to her, clasped her face in his giant right hand and gave her a huge kiss on the mouth. He didn't use his tongue, but his lips were wet, his whiskers were soaked with the smell of scotch, and Beth gagged, once again, her knees nearly buckled at the prospect of what awaited her. She was so terrified. She was so disgusted, but she would do her best not to show it. Scum like this fuelled themselves by shows of weakness.

Beth spat. "Ever heard of a toothbrush?" she said, looking at him with all the hate she could muster.

"Beth, Beth, Beth, my darling Beth. I'm going to enjoy this."

*

Mike, Lucy, Emma and Hughes all looked at the radio in horror as they heard Beth's cry for help. Hughes picked it up and tried to reach her several times, but to no avail. She was gone.

It was only a few minutes before a car screeched to a halt, just metres from them. Barnes climbed out and headed straight towards the barricade. "I'm going after her," he said.

"Barnes, calm down," replied Hughes. "We don't know what's happened, where she is or anything." He put his hand on the front of Barnes' shoulder.

"I don't care. I need to go after her. Let me through." Barnes grabbed Hughes' hand and pushed it away.

"Barnes, you'll end up dead, mate. You can't just go off into the night on a wild goose chase," pleaded Hughes.

"You think I've got anything to live for if she's gone? I'm going, and no one's stopping me." He shouldered his SA80 more comfortably and began to climb.

"Wait!" shouted Mike.

"Don't tell me what to do, Mike," said Barnes.

"Barnes! Stop!"

As Barnes reached the roof of the Luton van he turned. "This is something I've got to do Mike. You should understand that more than anyone."

"I do mate. That's what I'm saying. Barney...Beth's one of us. There's no way we don't go after her, but let's do it right."

"C'mon," said Lucy, signalling for him to come back down, "Let's figure this out."

Hughes shone a torch on Barnes' face and the stern, resolute expression mellowed. His head dropped and he began to climb back down. As he reached the floor, Emma put her arms around him. "Beth is family. We will get her back."

Mike smiled to himself, a few months before, his sister would have been talking him out of something like this, but now, she was ready for the fight as much as he was. He picked up the walkie-talkie. "Jules, it's Mike. We need George across at the pass right now!"

There was a pause.

"He's on his way. What's wrong?"

"Don't suppose you fancy coming across with him. I need a word?" asked Mike.

"We'll be there as soon as we can."

The broadcast went dead with a crackle.

Mike turned to the people gathering around in anticipation. "Okay, guys, we need to shift the barricade so we can get some vehicles through."

People immediately got to work. Hughes, Barnes, Lucy, and Emma all made a beeline for Mike. It was Emma who spoke. "Erm... You mind telling us what you're thinking? Or are you planning a surprise?"

Mike watched as people helped each other move heavy, cumbersome objects. The ones who were left, the ones who had not run out on them. They were good. They were decent. They were honourable. They were worth fighting for and alongside. He turned to his friends.

"I can guarantee they will have left guards where Beth was on watch. The first thing we do is capture at least one of them and get information," he said as if it was the most natural thing in the world.

"Say that's right. Say there are guards there and we capture them. What makes you think they'll tell us anything?" asked Hughes.

Mike looked towards Emma and then to Lucy in the light of the lanterns that had been lit to help the workers.

"They'll talk," he said and a grim smile appeared on his face.

"Okay," said Barnes. "What then?

"Then we go get Beth and the other look-out back."

"Jack... His name was Jack," said Hughes.

"Just as easy as that, eh Mike?" asked Barnes.

"Y'know what wins a war faster than anything, Barnes? It's being willing to do whatever it takes." Mike's eyes suddenly looked black as coal. "Beth is one of us. I don't care how many there are, I don't care how heavily armed they are, and I don't care what I have to do. She's coming back to us." There was a moment's intense silence, then Mike broke his gaze from the others. "I'm going to find Raj. Ask Jules to stay here when she arrives. I'll be back in a few minutes."

Mike walked across to the Ford Fiesta that Barnes had driven a few minutes earlier, climbed in and wheel spun away.

"No offence girls, 'cos I love the guy like a brother. But he's a real fucking head case," said Hughes. Lucy and Emma just looked at him and got to work with the others dismantling the barricade. Barnes walked across to join his friend.

"I've been a soldier a long time, Barney. I've never seen anyone command as much respect as Mike, I love him, but I'm scared that one day we'll all follow him to oblivion."

*

Mike hugged Raj and Talikha tightly as he entered the infirmary. All three of them sat down. Raj knew Mike wouldn't just show up for a chat. Not now. Not when they were about to go to war. He spent several minutes explaining what had happened with Beth and the first part of his plan, then there was silence.

"So, my friend, you have not come down here to discuss tactics with a veterinarian. What is it we can do for you?" asked Raj.

"Raj. I wouldn't ask if it wasn't important, and I hate this. Hate it. But, I know it will give us the best chance possible..." Mike looked at Raj, then at Talikha, then back to Raj. "I need Humphrey. He can sense when there are RAMs around and we will literally be in the dark. I also don't know if I might need him to track Beth. I would just feel a lot better having him with us than not."

Raj looked down at his hands as he pressed them together. He rocked back and forth in his chair before replying. "We are family Mike. After everything we have been through, we are family. Take Humphrey, I know you will protect him with your life."

Raj and Talikha both stood and headed out of the infirmary. Mike paused for a second to look back at Shaw who was fast asleep with half a smile on his face, then he followed them. They walked in silence down to the dock and boarded the yacht. They were greeted by the

Labrador Retriever's characteristic woof which always sounded like it came from a dog twice his size. Raj turned a light on and Humphrey bounded up to the three of them, getting fussed by each in turn. Talikha placed the leash on his collar and kissed him on the head whispering something into his ear before Raj knelt down in front of him. Humphrey licked Raj's face once, twice, three times, and Raj couldn't help but laugh, before kissing Humphrey firmly on his wet black nose.

"I love you, boy. Look after Mike," said Raj before taking the leash from Talikha and handing it over. "Take care, my friend."

"Thank you. Thank you both," said Mike as he turned and followed Humphrey along the dock. The pair of them continued; Humphrey was excited to be free from the small cabin, excited at the prospect of a fresh adventure. Mike looked back and saw Raj and Talikha holding each other close. He had asked the world of them and they had delivered.

"C'mon boy," he said, "we've got a lot to do before this night is over."

*

Fry's eyes were wild, mad, and it was not the whisky, it wasn't a figment of TJ's imagination as they caught in the glow of the lamplight. It was something he had seen before only in those men with the blackest of souls. Beth was sitting on the couch, the false bravado not fooling anyone for a second. Fry took another swig straight from the bottle and droplets of amber fluid dripped from his mouth and whiskers as he pulled it from his lips and offered it to TJ.

"No thanks, boss," he said, hiding revulsion.

Fry regarded TJ for a few seconds and then smiled. "TJ," he began, "I want you to head up to the north encampment. We attack tonight!" he said proudly.

"Erm... Boss...are you sure?"

"Sure? Of course I'm fucking sure," he spat, taking another drink. "Me and Beth are going to have a wee chat. Then I'm going to get on the radio to you, and you're going to lead the attack from the north, while I lead the attack from the east." His eyes bore holes into TJ. "Beth here is going to help us no end. I won't be able to shut her up before I'm done," he said beginning to laugh.

"Do you want me to get the men prepared before I go?"

"Let them eat and rest for a while. They're ready as needs be," replied Fry sinking down onto the arm of the sofa.

TJ didn't argue. He didn't question. He left the house and felt a pang of relief that he didn't have to stay in that room one more moment. As little as he didn't want to head to the northern encampment and launch a night attack, he would take any hell over what was about to happen to Beth. The more distance between him and that house, the better.

He climbed into his Land Rover and picked up a

large handset. He flicked it to channel 18.

"This is TJ. I'm on my way to you. Let the look-outs know. Over."

There was a pause then, "Roger that TJ, over and out."

Inside the house, Fry closed the living room door and pulled the curtains across. Before they shut, he glanced outside. His army...his men...how he despised them. He turned and looked at Beth. She still held her chin up. She still made believe she wasn't scared of him.

"Ohhh... you're a feisty one girl. I knew that the first time we met."

Fry walked through the inner door to the kitchen, only to reappear seconds later with two glasses. He placed them on the corner of the mantelpiece before sweeping all the rest of the small ornaments and photos off it. They crashed and clattered to the floor and Beth shook but tried her best not to show it. He poured large measures into each glass and then placed one on the table in front of her, before taking a large gulp out of the other.

"I knew back at the hotel that you were someone I could talk to. You have spirit, Beth. I like a girl with spirit. My Juliet has spirit." He took another drink and licked his lips, letting the dirty red whiskers tickle the tip of his tongue. There was nothing about the man that Beth didn't find revolting. "Y'see Beth, what it boils down to is this. The measure of a man is judged by his successes. Now, you beat me in that fucking village. Then what should have been a simple smash and grab when my men came up here ended up being the cluster-fuck to end all cluster-fucks." He began to raise his voice, but a weird feeling inside Beth told her, it wasn't for her benefit. "Do you know how much that cost me? How many men? How many vehicles? How much fucking standing? That fucking Don and his whore of a daughter, they mocked me. They ridiculed me." Fry was roaring now, and Beth began to shake. There was something at work here more than just anger. Her breathing trembled and she did her best to stifle a sob. She was going to die tonight.

Fry walked across to the holdall by the side of the armchair and picked it up. As he walked back past Beth, she breathed in the same sickly odour she had noticed when she first entered the room. He placed the bag down, unzipped it and with his wide back to Beth he removed two objects and placed them on the wooden shelf. When he spoke again, it was at a normal volume. "Now...even now...I feel them judging me," he said stepping back from the mantelpiece and revealing the heads of The Don and Lorelei.

Beth screamed, tears flooded from her eyes and she got up on shaky legs and started to run out of the room. In two long strides, Fry caught her and clasped her arm, flinging her back down onto the sofa. She landed awkwardly, banging her head against the arm. She let out a mournful yelp as she continued to cry like a terrified child.

"You're going to help me change all that. You're going to tell me what I want to know to make sure that nothing goes wrong this time. Your friends are all going to die, Beth. Let's be sensible here. I've got a bigger army than you can imagine. Some of them are ex-forces, experienced fighters. And you've got what? A handful of scared villagers?" His laugh boomed. "Your friends will die, but it's important that this victory is quick for me...and you, darling."

Beth brought her knees up to her chest and hugged them. Her crying continued as Fry took his glass and sat down next to her.

"All you need to do is tell me what I want to know, and this will all be over like a flash for you, and I promise you, your friends won't suffer either. They'll die quickly and with dignity. But if you don't tell me what I want Beth, then things will be bad." His eyes widened, he spoke with an eerie calmness. He took another drink before continuing. "Very, very bad Beth. Because me and Juliet will need to teach you a lesson, and Juliet's been in a really pissy mood lately. Haven't you, my love?" he said looking across at the armchair and smiling.

Beth couldn't believe what was happening. A thousand times before, she had heard people use the words mad man, but it was always just an expression. Now though, she was with a true mad man. She had never felt fear like this, not even when she was naked and tied up in that dark garage.

"You're fucking insane," she said.

"You do not disrespect me in front of them and my woman," he yelled, almost spilling his drink as he shot to his feet. He placed his glass down on the table and plunged down again next to Beth ripping her shirt open as he pushed her onto her back, and exposing her torso and bra. He pulled a knife from the back of his belt and cut the bra, she tried to shield herself, but he pushed her arms down and stretched them back over the arm of the chair. He straddled her and replaced the knife in his belt, while keeping her wrists pinned with his incredible strength. Then with his free hand, he placed his palm between her breasts.

"I can feel your heart. I'm no doctor Beth, but I don't think it's meant to beat that fast, darling," he said grinning again. He looked across to the armchair, "What?" he asked. Through her tears, Beth looked towards the empty chair. She looked to where Fry looked. There was nothing but an insane emptiness.

"Good idea my sweet," he said, removing his hand, and unbuckling his belt.

Beth started to writhe and kick, "What are you doing?" she pleaded through cries.

"All in good time, Beth, you'll see. All in good time," the grin reappeared on his face as he began to tie her hands together using his belt. When the knot was secure, he dragged her over to the door between the kitchen and living room. Reaching up he banged on the hollow wall above the frame with the butt of his dagger, to confirm his thoughts. "They don't build houses worth a shit anymore," he said, as he started gouging at the plasterboard through the ugly textured wallpaper. Within a minute there was a hole through to the other side. He threaded the belt and tied it firmly leaving Beth on tiptoes, with her arms stretched above her. Her torso and breasts only partially covered by the torn shirt. Fry walked across to the mantelpiece and turned the heads of The Don and Lorelei towards the doorway. Beth dropped her head and continued to weep. She raised her eyes again to see him angle the armchair round towards the door.

"There, that's better. My hands are free now," he said smiling before unleashing a fierce punch smashing into the bare flesh of Beth's stomach and making her wail with agony. "Yes," throwing another, "much," another, "fucking," another, "better." Bruise patterns began to appear instantly as the force of the blows left Beth wielding. The lack of breath stopped her tears for a while. "Now, Beth. Let's begin shall we?"

*

George made a beeline for Mike as soon as he arrived at the barricade. Mike put his arm around the older man and guided him out of earshot. "I need a couple of things from you, George," he said, as the older man pulled his pipe from his pocket and began to dab down the tobacco with his thumb.

"Go ahead," said George, positioning the pipe in the corner of his mouth.

"You remember those nail balls I asked you to make?" George nodded. "I need those. I need some protective gloves, masks, goggles, whatever you can get your hands on."

George nodded again, "I'll see what I can do." he

said, lighting the pipe.

"That's the easy part, mate," said Mike. George looked up at him in the lantern light, awaiting the next part of the favour. "I need you to come with us." He paused trying to gauge George's reaction. "We're taking one of the mangonels. Nobody knows those things better than you. We might get just one shot before the fun starts. We can't screw it up, George. Everything depends on us getting this right."

"So, you're going to launch an attack on a camp with God knows how many armed men in it... Just a few of you, backed up by me and a medieval siege weapon?"

"Yeah, pretty much," replied Mike.

George took a long suck on his pipe and ritually exhaled the smoke into the cold night air. "What makes you think for a second I would turn you down?" The older man smiled and began walking away. "Be ready in ten," he said, "I'll get what you need, then we'll set off."

Mike watched George walk away and he smiled to himself. He turned around to see Jules in conversation with Emma.

"Jules," he called, signalling for her to join him.

Jules looked at Emma with an expression of incredulity. "What the fuck stops him coming here?" She walked across to where Mike was standing. "What is it?"

"Sit with me a minute, Jules," said Mike perching on one of the rocks. She sat down beside him and the two of them watched as the flurry of activity at the barricade continued. Mike took hold of Jules's hand in both of his. "I know, I piss you off Jules. I know you don't like me much, but I have nothing but admiration for the way you looked after all those people back at the store. You are the only person who can take charge here. You are the only person who I trust to look after my family." Mike looked down at Jules's hand as he held it in his and squeezed it gently. "Since meeting you and your people Jules, I've realised that there is still good out there. That there are still good people. I was wrong all this time. I thought I had to do everything by myself, I thought I could trust no one. But, you, George, even your fucking idiot brothers. Your hearts are good." Mike's eyes became teary, and Jules slid her hand out of his and put her arm around him. "Promise me if it gets to that stage, that you'll take my brother and sister and get out of here... That you'll hop on a boat or something and just slip into the night. Find somewhere safe, make a new start."

Jules squeezed his shoulder. "Firstly, I fuckin' love you, y'daft prick. Second, of course I'll hold the fort down until you get back, but you will get back, make no mistake. And if for some reason, there's a bit of a delay, then yes, I'll take Sammy and Jake and we'll find somewhere safe until you find us... Good enough?" she said, still holding him as his tears fell onto the ground. He nodded. She leaned in and kissed the side of his head. "Now don't let anyone see you crying y'big girl's blouse. You're meant to be the fuckin' hard man around here."

Mike laughed through his tears. "Thanks, Jules."

"Why don't we all just slip away now? Get on the boats and go?" she whispered.

"One, they've got Beth and Jack. Two, a few might slip away unnoticed, but there is no way these guys don't want revenge for what happened in Inverness. But if it's blood they want, I'll give them blood, Jules."

"I know you will." She kissed him again and stood up. "Be careful out there. Bring our people back." She helped him to his feet and they embraced.

"Should I be concerned?" asked Lucy, smiling as she walked across to the two of them.

"Absolutely," replied Jules. "There isn't a second that goes by that this pug-ugly lunk doesn't concern the hell out of me." She let out a little chuckle. "Look after each other," she said to Lucy, who put her arms around Jules.

"We will, sweetie."

17

Barnes brought the Land Rover to a slow stop and Humphrey stuck his nose out into the fresh night air. There was a tied rubble sack in the back of the vehicle that was causing the dog no end of upset, but there was no room for him in the other vehicle. The mangonel was secured to the trailer and was pivotal to their whole rescue plan. Mike got out, as the Ford Fiesta carrying Lucy, Emma, Hughes, and George pulled up behind them.

"Okay, this is as far as we can go by car until we take the lookout point down," he said to the others. Hughes climbed out of the Fiesta and the pair walked to the side of the road.

"You okay, Mikey?" asked Hughes as they fell out of earshot.

"Listen, if we haven't signalled within the hour, abort. Get the hell back home as quick as you can. It's about ten miles from the east ridge to Dead Man's pass. They won't know where the shortcuts are to get around the roadblocks, so that will give you enough time to prepare."

"You listen. Fuck this shit! You're going to retake the ridge, we're going to get Beth and Jack, and we're all heading back home together," replied Hughes. Mike nodded and the pair hugged.

*

Mike and Barnes stayed low as they ran across the narrow shale ridge. All their plans hinged on getting this right, so every time a stray piece of rock cascaded down the steep incline on either side, their hearts jumped up into their mouths. The moon gave them just enough light. The path was dangerous on a clear day, hundreds of feet up, but, there was too much at risk for them to even think about failure. They were two hundred metres across the ridge when Barnes signalled for Mike to stop and crouch down. The soldier took his SA80 and peered down the scope towards the small flickering flames at the lookout camp where Beth had been stationed. As a sniper in Afghanistan, Barnes had been adept at evaluating situations, even in relative darkness without night-vision equipment. So, a campfire and half-decent starlight made things easy.

"Fuck, I count four of them," Barnes whispered. "About a hundred and fifty metres to go," he said, looking back towards his companion. "Y'know we can't have gunfire, Mike? But we need to take them out quick. Any thoughts?"

"Thoughts only get in the way, Barnes. Let's get our Beth back," he said pulling out the two machetes from his rucksack, edging past his friend and starting to sprint full pelt in the direction of the camp.

"Fuck!" Barnes said, shouldering his SA80 and pulling his hunting knife from its holster.

Mike burst through the thicket and hurled himself towards two men who had their backs to him. Before they could even respond to the looks of shock that appeared on their friends' faces, the crack of their skulls as two heavy blades entered their brains, echoed around the small opening. As the two men on the other side of the fire began to reach for their weapons, a knife flew through the air, its blade reflecting hellish orange flames before slicing into the stomach of one.

"Don't even think about it," said Barnes, already pointing his sidearm at the last remaining guard.

Mike grabbed the survivor by the hair, dragged him the few feet to the campfire and plunged one side of his face into the flames. His howl was inhuman, and even Barnes was disbelieving. Mike threw the man onto his back, while the now weeping figure tried to extinguish the flames burning his hair and scalp. Mike pushed his boot down on the guard's neck, pinning him as he gasped for air. Mike's eyes glistened red in the glow. "Make no mistake, you die tonight. It's just a matter of how much you want to suffer first," he almost spat the words.

The guard was Mike's age, give or take. Tears were streaming down half his burnt blistered face. When he spoke, it was barely intelligible at first, but then Mike released a little pressure. The figure looked towards Barnes to see if there were two of Hell's demons visiting him this night, but Barnes just looked away. Horror, revulsion, guilt, all playing on his emotions, but none could compare to his deep need to see Beth again.

After just a few minutes, Mike put the wretched creature out of his misery once and for all with a machete chop cutting through his skull. He pulled the flare gun from his rucksack, walked to the edge of the ridge and fired, not up, but straight, making sure, his people were the only ones who would see the signal. Within a minute, two lots of vehicle headlights came into view winding on the twisty mountain road.

"I hope he was telling the truth," said Barnes, still shocked at the brutality of Mike's interrogation.

"He was," replied Mike. "C'mon Barnes, we've got a lot to do."

Barnes nodded, then something caught his eye. "Jesus, Mike, wait a minute," he said shining the torch beam onto some equipment that was just out of the arc of light created by the small campfire.

"What is it?"

"Bloody Hell, Mike," He said, reaching down and picking up four pairs of night-vision goggles. He flung them to Mike, before reaching down again and grabbing a heavy, long rifle.

"What's that?" asked Mike.

"This mate, is an L115A3. Standard issue for snipers. He pointed it into the distance and peered down the viewfinder. And it only bloody comes with a night-vision scope. And three boxes of ammo. I tell you...Christmas." Barnes looked around at the bodies. "These guys were either military, conscripts, or they found a good cache somewhere. I suppose it's about time we had some luck," said Barnes, placing the strap of the heavy gun on his other shoulder and putting the boxes of bullets in his pockets.

"We make our own luck, Barnes," said Mike before beginning the steep descent to the road and approaching vehicles.

*

Fry drained his glass and refilled it before putting another fat cigar in his mouth. He pulled a lighter out of his pocket, and lit it, blowing the smoke in Beth's face. She coughed and spluttered, nearly gagging at the foul-smelling mixture of fumes. Fry took a step back and looked at her, his eyes leery and menacing. She gulped and turned away, but Fry grabbed her chin, pulled it to face him and slapped her hard, making her yelp and start sobbing once again.

"You never turn away from me," he said, slapping her a second time. "Y'fucking bitch. No heroes to save you now." He grinned and the hairs on the back of her neck stood up. There was madness in his eyes. This really was the end for her. Tied up like an abused animal. Even if she told him everything he wanted to know, she knew that he was going to make her pay for what happened in Candleton. So... she would tell him nothing. She would protect Barnes, she would protect her friends, no matter what he did. As if sensing her thoughts, he unleashed another vicious slap causing her cheek to turn bright red.

"Now," he said, beginning to pace up and down like a lawyer in court. "How many of you are left?" Beth said nothing, she just cast her eyes to the floor. He stopped pacing, walked across to her and pressed the end of his cigar against the bare skin of her belly. Beth screamed and started crying once more. "Answer my questions and this all stops," said Fry moving his face close to hers.

"Fuck you," whispered Beth through her tears.

"What did you say?" demanded Fry, pulling back from her.

"I said, fuck you," she repeated.

Anger turned to a smile on Fry's face, then the smile turned to a laugh, but the laugh suddenly stopped as he heard a sound.

"What?" he said.

Beth was suddenly not the focus of his attention anymore, and she watched in confused horror as he began a conversation with himself.

"She will," he said with irritation in his voice. "She will, and then they'll see." He walked over to the two heads on the mantelpiece. "You'll see," Fry said, directing the conversation to them now. "I'll find out what I need to know from this bitch, and then my army will wipe every last one of them off the face of this earth." He suddenly grabbed the head of The Don by his comb-over, "No," it's my army now, he said as if contradicting a taunt. Fry's gaze shot towards the armchair. "No one is fucking laughing at me, Juliet," he spat.

Beth looked on, terrified, as she began to understand the depth of Fry's psychosis. As if he sensed her eyes on him he rushed towards her, putting the cigar back in his mouth, holding the glass in one hand, he wrapped the other around her throat and squeezed. Beth began to turn redder as her windpipe became more constricted.

"It better not be you she's talking about, Beth. You wouldn't be so stupid as to laugh at me, would you darling?" he said, clenching the cigar in his teeth as he spoke. He moved in towards her face, and she could feel the heat of the cigar, but all her efforts were focussed on trying to breathe as she wriggled and writhed in an attempt to free herself from his vice-like grip. Her eyes began to lose focus and there was a dripping sound which made him look down to the old fashioned carpet. A wet patch was forming on the floor, and he realised it was coming from Beth, as the fear of her impending death made her lose control of her bladder. He pulled back and began laughing. It empowered him to see how much fear he had put into her. Beth choked and spluttered as she gasped for oxygen. Her sobbing made it harder, but she couldn't control herself. She wanted to put up a front, to show him she was not scared, but she'd just revealed the true depth of her fear to him. He owned her now. This was only going to get worse.

*

George had taken all the bulbs out of the rear lighting panels on the vehicles. All they would do is alert the enemy to their whereabouts. The two cars pulled up on the dark road and preparations began. They could see the lights and small fires around the camp, it was a few hundred metres away, but it stood out against the surrounding blackness.

The four men wheeled the mangonel off the trailer. It wasn't an easy job at the best of times, but in darkness, it took more effort than anyone wanted. George stood back while the others positioned it to his requirements, then they retrieved the two bins full of the balls with nails through them that Mike had commissioned George to manufacture. Mike lifted out the tied rubble sack and when he undid the tie, the stench of foulness exploded into the night air making everyone gag.

"There are gloves and masks," he said talking to everybody. "We mix this stuff in with those," he said signalling for the offal to be combined with the balls. "Be very, very careful not to get scratched. I brought a couple of shovels. There's a baseball bat in the back of the Land Rover. Use that to swirl the stuff around."

"I don't understand," said George.

The others knew. They had done something

similar in Candleton, this was just the medieval version.

"It's simple George," replied Mike, "We fire these at them; the nails break their skin, they get infected, they turn, they start attacking their former pals."

"Oh my God! Tell me you're not serious. You're talking about deliberately turning people into those things? It's inhuman! It's monstrous! I won't do it," said George, starting to fish in his pockets for the car keys.

Mike took a pace towards him. "So let me get this straight. These men are going to torture, rape, and kill our friends, our families. And I'm the fucking monster?"

"It's unholy what you're talking about doing, Mike," replied George.

"Unholy?" Mike said, raising his voice. Lucy and Emma immediately stepped towards him as he moved further towards George.

"Oh, God," Emma muttered to herself.

Both she and Lucy put their hands on Mike's arms, not restraining, just reassuring.

"George, listen to me," began Lucy. "We did something similar to this when we got ambushed by these men in Candleton. These are bad people. What they do to women...to anybody who gets in their way... it's evil." She took her hand from Mike's arm and stepped between him and George. "We are vastly outnumbered and outgunned, and they've got two of us in there, two of our people. God only knows what they're doing to them, but they're our people. We do whatever—and I mean whatever—it takes to protect them. I'm sorry, this is the way it is. I'm sorry we have to do these things. But we do *have* to do these things, George." She couldn't see facial expressions in the light, but she could feel the tension ease.

"I... I..," began George.

Lucy reached out, hearing the sadness in his voice as he came to terms with what he had to do. She put her hand on his arm and spoke softly. "None of us are the people we once were. The world dying kinda changes that. We can still be the same people to family and friends, but to the rest of the world, we're someone else. We do whatever it takes to protect our own." She felt his hand reach for hers. "They've got our people, George. We need to get them back."

George released her hand and without saying a word began to shovel the spiked ammunition into the mangonel. The bucket was a quarter full when he put on a face mask, goggles and gloves, and lifted one of the thick rubble sacks pouring out a bloody, sloppy mixture of organs and entrails. He gagged despite the mask. He used the baseball bat to mix the deadly tissue with the ammunition, before adding more and repeating the process.

"Well done, Luce," said Mike as the two of them stole a moment away from the rest of the group.

"I love you, Mikey, but pummelling somebody until they do what you say isn't always the best way," she said. He couldn't see her face, but he could hear a smile in her voice, before it disappeared just as quickly. "Be careful," she said, putting her arms around him and squeezing him tight.

"I'll be fine, you need to be careful. They might have a couple of guards kicking around, but they won't be expecting an attack. When it all kicks off, they're going to figure out pretty quickly where the attack came from, though. Remember the plan," he said to her and kissed her on the lips. "I love you, Luce."

How many times had they parted like this? How many times could their goodbyes have been their last? "I love you too."

"Remember, don't let Barnes off the leash. With that sniper rifle, he's more vital than ever."

"I don't really think I can stop him if he wants to change the plan."

"Give him a speech about family and shit, that'll work," he said. This time, she could hear the smile in his voice.

"Wise-ass."

*

Mike kept Humphrey on a long lead as they ran low across the field. There were at least two chest-high dry stone walls in between them and the farm encampment, but they didn't want to take any risks. Hughes followed the two of them. He had traded his heavy SA80 for a Glock 17 and he was just managing to keep up. The three of them ran in an arc, circumnavigating the camp by a few hundred metres and ending up far from any roads, at the rear of the farmhouse. From their position, they could see the lights of the house. There were no growls from Humphrey, there was no danger of any RAMs out here. Not yet.

"Okay," said Hughes, "We need to slow down a bit," he said, trying to catch his breath. "Slow and steady Mikey, until we're there."

The three of them moved off again, Hughes kept raising his night-vision goggles as the glare of the house lights dazzled him.

Mike reeled the lead in further and further as they got closer to the house. There was a smell of smoke in the air as campfires burned at the front of the farmhouse, where over thirteen hundred men, all but for a handful of guards were beginning to bed down for the night. There was a waist-high wall enclosing the garden, nothing like the things, Mike and Hughes had lifted Humphrey over. Mike straddled it, Humphrey jumped on top and down in a fluid movement, and Hughes clambered over it, scraping his belly.

There was a post for a washing line and Mike wrapped the lead around it. He crouched down, kissed Humphrey on the head, who reciprocated with a sloppy lick of his friend's face. Mike smiled.

"Stay boy," he said and the dog sat down.

Mike and Hughes crouched down, working their way along the windows. Then they saw one partially illuminated. It was the kitchen. It was dim inside, but light was travelling from another room. The pair had to do a double-take as they looked in, realising Fry had Beth strung up by the arms in between the doorway to the kitchen and living room.

*

Fry hurled The Don's head across the room like it was a football. It made a splat against the wall, leaving a gory mark as it fell to the carpet. "I'm sick of you all laughing at me," he said, striding to where Lorelei's head perched. He forced his index and middle fingers into her eyes, pushing them into the sockets and forced his thumb into her mouth like her head was a macabre bowling ball. He flung it at the panelled glass door separating the living room from the hall, and one of the panes of glass smashed before the once pretty head hit the floor with a heavy thud.

Fry lurched towards the armchair and gripped the rests, pinning his imaginary audience down. "And I'm telling you now, I've had enough from you, my girl. Unless you want to end up like them, you'd better just stop it with your smart little comments." Beth began to cry again, which enraged Fry further. "Y'see what you've made me do? Y'fucking whore," he yelled and punched her in the stomach, making her whine and howl with pain once more. He closed his fist around her hair. She grimaced as she felt his nails dig into her scalp. She clenched her eyes shut as he brought his face up to hers. She could smell the tobacco and the whisky. She wanted to vomit. He moved his face closer. "Well, no point letting a good whore go to waste, I might just give you one last hurrah before I put you out of your misery," he said beginning to move his finger around the elastic of her panties.

Beth started screaming, which gave Fry great satisfaction. He began to laugh as the look of panic etched itself on her face.

Fry stopped. The black night beyond Beth's shoulders and the kitchen window suddenly had a tinge of green. He barged past his captive and into the other room. Walking to the window, he looked up to see a green flare lighting the night's sky. His laughing stopped, confusion reigned on his face. This intensified when he heard pops, thuds and screams erupting from the camp at the front of the house. He stormed back through, pushing Beth out of the way, and went straight outside to see for himself what was going on.

The confusion intensified as small objects rained down on the camp. Some bounced, some stuck in mud, some ripped through tents and smashed vehicle windows, and some lodged in bodies, shoulder blades, backs, stomachs, legs.

"What the fuck?" said Fry, rushing to his vehicle. He opened the door and grabbed the radio. "TJ!" he yelled, anger consuming him.

A few seconds passed. "This is TJ, what is it?" he asked, hearing the venom in his voice.

"Attack! Attack now!"

"Okay, Fry," came the sombre response.

Fry put the radio back in its cradle and was about to shout the same command out to his troops, when one of the falling objects cracked his windscreen, piercing the glass and sticking. He pulled it out. "A fucking tennis ball with nails through it? What's this fucking shit it's covered in?" He brought it up to his nose but pulled it back just as fast. Then he heard it; that familiar sound, the guttural growl of a RAM. He looked up to see one of his men, only it wasn't one of his men any more, leaping on another and tearing a chunk out of his face. He turned and saw another RAM attacking someone else, then everything fell into place. What he held in his hand was a biological weapon. He heard more screams, then even more as the attacks multiplied.

"Get into your vehicles, we're moving out," he yelled at the top of his voice. Some men heard what he said and dived into the nearest thing with four wheels. But many were fighting off attacks or running into the night. Fry marched back into the house.

"We're going to have to cut this short," he said bursting into the living room, "Your fucking friends have..."

His mouth dropped open as his eyes fell on Mike. "You?" he said, remembering back to the hotel in Candleton; the bluff that was played on him, losing him the battle, starting all his problems. "You!" disbelief turned to rage as the same thing was happening again.

"You like torturing girls, do you? You piece of

shit," spat Mike.

Fry was a lot bigger than Mike in height and girth, but this was a fight that the younger man wanted. The big man ran towards him, roaring like a rabid animal. Mike unleashed a powerful blow to his gut, winding him and making his eyes flare with even more hatred. As Fry doubled over, Mike grabbed the bigger man's ginger hair and pulled his face down hard, while bringing his own knee up even harder. The crack echoed around the living room and Fry fell back, his face, awash with blood as his flattened nose oozed and pulsed red. Without pause, Mike leapt on top of him, straddling his dazed body, and pounded his fist into the bloody mess that was Fry's face, time after time after time. Mike would have continued all night, but then one of his own missiles smashed the living room window, causing him to pause and look up. Fry took advantage of the distraction and laid a punch on Mike's chin, knocking him off balance. The mad man's power was immense and even dazed and battered, he could deliver dangerous blows. Mike started to pick himself up, suddenly noticing the heads of The Don and Lorelei on the floor. His confusion cost him another strike, as he felt a small side table crash over his back and head making him collapse to the floor once again. He took a breath and started to rise, but then a boot smashed into his ribs, once, twice, three times. He felt one crack, maybe two. The assault was becoming more vicious by the second as Mike realised he had underestimated the agility and speed of his opponent. He felt himself being lifted up and before he could scramble to his feet, he was thrown, head first, into the wall. He felt the top of his head dent the plasterboard. He started getting up again, only to have his legs kicked from under him and something hard batter his back, repeatedly. In between hits, he rolled onto his side to see Fry had a thick table leg that he was using like a caveman. He brought it down with a heavy blow and Mike felt another rib crack. He growled with pain much to Fry's satisfaction, who backed it up with another good kick.

Fry's face was covered in blood from his splattered nose. It dyed his ginger and grey beard red and the blood dripped over his lips and stained teeth as he broke into a smile. He looked towards the armchair, "See who's laughing now, Mummy?" he shouted and began to cackle.

Although Mike was in pain, the furrowing of his brow had nothing to do with that right now. When he had freed Beth and she had said, "he's insane," he didn't realise she meant literally. Mike used his feet to push himself to the wall and slowly, shimmied up.

Fry broke his gaze away from the armchair and set his eyes back on Mike. "Right y'little fucker," he said, waving the table leg in one hand and pulling a hunting knife from his belt with the other. "Time I had me a little carve-up," he laughed, as he stormed towards his foe.

Mike cursed his own stupidity. He had left his gun in the other room deliberately. He wanted to exact his pound of flesh from this monster by hand and he thought he had the strength to do it, but this guy was like a rhino. Fry was almost on him when Mike pushed back against the wall, and kicked out with the flat of his foot, sending his assailant toppling backwards with his arms flailing. All hell was breaking loose outside, but that was nothing compared to the hell Mike felt he was in at that moment. He was in pain all over his body. His ribs were in agony and his breathing wasn't great as a result. Fry was not only mad, but seemed unstoppable. What Mike had done to him earlier would have put out ninety-nine point nine percent of men, but this freak just laughed it off. It was as if he liked the taste of his own blood.

Fry scrambled to his feet and made a beeline towards Mike again, who this time, swung a hammer punch at Fry, dazing him for an instant. Mike pulled his own knife from his belt and the two began to edge towards each other again. Who would strike first?

Fry lurched towards Mike with the knife outstretched. Despite the painful movement, Mike jumped to one side, dodging the blade, but Fry played it to his advantage and swiped with the heavy table leg. Mike toppled backwards, over the sofa and crashed onto the hard floor sending a jolt of pain throughout his body. His knife spun out of his hand and a raucous laugh erupted from Fry.

"Don't worry, Mummy, I'll save you the head," said Fry, looking towards the armchair, as he walked to where Mike was laying. He loomed over him menacingly, staring down from his ugly, bloody face with malevolent eyes. "I've been looking forward to this ever since that fucking hotel," he said breaking out into an ugly grin. "Thought you were clever, didn't you? Thought you'd beaten me. Well, do I look beaten now?"

Mike knew, with the pain he was in and his cracked ribs that he was in trouble. He needed a weapon.

This bastard had two, and he wasn't afraid to use them. Then he saw it, just a hand's length out of his reach. It was the gruesome, homemade missile that had smashed through the window.

"Well boy. It's been fun, but I've got all your friends to butcher before this night is over. My men are on their way to your place right now, so it's time to say goodb—"

Mike shoved his heel down hard onto the floor and pushed, he slid far enough to get the ball in his hand. He held it carefully, making sure the spikes wouldn't so much as graze him, then threw it with all his strength towards Fry. It lodged in the ample flesh of the Fry's stomach. Looking down, the grin disappeared from his face. He dropped the table leg and grabbed the ball, yanking it from just below his rib cage. No pain registered on his face as chunks of bloody gristle followed the spikes out. He just looked, dumbfounded. He staggered back, one step, then two, as the realisation of what was happening swept over him.

Mike wasted no time and slid away across the floor, before clumsily struggling to his feet. He winced as pain shot through his ribs. The shock on Fry's face turned to anger as he threw the ball back towards Mike with all his power. It missed by a way and went clattering off the wall. "I'm guessing cricket wasn't a big thing where you came from?" said Mike, smiling through his discomfort. "Lucky for me, we live and breathe it in Yorkshire. Now who's laughing, you prick? This is the last lesson you'll ever learn, but it's one you should have learned a long time ago.

Never mess with my fucking family."

"Aaarghh," yelled Fry, grasping his wound. He fell to his knees, grimacing in pain as his eyes began to lose focus. Growls began to emanate from the back of his throat and he collapsed to the floor, his body shaking and convulsing.

Mike stepped around him and through to the kitchen. He picked his rucksack off the kitchen work surface and headed out into the enclosed garden. Humphrey was edgy and straining against the lead as Mike approached him. The dog whined as if showing concern for his battered friend.

"It's alright boy, I'm alright," he said. Just then, the Lab Retriever started barking. Mike turned to see what was once Fry coming out of the kitchen door and hurtling towards them.

"That was quicker than I thought it would be," said Mike as he pulled a machete out of his rucksack and sliced it through Fry's forehead. The creature stopped dead in its tracks and fell to its knees, then onto its face. Mike released the blade, wiped it on the RAM's clothes, replaced it in his rucksack and bent down to untie Humphrey's leash. "C'mon, Humph, our night's not over yet."

18

Emma was loading the siege machine as George adjusted it ready for the next shot. Barnes was staring down the night scope of his sniper rifle, and Lucy stood on the Land Rover's roof watching the mayhem unfold with a pair of binoculars. The first vehicles screeched away from the freshly made war zone.

"Okay, that's our cue, guys," said Lucy, climbing down.

"Ready?" asked George.

"Ready," replied Emma, backing away from the mangonel.

George pushed down a lever, setting the mechanism in motion and instantly a throng of deadly missiles launched towards the encampment.

"Ok," he said, and the four of them converged

on the leaden machine to angle it down the road. George did some more adjustments, while Emma and Lucy emptied the remainder of the first bin into the mangonel's bucket. They opened the back of the Land Rover and lifted the unused bin back inside. The seats had been folded down to create room, and Lucy climbed in with it, and Barnes joined her. Emma dived into the driver's seat and started the engine.

The first vehicles appeared on the road just three hundred metres away. "I'm not ready," shouted George.

"Okay, George, stay calm, I've got this," said Barnes, as he knelt on one knee, bringing the other one up for support. He placed his elbow on his thigh and brought the sniper rifle night-vision scope up to his eye. He remained composed as he got the driver of the first bus in his crosshairs and squeezed the trigger. A boom echoed and a second later, the vehicle veered off the road and smashed through a fence before going down a small embankment and toppling, coming to rest on its side. The van behind slowed before its engine revved wildly, and it shot forward at breakneck speed in order to reach the stationary vehicles before the next shot rang out. The one behind it did the same and, what was now a convoy came speeding towards them.

"I'm ready," said George.

"Then don't piss about," replied Barnes, "Fire for Christ's sake."

George released the lever and a wall of missiles launched towards the oncoming vehicles. He ran around the Land Rover and to the Fiesta, jumping in, he started the engine and drove away. Lucy and Barnes watched as the spikey missiles smashed the windscreens of the first and second vehicles before they punctured tires causing a pileup. One vehicle flipped and within a few seconds was on fire. It wouldn't be long before the growing population of RAMs at the farm became interested in those flames. That part of the plan had gone better than anticipated. Lucy shovelled a few of the spiked tennis balls onto the road as they drove, just in case, by some miracle the odd vehicle managed to get past the wreckage.

They pulled up behind George at the rendezvous point which was just around the corner from where they had launched the attack, but was guarded from view by a thicket of trees.

Now came the hard part—waiting.

A small explosion resonated through the night air, as a petrol tank combusted, somewhere in the pileup. Barnes placed the rifle down and got out of the vehicle. The cool breeze refreshed him, and he rubbed his hands over his face. He hadn't allowed himself to think about anything but the mission. Once a soldier, always a soldier, but now, he thought about the reason they had launched the mission.

"She'll be alright," said Lucy, placing a gentle hand on his shoulder.

"I hope to God you're right, Lucy," replied Barnes. Emma and George joined them.

The four of them stood in silence looking into the darkness, trying to anticipate where their loved ones would emerge from. With each minute that passed, the tension grew, until they heard the snapping of twigs. Emma and Lucy immediately pulled Glocks from the back of their belts, while George shone a powerful torch towards the noise.

"It's us," called Hughes, "Me and Beth," he said. The Glocks were instantly re-holstered and the four of them ran towards the emerging figures. Beth was being supported by Hughes as she stumbled into the clearing. Barnes immediately grabbed hold of her. In the light of the torch he could see the pain on her face, the cuts and bruises. He could see the dried trails of tears, and he held her gently, but gratefully, not knowing the full extent of her injuries. She burst out crying and Barnes did too. He had her back. Whatever happened from now on, at least he had her back.

Emma and Lucy both hugged Hughes, but then pulled back, looking at him expectantly. "Mike's on his way," he said.

"What do you mean?" asked Emma

"Time was a thing. I couldn't stop him, Emma. He saw that Beth had been tortured, and he got that look in his eyes...I had to get Beth to safety."

She put her head in her hands. "That fucking idiot brother of mine is going to be the death of me, I swear to God," she said, pulling the Glock 17 back out and starting to walk in the direction from where Hughes and

Beth had emerged.

Lucy grabbed hold of her arm, "Wait a second," she said, turning to the rest of them. "Head back home, we'll take the 4x4. Be careful."

"Hang on a minute," said Hughes, "I'm coming with you."

"And me," said Barnes. He kissed Beth; knowing that she was safe again was all he wanted. Mike had saved her, and he'd set out to punish the man who'd hurt her. There was no way he wasn't going to have his back. "George, take her home. Get her to Raj, we'll be there soon enough.

George took Beth's weight and guided her back to the waiting car. All their heads turned as a dog's bark cut through the night. It was followed by rustling and finally, Humphrey emerged, pulling Mike behind him. Emma and Lucy both ran towards him. He released the leash and Humphrey went happily bounding up to Hughes and Barnes who made a loving fuss of the dog. As Mike hugged the two women, and as they reciprocated, he let out a grunt of pain. Lucy and Emma both backed away and looked at Mike in the torchlight. He had obviously been in a real fight.

"We've got to get home. His men are on the way to the north ridge," he said through laboured breaths.

"Oh, shit," said Lucy. "We won't have a radio signal from here, we need to get past the east ridge, before we'll be able to pick one up"

"Let's go everybody," shouted Hughes as they all climbed into the vehicles and sped away.

It was only a matter of minutes before they managed to get a signal. "Jules, it's Emma, do you read me? Over."

"The signal flare's gone up, Emma. I'm heading to the north road barricade now, over."

"We'll meet you there Jules. I'm sorry, Jack didn't make it, over," said Emma.

There was a pause. "He might be the lucky one," replied Jules. "I'll see you at the barricade, over and out."

"See you soon, good luck, Jules, over and out," replied Emma.

"This night just keeps getting better and better," said Lucy as she put her foot down hard on the accelerator.

Mike took two painkillers with a swig of brandy from the hip flask George had given him. "Don't worry, I've got another good fight in me before I turn in," he said grimacing. "These fuckers really picked the wrong night."

*

TJ didn't want this fight. It wasn't that he thought they couldn't win, he just didn't see an upside. Yes, they would vanquish an enemy once and for all, but they had already taken all they had, so what was the point? What was the point of risking men and equipment for no reward? It was foolhardy, but it wasn't something he could argue. Fry had become less and less approachable as of late. He had confided in TJ less, preferring Juliet to be his confidant and advisor. Bedfellows might be fun but rarely do they make good generals. TJ had earned his position in this army. He had the respect of the men. They didn't fear him like they did Fry, but he had their loyalty. Well, as much loyalty as you could get from a huge gang of marauding thieves anyway.

When he had given the order to attack, there were no questions. The men all knew what they were doing. They mounted the vehicles and started the engines. The convoy consisted of a variety of adapted vehicles. Buses had panelling welded over the windows with peepholes cut out, big enough for rifles and shotguns to slide through. They were down to just one mortar now the army had split in two, and that was on the back of a Toyota Navara pickup. Once again, metal sidings had been welded into place, making it impossible for anybody at ground level to get a view of the mortarmen. They had a dozen bikes for speed, a couple of army jeeps, minibuses and one all-singing, all-dancing Winnebago, which was TJ's mobile command centre. Much to the disappointment of the men, this trip hadn't included an entertainment wagon. All the women had been left under a minimal guard back at Loch Uig. In total, there were thirty-one vehicles in the convoy with just over eleven hundred men. The other part of the army had a few hundred more than that, but negotiating the pass would be a harder task. TJ had the easy part, the coast road. It was a little hilly, but nothing unmanageable. His mission was to sweep down the coast, taking out the small band of survivors who remained, then meet up with Fry.

The women who had escaped the raiding party had been smart and capable, and both Fry and TJ knew that they would put up some resistance, but Fry wanted to make a statement, which was, you mess with his army and you will be annihilated. That was the simple purpose of this mission, to obliterate this area of coastline.

TJ felt the vehicle come to a halt. He stepped down from the Winnebago as two of his men approached.

"There're a couple of croft houses set just back from the road there, but it doesn't look like anyone has been living in them for a while," said one of the men.

"Doesn't matter," replied TJ, "Fry wants it all gone."

The men nodded and walked up to two waiting bikers. The bikes headed up the incline and within a minute, flames could be seen lighting up the night sky as muffled explosions sounded. The bikes rejoined the convoy, and TJ climbed back into the Winnebago before the convoy rolled off once again.

"Doesn't this all seem a bit...much?" asked Jason, the driver of the lumbering motor-home, as TJ climbed into the passenger seat.

"Fry wants to send a message," he replied. "He's the boss, we do what he says."

"Y'know the men would follow you anywhere, don't you TJ?" said Jason.

"That's good. The men follow me, I follow Fry's orders, the job gets done, and everybody's happy," TJ replied.

"People are talking about what happened to The Don. A lot of the men are...unnerved," said Jason, glancing towards TJ before looking back to the road.

The convoy of vehicles slowed again, and the bikes went off in different directions. One of the houses was close to the road, and TJ and Jason watched as a Molotov cocktail arced through the air, smashing through a downstairs window exploding into a ball of flames as it washed everything in the room with a fiery coating.

"Oh?" said TJ. "Who exactly?"

"Erm... no one really, erm... y'know, it's just talk," he said, putting the vehicle into gear again and avoiding further eye contact.

"Loose talk does nobody any good," replied TJ. "It can get people killed around here. We have some good guys, I'd hate to see them coming to a bad end because of chit chat."

They continued the drive in silence. TJ looked in the wing mirror. The convoy had been climbing for a while, but now they were on a straight stretch. There was a steep incline to their left, way too steep for the possibility of any housing plots.

"Bloody hell," said Jason, craning his neck and looking down at the shimmering water forty metres below.

"What?" asked TJ.

"It's a sheer fucking drop, I bet this road sees a few nasty accidents in winter."

"The council would have been obliged to keep it open. There'll probably have been more grit used on this stretch of road than they used in the whole of Newcastle centre," replied TJ.

"Yeah, but still, it's fucking st..."

Jason stopped as he saw a flash in his mirror. TJ saw it too and leaned closer to the wing mirror to see what it was. The flash became a fire, and then he saw a small flame travelling through the air, before another blinding flash.

"What the fuck is that?" demanded TJ looking out at the bay.

Jason put his foot on the brake as he saw flames in the middle of the water. Suddenly the flames appeared to turn into flying balls of fire that were scorching a trail through the night in their direction. The lead bus exploded into a rolling inferno as two of the burning missiles hit it. A third crushed two bikes before splitting into a hundred blazing pieces, spreading the fire further. The parade of vehicles came to an abrupt halt, blocked to the front and blocked to the back by burning wreckage. TJ and Jason sat frozen, their mouths agape. This was meant to be a pushover, a walk in the park, just a handful of escaped women and maybe the odd one they'd missed from before, but nothing like this. They'd seen the signal flare go up earlier, but they thought that had been a warning to the survivors to run.

TJ ran into the back of the motorhome and grabbed the radio. "Fry, we're under attack!" There was no response, not even static. TJ checked the battery and hit the test button. The radio was not faulty. "Fry for fuck's sake!"

"Boss!" shouted Jason.

TJ looked out of the window to see more flames flying through the air towards the convoy. He opened the door and climbed out just as another bus close to the back exploded. He heard the whoosh of flames and the screaming men despite the distance. He ran around the Winnebago to get a look at the weapon that was firing at them. All he could see from this distance was the fire and possibly the outline of a boat. TJ ran to the pickup carrying the mortar. The men were already climbing into the back, they realised what was happening.

"Can you take it out?" TJ shouted over the increasing volume of the spreading panic.

One of the men was already looking through a night-vision scope. "Too fucking right we can," said the other as he picked up one of the mortar shells.

Just then there was a rumbling sound, and TJ turned to look at the steep incline to the left of the road.

"Oh fuck!" he whispered as he saw a huge cascade of boulders and logs thundering down the hillside.

On a darker night, he would have seen nothing. How he wished for a darker night now. Then, the air above the full length of the convoy lit up as a flurry of Molotov cocktails were launched. He heard some of his men begin to fire shots, but it was pure panic. There was no way they could pick a target.

The missiles landed setting vehicles and men alight, and the whole stretch of road glowed brightly enough for the invaders to see the wall of debris as it collided with them, crushing men, crushing vehicles, forcing others from the road, over the edge of the cliff face to smash and burn on the rocks below before eventually being washed out to sea. It was carnage. TJ stood for a moment taking in the full extent of the destruction. When he saw the huge bouncing pine log heading towards him he did not even bother moving. He just lowered his head and closed his eyes as it smashed his torso to a bloody pulp, wiping him and the surrounding vehicles from the road and to their end.

Shots rang as Barnes took out a couple of the bikers who were trying to get around the burning wreckage of the lead bus. More Molotov cocktails were thrown, exploding against anything that hadn't been swept from the road by the avalanche. The victory was emphatic. Brutal, unforgiving, but emphatic.

When all movement ceased, when there was no man left to kill and no vehicle left to burn, Jules launched a red flare into the air. Red to stop. They had won.

They were safe for now.

*

Dawn was breaking and the air was thick with the smell of burning vehicles, burning logs and burning flesh. The clean-up was going to take some time. They were cut off by road for now, but that meant nobody could get to them as well. They would have time to rebuild, to fortify. They were few, but eventually, more would come. They would build a proper community, a proper life. Whatever difficulties they would have to face, they would face them together.

Epilogue

It had been a long time since people had been to a party, but everybody, everybody but the lookouts anyway, was present.

Lucy gave Mike a big wet kiss and laughed. He rolled his tongue around his mouth to try and figure out the taste.

"What have you been drinking?" he asked.

"Blackberry brandy," she said with a wide smile on her face. She pulled him towards her and kissed him again. "Just so you know, I think you might get lucky later," she said and giggled.

"I'll hold you to that,"

"To what?" asked Sammy as she crept up behind them, only hearing the end of the conversation.

"Sammy Bear," Mike said, lifting her into the air

and twirling her around. "You're like a ninja." Sammy laughed, as did Jake who had joined them. Lucy laughed loudest and winked at Mike playfully putting a hand on her breast and moving it down her torso. Mike's eyes nearly popped out of his head and Lucy doubled over laughing before taking another drink from her glass. "Sammy Fletcher, Ninja Warrior Princess. How does that sound?" he asked.

"That sounds like trouble," said Emma, as she and Sarah walked up together holding hands. Mike put Sammy back on the ground.

Richard, David, Ruth, and George came up to the growing gathering. Ruth had her arm looped around George's. "I think everybody is here," she said.

"I'm not used to giving speeches Ruth, just give me a minute," said Mike.

She let go of George's arm, took hold of Mike and kissed him on the cheek. "You'll be fine. There are no enemies here, only friends. Proud friends."

"I couldn't have said it better," said Jenny who had walked across to join them.

Mike nodded, "Thanks, Ruth. Thanks, Jenny."

"C'mon then, Mikey boy, we're wanting to get to the grub," said Hughes, nodding towards a line of trestle tables filled with an array of items no one would have thought possible. But everyone had contributed. Some had gathered, some had fished, some had picked, some had cooked, some had baked. It was a community. That was the whole point of this day.

Shaw had a walking stick for support, but he was getting better every day. He walked up to Mike and put out a hand in friendship. Mike knocked it away and put his arms around Shaw.

"You saved my sister, you were there in the school when I needed you. We're good, you and me."

Shaw didn't say anything but returned Mike's firm embrace.

"Good luck," said Beth kissing Mike on the cheek. Barnes didn't say anything, he just grinned and gave him a bear hug, before ruffling his hair. John and Annie went to join Jake and Sammy and Sarah's pupils all came to stand with them.

Jules's brothers all nodded as they passed Mike and Jules walked up to him and straightened the collar of his polo shirt. "Jesus, look at the state of you, y'bloody scruff."

Mike laughed. "My throat's gone dry. I hate this stuff."

"Who're you trying to kid?" said Jules. "In my life, I've never met anyone who loves the sound of their own voice so much,"

"You are such a cheeky cow," he said smiling and shaking his head.

Jules broke out into a huge smile. "Give us a kiss," she said before pecking him on the cheek. "Proud of you Mike," she said and went to join her brothers.

Mike climbed onto the big rock that was to act as the podium, and everyone assembled suddenly stopped their conversations and looked in his direction.

He looked around at all the faces. Ruth was right. He was talking to friends—no, they were closer than friends.

"It was just three months ago when we faced the fight of our lives. I remember that night like it was yesterday. I think I always will."

He swallowed and signalled for Emma to pass him a drink. He took a few gulps and handed it back.

"We did what many thought would be impossible...but impossible starts with believing you can't, not believing you can. A lot of people have said to me time after time that I've done the impossible, but I haven't, I've just believed." Mike looked around at the faces and saw that all eyes were fixed on him, he gulped again. "Belief is a powerful thing. It makes some people do terrible things and some great things. It all depends on the person and the belief. My belief was in my family and one simple truth and that is there is no greater weapon than the will to fight for the ones you love."

People in the crowd began to look around at each other and smile. A few clasped hands, a few others put their arm around family members. The love radiated off these people, and Mike could feel the warmth wash over him. These people were his family in every sense of the word. This thought stirred painful old memories, and an idea formed in his mind.

"We had no mortars, very few guns and just a handful of people compared to a huge army. But we knew we would fight to protect our own with everything we had. Em and me didn't have a great childhood."

Mike looked towards his sister. The pair of them locked eyes and smiled—a sibling's smile, all-knowing. Lucy suddenly sobered up, Mike had practised the speech on her and this was a definite deviation.

"We had a real bastard of a father," he continued, "and so many times when I was ashamed of him or enraged by him, people would say to me, *you can't choose your family, Mike.* But that's not true is it?" He said looking around at the crowd. "Because I chose, Lucy. She's my family. I chose Ruth and Richard and David. They're my family. I chose Beth and John and Annie and Barnes and Bruiser and George and Sarah and all the girls and now...now I'm choosing you. You're all my family, and I'm yours. And we might argue, and we might get on each other's nerves. But if we aren't family after what we've been through together, then it's time to rewrite the dictionary."

People applauded and cheered and shouted, and Mike choked up at the outpouring of emotion. It was a few minutes before the commotion died down enough for him to continue.

"Today, we're continuing to do the impossible, you and I. Today we're establishing a town."

He stepped down off the rock and picked up a fence post mallet before walking across to the roadside. Everyone followed him and watched. Hughes grabbed a six-foot fence post with the spike already attached. There were two signs nailed to it, covered by blue towels. Mike hammered the post into the ground and stood by the side of it.

He waited until he was sure he had everybody's attention and then pulled away the bottom towel. It read POPULATION 138.

"Ladies and gentleman," he said pulling away the other towel. "Welcome to Safe Haven."

THE END

A Note from the Author

I really hope you enjoyed this book and would be very grateful if you took a minute to leave a review on Amazon and Goodreads.

If you would like to stay informed about what I'm doing, including current writing projects, and all the latest news and release information; these are the places to go:

Join the fan club on Facebook
https://www.facebook.com/groups/127693634504226

Like the Christopher Artinian author page
https://www.facebook.com/safehaventrilogy/

Buy exclusive and signed books and merchandise, subscribe to the newsletter and follow the blog:
https://www.christopherartinian.com/

Follow me on Twitter
https://twitter.com/Christo71635959

Follow me on Amazon
https://amzn.to/2I1llU6

Follow me on Goodreads
https://bit.ly/2P7iDzX

Other books by Christopher Artinian:

Safe Haven: Rise of the RAMs
Safe Haven: Realm of the Raiders
Safe Haven: Reap of the Righteous
Safe Haven: Ice
Safe Haven: Vengeance
Before Safe Haven: Lucy
Before Safe Haven: Alex
Before Safe Haven: Mike
The End of Everything: Book 1
The End of Everything: Book 2
The End of Everything: Book 3
The End of Everything: Book 4

CHRISTOPHER ARTINIAN

Christopher Artinian was born and raised in Leeds, West Yorkshire. Wanting to escape life in a big city and concentrate more on working to live than living to work, he and his family moved to the Outer Hebrides in the north-west of Scotland in 2004, where he now works as a full-time author.

Chris is a huge music fan, a cinephile, an avid reader and a supporter of Yorkshire county cricket club. When he's not sat in front of his laptop living out his next post-apocalyptic/dystopian/horror adventure, he will be passionately immersed in one of his other interests.

Printed in France by Amazon
Brétigny-sur-Orge, FR

10199372R00181